IDENTITY X

MICHELLE MUCKLEY

For the people who support me, in whatever simple or complex way that might be.

Special thanks go to Dr George Vassiliou for his help and advice. Any mistakes regarding the science in the book are mine and mine alone.

"The end of a melody is not its goal: but nonetheless, had the melody not reached its end it would not have reached its goal either."

Friedrich Nietzsche (1844-1900).

Other works by Michelle Muckley

The Dawn (five book series)

Psychophilia

Containment (short story)

Escaping Life

The Loss of Deference

PART ONE

NEMREC

(Nuclease Mediated Recombination Correction)

ONE

SIXTEEN EYES GAZED BACK AT him, twelve of them through heavy rimmed glasses. They stood there silently waiting for him to speak whilst clutching their plastic cups, shuffling first left, then right. Graham was still holding his pipette, his fingers poised and willing, trained for nothing but repetition and tedium. Even in a moment of glory Ben could see that he was desperate to get back to his workspace. Alan was pulling up a stool, rubbing the base of his back like a woman in the third trimester of pregnancy who had reached her daily limit. Ami stood behind them, her open lipped smile full of reassurance, staring at Ben as if they were the only people in the room. Right now he was the centre of the world. He was the centre of Ami's world. It felt good to have her approval.

Phil finished pouring the cheap champagne into his own crumpled cup before tipping the remainder of the bottle, which seemed to constitute little more than froth, into Ben's. He stood nonchalantly at Ben's side ready for the celebratory cheer, the empty bottle swinging low. He nodded to Ben to speak, a quick come on, we're waiting.

"Well, it has been a long four years," Ben began, pausing for breath after almost every word. It was hard to concentrate over the distracting sound of his wine fizzing in his cup, and the whirring of the air conditioning rattling above him. His eyes were tired and gritty from the dry atmosphere. It was seven thirty at night and he

1

had been in the lab for over twelve hours already. He had known by late morning that today would be the day. As soon as the first results came back, he knew it had worked. He gazed out from behind his glasses to see them all waiting for him to say something momentous. He felt an uncontrollable need to find something meaningful and poignant to say; to mark the life changing occasion with something that would never be forgotten. He had to find something inspiring. Something they could regale to their families, who in turn would tell the tale to their friends. A story that would stand the test of time.

He felt the weight of all great men before him who had stood on the same precipice of achievement, the moment before the world learns what has been accomplished. All that came to his mind were the fuzzy, static heavy words of Neil Armstrong as they beamed back from the moon all those years ago. People still spoke about that moment, even kids like Ben who were born years after the event. It was impossible to forget the significance of that first footstep. His success today may not have the same intergalactic stretch, from one celestial body to the next, but he felt the same sense of weightlessness. This moment was the joy. This moment was his, just before the curtains are drawn to reveal the expectant audience. Standing there in his lab coat and shoe covers in front of a sea of tired faces, he felt as overwhelmed and excited, he imagined, as the first man to step foot on the moon.

"We have done it together. This is our success, and it will change the world. Raise your glasses." Ben held up his plastic cup, and a series of hands rose up before him, including Graham who had finally relinquished his pipette to the bench.

"Here's to us. And here is to NEMREC. We did it." They all nodded their heads, their plastic cups in the air in muted celebration before knocking the liquid back. He saw a couple of smiles. Several of them patted their nearest colleague on the shoulder in a display of professional appreciation and admiration. If he could have done so without automatically assuming an air of inflated self importance, he would have patted each of them on the back himself, and thanked them for their individual efforts. Instead he settled on a submissive handshake with each, as the formal line of scientists disintegrated into a casual crowd.

2

He had wanted to emphasise the joint effort today. He knew in the whirlwind of media attention and fervent celebration that it would not be his team appearing on the television. Nor would it be them who would be whisked away, by business class no doubt, to the next conference for genetic research - a six day stint in Dubai. It would be Ben Stone. Revolutionary Scientist. The one that cured genetic disease. He rolled his self-awarded title around in his head enjoying the way it sounded, getting drunk on the dizzy heights of accomplishment. It sounded good. Seeing that during his momentary lapse into daydream the rest of the team were either finishing up at their work benches or had already discarded their lab coats, he took a step towards his own office.

"Don't forget, drinks at Simpson's tonight," he called. A couple of them nodded in enthusiasm. Ami nodded too. "Eight thirty, I'll be there." He turned and opened the door to his office, and sat down into the green leather chair. It was always darker in here, although in theory there were the same number of lights as the main laboratory. The trouble was that there were so many papers and so many books that the light literally got sucked into the heaving mass of a lifetime of research. Every surface had been utilised to hold some item of importance, including the uncomfortable looking couch that had on occasion formed an impromptu bed when he missed the last train home.

He had read every page of every book in here. He had spent the majority of his life huddled over a test tube, or with his head buried in a book. He had decided upon his life's path the same day he learned of his family's genetic flaw. His mother had sat him down to explain the basis for his father's mood swings. They would likely get worse, she said, until one day when they might not be able to recognise the man they knew anymore. Until then, Ben had been happy to play the role of a teenager. But that day changed everything.

Consumed in his daydream he hadn't seen Ami approach, and when she tapped her knuckles on the glass door she startled him. As he looked up from his desk he saw the cascading mass of jet black hair, released and flowing like a waterfall across one shoulder, pooling in the crevice of her elbow. Her eyes were set as endless jet black saucers, so different to the Ionian blue of his, and her skin was the perfect shade of honey. When she joined the team just over a year ago, he could barely believe his luck. He motioned with a smile and a quick wag of the fingers for her to open the door. In a single fluid motion, she pushed the door ajar, and leant like a ballerina, curling the top half of her body around the half open door.

"We are all leaving now, Ben. We'll see you there?" Her hair fell forwards, spreading the scent of dried rosebuds across the office. Ben wondered if he looked as foolish as he felt in her presence when it was just the two of them. He sat himself upright, his chair creaking as he shifted his weight around uncomfortably. He pulled the nearest research journal in front of him and began leafing through the pages in an effort to look casual and unflustered.

"OK, yeah. I'm right behind you, just finishing off here." He motioned to the research journal and glanced down at the page. He had undesirably opened the journal at a location that detailed a new stem cell treatment for erectile dysfunction. An article complete with diagrams. He caught her glancing down at the journal. He closed the cover, hoping that she hadn't deciphered the subject matter. "I just need to make a telephone call."

"Shall we wait for you? It's not a problem." She either hadn't seen, or was too polite to joke at his expense. He was grateful for either possibility, with a heavy preference for the former.

"No, go on ahead. I'll meet you all there." She smiled with pursed lips and tucked her chin in. It made her look cute and sexy at the same time. She closed the door behind her with her perfectly manicured hand. He leaned back in his chair, adjusting his position to watch her cross the laboratory floor. He wondered if she swung her hips like that on purpose, or if when he looked away they would rest into a more natural rhythm. He took the offending journal, shook his head in disgust and tossed it with revulsion into the waste paper bin.

He kicked his chair out from under the desk and put his feet up on top of the papers. Resting his head of thick blond curls back onto the top of the chair he took the arms of his glasses in his fingers and slid them from his face. He could barely believe that all his years of work had culminated in this solitary moment. He was surrounded by brilliance in his laboratory, and his team was made up of the best of the best in their field. Yet now, when it was quiet and he was alone it was impossible not to go back to that day when his mother explained to him what a genetic disease was. He would have loved to pick up the telephone, dial her number, tell her one simple thing. He would tell her that he had done it. That nobody else would suffer, and that their past would never be repeated. He glanced over at the telephone, playing her long since redundant number over and over in his head. The answering machine was flashing on the far side of his desk and it brought him back to reality. There were three messages. Swinging his legs back down he propelled himself forward and hit the play button, leaving thoughts of his mother in the past where they belonged. The first was from a supplier of gene chips to let him know that Monday's delivery would be late.

"I don't think we need to worry about that," he laughed to himself. The second was from Hannah, asking him what time he expected to be home. Her words sounded bitter, and he could hear her mumbling to herself as she hung up the telephone. He wouldn't let it spoil the moment though, and he put her message to the back of his mind. The final message was from a Mr. Saad. Ben still had no idea how he had managed to get hold of his direct telephone line. The familiar and gravelly accent needed no introduction.

"Hello, Mr. Stone. I do hope you will do me the courtesy of returning my phone call this time. I want very much to discuss your research with you. I am able to offer a very substantial contribution to your funding which I know that you will need very soon. My personal contact number is...."

"No, thank you." Ben hit the delete button before he finished listening to the message. He had done it. The compound worked. NEMREC was ready to go. It was only a matter of time before support from a large pharmaceutical developer would roll his way. He had a month until the National Genetics Conference, and that was more than enough time to collate his results into something presentable. After that, the funding and everything that came with it was virtually guaranteed. He could almost feel the heat of the

Dubai sun on his face. He wondered if any sponsor might let him take an assistant, but with the same speed he considered it he reminded himself of the inappropriateness of his intentions. He stood up from his chair and grabbed his jacket from the coat stand as the falling rain hit the flat metallic roof.

He made his way towards the door but from the corner of his eye he caught sight of the brown wooden photo frame on the edge of the desk. It had been gradually pushed to the side over a period of time by an ever increasing volume of paperwork. He picked up the photograph with both hands and held it closely to him but angled it so that he could see it. Staring back at him was the past, another time and another life it seemed to him now. It was his own eight year old face, smiling and happy, pressed up against the aged face of his father. Seeing this photograph reminded him that it wasn't the celebration, the glory, or the admiration on Ami's face that he was looking for. He didn't need the all expenses paid trip to Dubai, as nice as it might be, especially if he got to take an assistant. He didn't need the nod to significant and overwhelmingly important prizes. All the recognition he needed was here in the eyes of his ageing father. He tapped the photograph with the back of his fingers.

"We did it, Dad." He sat the photograph back down on the desk, clearing away a selection of papers to place it centrally, and where tomorrow he would see it again. He picked up the telephone and tapped out his home number. Hannah answered, and the annoyance in her voice regarding his recurrent lateness was tangible.

"Yeah, I'll be late. I'm finishing up at the lab." He paused briefly to listen. "Just waiting for the machines and the final run. I'll be home by ten thirty. Yes, you too. See you later."

He hung up the telephone and grabbed his briefcase. He glanced at the piles of handwritten notes on his desk and considered taking the latest of them with him. Instead he agreed with himself that he deserved at least one night off and so left them undisturbed. He made for the door and turned off the lights, and as the air conditioning units slowed to a halt the sound of the rain grew louder as it hit the roof. He was close to the underground station but doubted he would make it without getting soaked through. He grabbed his raincoat from the hook and threw it across his shoulders, wriggling his arms into the sleeves. He pressed the button and the entrance door slid open as a quick shot of air squeezed out from the pneumatic mechanism. He made his way downstairs towards the chill of the early spring rain.

TWO

HE WAS RIGHT ABOUT THE weather. The rain was falling as a deluge of giant droplets, the biggest that he had seen since the great floods twenty years ago. The combination of old Victorian and Georgian homes that lined up proudly alongside each other became swamped under the rush of water. Cellars became unwanted indoor pools as they swallowed up the cascading tide. The following morning was total chaos, and tonight seemed no different. A barrage of water submerged the streets, and the edge of the road where it met the pavement was flowing fast as a swollen river. Through the glare of the headlights from the cars Ben eyed up the entrance to the underground station. After making a mental calculation as to the best route of passage, the variables of distance and pooled surface water weighed against each other, he pulled his rain coat above his head. He darted out from underneath the shelter of his office entrance door, dashing across the road.

The entrance of the underground was packed with commuters, people refusing to attempt the final leg of their journey, sheltering themselves in the tight entrance. Ben pushed his way past the crowd of bodies. The humidity hung uncomfortably low in the air, courtesy of all the warm damp clothes of the people huddling together. Shaking his legs and his jacket behind him, he reached into his inside coat pocket and pulled out his identity card. He held it against the screen that controlled the movement of the entrance doors. The red light immediately changed to green, and underneath it in small green lettering the words *Good evening, Mr. Stone* flashed up to greet him. He had never managed to become accustomed to this level of regulation. He knew of people that would say how they quite liked the personal greeting when boarding the train, paying for food at the supermarket, or when you put petrol in your car. Some of these devices would even talk to you and ask if you had had a nice day. Ben saw through the facade of propriety, and knew that it was just a way of tracking people's movements. He couldn't understand why society had accepted it so readily. He cursed the androgynous voice under his breath, stowed his identity card back in his pocket. He made his way through the tunnels, facing the oncoming breeze. It delivered an unwelcome chill, but to its credit, also began drying those of his hairs which had not escaped the torrential rain.

By the time the twenty minute journey across the city was complete his hair was almost dry. Ben usually swept it back into a semi-straightened style with a slick of the sweet smelling paste that promised more in its advertising than the offer of a good hairstyle. But now his blond curls had worked loose. Under his raincoat he was wearing a crisp white shirt and black tie, loosened progressively throughout the day into its current casual position. Combined with his raincoat he looked more like a city lawyer than a scientist. Most of the people he worked with dressed in jeans and jumpers that looked as if they had been pulled from the bottom drawer every winter since the day of their graduation.

As he made his way towards the exit of the station he could hear that the rain had subsided, and there was a steady stream of people on their way out. The corridor was quiet, and as he approached the exit gate he could see a man having trouble with his identity card. It wouldn't permit him access to the station and there was a pulsating mass of people behind him that appeared to be growing progressively angrier at the delay. All it would take was an unpaid bill, a trivial criminal misdemeanour. Even an unfounded complaint against you could be enough to get your identity card deactivated. There was only one way of getting it reactivated and that was to go in person to the Central Government Offices and deal with whatever problem had caused the deactivation, and nobody wanted to have to do that.

Ben flashed his identity card in front of the screen and the door slid open. He cursed the courteous computerised greeting as was customary, and watched as the guards made their way over to the troubled man. He was protesting his innocence but it was no use. He already knew the guards wouldn't listen to any of his reasoning, no matter how logical he made it seem. They would never oblige by opening the doors at the hint of a convincing explanation. If your identity card failed you, you were out of the station on your heels.

The streets were quieter with the passing of the rain, and the syrupy sweet smell that it left behind permeated the clear air. It was early April, and as much as people expected the bad weather, the first proper downpour always caught the world unawares. There were people walking home in rain soaked suits, their expensive shoes soaked through to the sole. Aside from his own rain soaked shoes, Ben enjoyed the purity and cleanliness of such an atmosphere and inhaled it deeply as he walked through the streets. As he approached the bar, the glow of the lights from inside licked at the oily streets. Shaking off the last drops of rain from his coat, Ben stepped into *Simpson's* and could see Mark standing at the side of the bar. Ami was stood to the side of him and waved over for Ben to join them. Ben shuffled his way through the crowd, walking sideways and dodging the hoards of wayward elbows. Mark was the first to speak. He was Ben's oldest friend, his boy, his wing man, and the first person he called when he saw the first positive results earlier on that day.

"Hey, buddy. Congratulations are in order. You did it." They greeted each other with open arms and embraced, ending with a simultaneous slap of each other's back. It was a stereotypical male embrace, but genuine nevertheless.

"No, that's not right. We did it," Ben said, breaking away from Mark and playing to the crowd. Ben turned to look at his colleagues, eager to include them in the success after their effort in turning up at a bar. In comparison to the rest of the clientele, his crowd of colleagues looked out of place in their jeans and threadbare jumpers. Ami was the only one who looked like she might have come to this bar of her own accord. The others looked like they might be part of an organised group outing, rounded up and dragged into somewhere they would neither choose or wish to be.

"Yeah, but they're not going to get to go to Dubai are they?" Mark was laughing as he said it, and looking at everyone except for Ben, playing to a tough crowd. A few of Ben's geeky-looking colleagues raised a smile, but Ben could also hear the rumblings of discontent as they considered that indeed there would be no foreign trips for any of them. He wanted to give Mark a good dig in the ribs for mentioning Dubai, but also found himself wondering if Ami had heard. *Surely she would like a trip there?*

"Take this, and raise your glass." Everybody was already holding another glass of champagne, only this time the bottle cost six times that of the first and people were holding up crystal flutes rather than paper cups. Ben took the glass from Mark and raised his hand as instructed. "Ben, very soon people will know your name. You will present in London and then Dubai, and the world will learn what you have done and it will be a better place for it. Here's to my man, Ben."

"To Ben," they all cheered. As Ben glanced around, they all smiled back, tipsy from another alcoholic drink when most hadn't eaten since lunchtime. He caught Ami's eye, and she tipped her glass and head in unison towards him in recognition of his success. A vision of white sand and blue water flashed through his mind once more. One by one they sipped on their drinks and began their own private conversations.

Mark motioned to Ben to sit at the two empty spaces at the bar. They pulled out the leather stools and set their champagne flutes onto the glass topped bar. Mark raised his fingers and the barman poured two Whiskey shot's over brilliantly transparent ice. Ben shuffled off his raincoat and loosened his tie as they both sat down on the stools, their legs turned to face each other, their elbows resting onto the surface of the bar. Ben picked up the Whiskey shot and prompted Mark to do the same. They tapped their glasses together and knocked back the shots.

Mark nodded his head towards the crowd who were all just out of earshot above the humdrum of the background soul music.

"So, how many of these guys do you think are saying that had it not been for them you wouldn't have succeeded?"

Ben laughed as he sat back in his stool, stretching out his legs. "At least fifty per cent of them. The others are just waiting their turn," he grinned. He raised his hand to the barman and motioned to the empty glasses. The barman set down another two perfectly poured shots.

"So, what now? Is that it?" Mark asked.

"No. I have to prove that we can succeed across a whole spectrum of disorders. I think we will be well on our way by the conference next month."

"I still don't understand exactly how you have done it." Mark leaned in a little closer to encourage him to continue.

"You have to remember the past research, Mark. You remember, when you were still a good scientist and not just about the money." They both smiled before Ben carried on with his explanation. "Remember what Yamanaka did. It was brilliant in theory to make stem cells from skin. He reprogrammed genes to create a pluripotent stem cell, a cell capable of becoming any type of cell in the body. The problem was, when they remodelled the cells by inserting new genes, they delivered them to the host via a virus. The new genes got inserted in an arbitrary position. If this happens to be in the middle of an original gene, it gets disrupted." Ben stopped to take a sip of his whiskey, and Mark did the same. "If that gene modifies cell division for example..."

"You cause cancer," Mark finished on his behalf.

"Exactly," Ben smiled, as if to say *so you do remember some stuff.* It was their usual banter and they had slipped into their usual roles, Ben the genius and Mark the sell-out who had traded a workbench for a desk. "So adding in new genes was problematic. They did a lot of development, and the oligonucleotides went a long way to help, but the real magic was to correct what is already there. Instead of trying to cleave out mistakes and replace faulty bits you just repair the fault. That's what NEMREC does."

"Replace one DNA base with another?"

"No, not replace. If we know what a normal genome looks like, one without any genetic mutation, then we can model NEMREC to hunt down the faults in the code and repair it. Nothing is inserted, nothing is removed. Just repaired."

"Wow," Mark said as he shifted in his seat, as if the weight of such a discovery had made him physically uncomfortable. "It is quite something you have created here, Ben." Mark sat recumbent on his bar stool swirling the ice around in his glass before knocking back the remaining liquor. "It could be very valuable."

"It's not about that, Mark. You know that. You know what it's about." The memory of his father mixed with the intoxicating whisky was a heady combination, and he felt the effects of both.

"Don't be hasty. Just let your mind wander a little bit," Mark pushed on. "I know it's about your father, and Matthew. But just think what this is capable of. Think of the capabilities of a product like this; to the cosmetics industry, to the food industry," Mark dared push on, "to the military."

"The military?" Ben looked up and tried to determine which undulating outline was the actual embodiment of Mark. "What the hell would the military want with it?"

"I'm just saying that the ability to alter genetic code stretches further than medicine."

"It's all about disease, Mark," Ben chuckled as he knocked back the last of his whiskey and slid himself forward from his chair, his feet unsteady, his vision not far behind.

"And what about her?" Mark nodded towards Ami who was standing in the corner, attempting to look like she wasn't paying Ben any attention. "She's got to be a pretty valuable researcher, right?" Ben knew their conversation had already moved on. Mark's interests in the capabilities of NEMREC had no chance of frustrating his other, primary interest. Which at this moment was Ami, or in her absence, any willing and typically beautiful female.

"For God's sake. After the last time, do you think she's even going to talk to you tonight?"

"She already did," Mark said as he too stood up and slid along the bar towards Ben, nudging him in the ribs with his elbow. Mark was smiling broadly at Ami, who had realised that she was now their topic of conversation. "What did I do that was so bad the last time?"

"Mark, you spent the whole night talking to her and then at the end of the night she found you outside with that blonde getting into a taxi."

"And what exactly is your point? Ami made it quite clear that my efforts were going to waste." Ben dropped his head back in frustration at Mark's lack of understanding of the female disposition, or the inappropriateness of his bullish behaviour. He raised his hand for another two shots and knocked the one in front of him back.

"How's Beth, by the way?" Ben reminded Mark of his real life by overemphasising the name of his wife.

Mark scowled as he said, "She's fatter."

"You're such an arsehole." Ben had known Mark since high school. They had sat next to each other on the very first day. Since that first meeting when a forthright Mark had offered out his hand to Ben, nothing had changed. They became inseparable. Where you saw one, you would surely find the other. Like the moon and the earth they were different, but yet totally dependent upon each other.

"That I might be, but it's not me she's interested in," Mark said, as he turned the conversation back to Ami. "Just like everything with us, you're the star. It's you she wants."

"What do you mean?" Ben said, sipping at his drink.

"Don't tell me you haven't noticed it. She is crazy about you. Are you trying to tell me that you never got a bit close when you were working late, putting in extra hours? Come on man, she's gorgeous. I would have."

"I know you would have. You don't need to tell me that." Ben had accepted Mark's flaws. He had known him so long that all flaws, including the inability to remain faithful to anything, namely women, were just part of his character, like the fact he liked a good whiskey or enjoyed a game of football. It didn't affect Ben, so he turned a blind eye. But Mark was still staring at him, waiting for an answer, a half grin on the left side of his mouth in reference to Ami. His face was saying, *there is a space on my team if you want to play my game.*

"Yeah, I like her," Ben admitted as he averted Mark's non-judgemental gaze, "but, I'm married." Ben tried to sound firm in his stance, unwavering and committed. He didn't share Mark's values. That's what he told himself anyway, but recently he found himself cruising along dangerously close to the edge. He soon discovered another Dubai based scenario formulating in his mind, and berated his thoughts and words for behaving like the polar ends of a magnet.

"Yeah, you seem really happy." Mark's words were flat and overstretched like a deflated balloon. Ben knew that he wasn't happy, and he knew things had been tough. But still, it wasn't that simple. Getting involved with Ami, no matter how tempting it was, would be career suicide. It could kill his work in the same amount of time it took for him to hoist her up and lift her skirt.

"There are more important things going on in that office. You know that. You know why I do what I do. You watched him die too," Ben said. Mark was quiet. There was nothing more to say. Ben shuffled his arms into his jacket in a series of stuttering movements. He held up his hand and Mark hit him with a sideways high five, their hands gripped together, their thumbs interlocked. "We still on for Saturday?" Ben asked.

"Yeah man, I'll see you there." Their eye's met for a moment, and Ben didn't know if it was the alcohol that they had drunk in too quick succession, or if Mark was thinking back to the time when Ben's father died. His eyes appeared glazed. As Ben began to pull his hand away, he felt resistance as Mark held onto him, counteracting his departure.

"Always better than me. Always get it right where I fuck up." There were lots of things Ben could have said in response. But he remained silent. The alcohol had whipped into Mark's system, done its best work, and left a usually well composed man on the brink of what looked suspiciously like tears. The last thing Ben wanted to see now was Mark crying.

"You're full of shit. And you're pissed," Ben said. Mark nodded in agreement, and finally let go of his friend's hand. "Don't let me down on Saturday," Ben walked away pointing at him as if his fingers were a rifle. "Matthew is looking forward to it."

After stepping back outside and into the evening chill which whipped annoyingly at his damp trousers, he realised that he hadn't said goodbye to Ami. Postulating that perhaps that wasn't such a bad thing, he turned, permitting himself one final look into the bar. His blurred eyes found their way through the crowd. They settled upon Ami and Mark who were deep in conversation, and Ami looked angry. Ben took a glance at his watch, finding it hard to focus on the hands, before taking the first steps towards the underground station. He found himself wondering whether Ami had really looked angry with Mark, or whether in his own inappropriately jealous mood, it was just his own wishful thinking.

It had got colder outside, and he pulled his jacket up around his neck. There was silence in the street, with the exception of the occasional crawl of rubber tyres gliding over rain soaked tarmac. The sky had cleared, and the few grey clouds that dawdled lackadaisically in the tail end of the storm were swept along by a high wind. Ben darted across the road and ducked back into the entrance of the station. He was too tall for most of the archways and always had to lower his head as the tunnels to the platforms grew narrower and more diminutive in height. The rumble of the approaching train clattered up through the black of the tunnel, and as the wind raced past, Ben felt his coat tails whip up behind him and he steadied himself against the shiny white tiled walls. He sat down on the first empty seat, his eyes heavy and head swimming from the whiskey shots. In the warmth of the bar he had still felt clear headed in spite of his difficulties with his vision. Now, sitting on the train as it rumbled along the tracks, sloshing the contents of his stomach about with every bump, he felt more than a little drunk. He could feel the contents of his stomach somersaulting back and forth. He considered the humiliation that would ensue if he vomited into the small metal grooves on the floor in front of him. The vision of being escorted from the station was a sobering idea, and he clenched his jaw together and clung onto the silver pole next to him. The sight of the pole made him consider where Mark might be going later on in the evening if he didn't manage to sweet talk Ami into leaving with him. For an unjustifiable reason, Ben hoped that would be the case. Mark ending up in another type of club, a couple of hundred pounds poorer would be the best outcome as far as Ben could see.

He rested his head back onto the graffiti covered window and stretched out his legs in the almost empty carriage. His only companions were an old man with a deeply wrinkled face, and a boy probably no older than eighteen. He wore his hood pulled up loosely over his head, and his oversized headphones silenced the world around him. Ben thought about the first results from earlier on that day, and how many diseases he already knew he could cure. If he could repair genetic code with just a simple injection there would be no end to the possibilities. Pharmacy would be redundant in many cases. Lives would go on normally without hospital visits and surgery. Children would be born and screened, and treatment could be given before even the first sign of disease would show. Nobody would have to die because of genetic illness. Nobody would suffer the fury of their father's fist because he couldn't comprehend his own actions anymore. Nobody would have to wait to see if their own child would develop the crippling illness that cursed through their family like a malevolent fault line. All of his years of hard work, and all of the hours of effort had finally been rewarded.

He closed his eyes and let his mind travel to Dubai, where Ami reclined on a sun lounger next to his own with a bottle of sun lotion ready in her hand. His dream was interrupted by the vibration of his telephone, and he fished it out from his inside pocket. It was a picture message from Mark of a woman wearing a tight pencil skirt that he assumed based on the perfectly formed shape of the enclosed rear-end must belong to Ami. The caption read, *early night?* Ben's finger lingered over the delete button for a while and after wrestling with his conscience and telling it no, decided to leave the message, and placed his telephone back in his pocket. Five minutes later he took it back out and took another look before pressing delete. It was definitely Ami, and he wondered how such a small thing as a message combined with a lot of imagination could place a blot on an otherwise perfect day.

THREE

BY THE TIME BEN WAS walking up his front steps the sky had cleared, and the streaks of cloud had passed to reveal a blanket of twinkling stars. He was already regretting deleting the photograph, and wished that he'd had the clarity of mind to at least email it to himself for another look tomorrow.

After the train ride he had a ten minute walk home and it had worked wonders for the heavy eyes and swirling head. On the train, his eyes had felt like they were moving independently from his head, swirling around in their sockets like a psychedelic kaleidoscope and as heavy as lead balls. Manoeuvring across the last steps to his house, he inserted the key into the lock on the third attempt. He pushed open the thick wooden door and slipped into the hallway. He pushed the door closed, shutting out the night behind him.

The hallway was dark, and he could only just make out the stairs. The only light was a strip of flickering illumination that snuck out from underneath the door to the living room, and was accompanied by the laughter of whatever television programme Hannah was watching. He pulled the cord of the lamp that sat on the hallway table and the bulb shone softly to light the hallway, the glare still managing to startle his eyes. Before him, above the ornate polished wooden handrails of the old banister the wall was lined with certificates. Over twenty framed papers that documented his rise from top of his class university student researcher of the year. Then his latest accreditation from the Genetics Society of Great Britain. In his own world, he was quite the celebrity. He put his keys into a small china dish which sat atop the table, and dropped his jacket onto the wooden ball of the banister. He set his right foot on the first stair, planning to head straight up to watch Matthew sleeping. Before he took another step, the door in the hallway opened. The light from the lounge poured through, and Hannah was standing on the other side of it.

"Were you not even going to say hello?" The stern and empty look on her face communicated her displeasure at finding her husband creeping up the stairs before even speaking to her. "I heard you come in." This neither surprised nor concerned him, for in his less than lucid state, he had never once trusted that he held the ability to creep anywhere.

"I did it, Hannah," he said, ignoring her question. He turned to face her, cupped her cheeks in the palms of his hands. He hoped the significance of the day would be enough to stifle any argument that might be heading his way. "I made it work." For a moment she looked alarmed, surprised even. Her eyes darted around looking at nothing in particular until they eventually found his gaze. "NEMREC works." She reached up with both hands and took his wrists, pulling them down from her face, and rested them together just beneath her chest. She looked away for only seconds, but as he stood watching her reflect on what he had just told her, it seemed like almost their whole lifetime passed before them. He knew that his work was destroying their relationship. He knew only a fragment of the closeness that they once shared remained. He knew from her breathing that when she closed her eyes in bed at night she wasn't really asleep when he spoke to her. He knew she was just pretending, choosing not to answer. He did love her, and he wanted their relationship to survive, but the structured and dedicated functioning of his brain could not be altered to suit his personal life. He knew they were hanging on by a thread.

"I'm proud of you. Well done," she said quietly. It was a simple response, and as she was saying it she was already walking towards the back of the room and towards the kitchen. He heard her calling out to him, asking if he was hungry or not. In fact he was starving. He was sure that was why the whiskey had taken such a tight grip on him. He loosened his tie and pulled it out from underneath his collar as he followed her towards the kitchen, tossing it casually down onto the sofa. Unbuttoning his shirt he opened the fridge and pulled out a beer. He sat down at one of the stools that were tucked neatly under the island worktop. As Hannah placed a plate of food down near to him he pulled it closer with his fingertips. It was a plate of pasta in an unidentifiable sauce which was starting to dry at the edges. He opened the far drawer whilst balancing on his stool, placing more trust in his ability to counter balance with an outstretched foot than he should have afforded himself. He gripped onto the granite work bench to stop himself from toppling down as he felt the legs of the stool wobble. As he righted himself, he used the fork that he had risked a fall for to mix the pasta together, and took a mouthful. It tasted good, although too creamy for his already curdled stomach. From the other side of the kitchen he could hear her telephone beginning to ring. Hannah was standing in front of him propping herself up on her elbows with her hands underneath her chin watching him as he ate the first mouthfuls of pasta. She didn't seem to hear the telephone, and remained in position. The fondness on her face, evident in her simple and effortless smile and the tissue-paper wrinkles underneath her eyes which did nothing to dilute her beauty, made him feel guilty for considering the photograph for a second time. Even more so for wishing he had emailed it to himself.

I'm no better than Mark, he thought.

"Are you not going to answer that?" he suggested, finding the call a welcome diversion from his own thoughts. She turned to look at the telephone, her previous gentle expression now wiped to reveal a blank, and if he was honest with himself, nervous appearance. She turned back to him, her face unchanged. "Shall I get it?" he asked. He began to stand up, and he wiped the corner of his mouth on a napkin which he had also pulled from the drawer. As he did so she too stood upright and smiled at him, resting her hands on his, encouraging him to sit back down.

"No, I've got it." She walked over and picked up the telephone. "Yes?" She listened for a while, and Ben took a large swig on his beer. Eventually she spoke. "Sorry, you have the wrong number." Setting her telephone back down she returned to face him and picked up his beer. "You know, tonight is not a night for beer. We are celebrating, right?"

"I believe we are," he said, smiling through a mouthful of pasta. She took his beer and poured it into the sink. She opened the cupboard from beneath the island at which he sat and took out two glasses and a bottle of expensive looking champagne. In truth he had already drunk just about all the champagne that he could handle for tonight. But such a truth could easily shatter this fragile and unexpected ceasefire.

You don't give a fucking shit about me, you motherfucker! Or our son! I'm trying my best to keep us together and you couldn't give a shit!

He could hear the argument already, a replay of yesterday's, or the day before, or the day before that. He would drink the champagne whether he wanted it or not. "Wrong number?"

"Yeah, looking for a *Sally* somebody," she said, waving her hand to bat the idea away. "I got this a while back, when you thought you were close," she smiled. "I put it here ready for when you succeeded."

"I didn't even know we had a cupboard down there." He leant over to see the hidden cupboard but as he did so she popped the cork on the bottle, interrupting him, and he sat back into his stool. She handed him a glass and they drank together, toasting the success that had ripped a ragged line through their family, which had divided their time and rendered their relationship incomplete. Hannah always described the best relationship that Ben had as the one with his work. She told him at least weekly that he was never really happy unless he was in the lab, working every free hour that came his way. When he was at home she said, he was just killing time until the moment came that he could legitimately and without argument return. He resented it and he had argued his case, but he also knew that somewhere in amongst her words lay the truth.

They sat watching the end of the show that Hannah had been watching when he arrived, slumped together in front of the television in silence. Ben had chugged back his champagne within moments of Hannah setting down the glass, surprising even himself. Yet he could see hers was almost full and still on the table at her side. He offset the banality of the show by trying to recall exactly how many drinks he had enjoyed, and by calculating how many units they equated to. His eyes were open, but his vision was as blurred as his concentration. He felt the whirling of his stomach, the contents swirling around like water being sucked through a drain. He could feel his head dropping to the side, and he had slumped right down in the settee. Sensing Hannah was watching him he was trying desperately hard to stay awake.

How many whiskeys had he had? Two? Four? That's either two point eight, or five point six units, right?

He could hear the generic canned laughter coming from the television, but he couldn't hear the words properly anymore. He didn't understand the jokes. The sound of static was playing out in his head.

Is that rain?

As his head rolled first backwards and then forwards, he was certain that he could see Hannah's face in front of his. She was peering at him, and as incoherent as he felt his thought process to be, he was certain that his sleepiness would be the last piece of the jigsaw to finally get him in trouble.

"I'm, I'm awake," he heard himself saying unconvincingly.

"Yeah, sure you are. Let's get you to bed." He felt her lift up his arm and slide her own underneath his, around his shoulders. He knew by now that he was on his feet, perhaps after a small stumble, but he could barely feel them underneath him. As he bumped his way past the hanging certificates, sensing his feet clattering haphazardly against the steps, he was certain he heard one of the frames crash to the ground.

"Did I do that? Is it broken?"

"It doesn't matter." The warmth of the soft quilt underneath him felt good as she dropped him on the bed. He opened his eyes just in time to see Hannah, propping herself up with both hands splayed out above him as she sat on the edge of the bed. He reached a hand up and cupped her face as he had when he first came home earlier that evening. He was sure that he could feel her hand on top of his. It was warm and soft, and it felt comforting to have her next to him.

"I'm sorry Hannah." He was mumbling and his words were blurring together in a long string of unidentifiable sounds. Even under the cloud of intoxication he was aware that the succession of rank smelling and poorly executed apologies were not winning him any favours, but yet the drunken will of his subconscious overwhelmed his ability to control himself, and he continued to ramble.

"I had to do it. What if Matthew gets it?" His breathing was laboured and he was starting to huff and puff as the chemicals in his body made him feel sick all over again.

"It's alright. You don't have to explain." He felt her hand rubbing against his own. "I understand."

"You don't. You didn't see it. I can't bear to watch that all over again as an old man." His words cracked into tears, and he brought his left hand across his face and tried to wipe away the drops that were trickling across his cheeks. His movements had become uncoordinated and his hand butted up against his eyes. After more deep laboured breaths, he felt his hand drop away from Hannah's face and fall loosely over the side of the bed. In a matter of moments he fell into the deepest of sleeps.

FOUR

BEN WAS DREAMING. HE WAS dreaming about gobstoppers. He kept eating them, shovelling the first into his mouth, closely followed by the second, and then the third, until eventually there was no room left for any more. He could feel his jaw stretching and aching under the strain of the bulbous chewy mass filling his mouth, saliva running out in sticky streaks from the corners. He tried to spit them out, only to find that they were stuck, the edges softened into his teeth, too pliable to lever out with his tongue. In his dream he started to panic, frantically tearing away at the sugary flesh of the slimy gobstoppers, trying to pick it out from his mouth piece by piece. He couldn't breathe and his situation was becoming more and more desperate and he was pulling and pulling and coughing and coughing, and then he was gagging and before he knew it he was choking and.....

He woke in a start, the soft goose down pillow stuffed inside his mouth. He had no explanation if his dream triggered the insertion of the pillow, or if indeed the dream itself was a sensory indicator to wake up and remove the respiratory impediment. His throat felt drier than it ever had as he rolled onto his back, kicking his legs out from the duvet. His head was throbbing as if it had been gripped in a metallic vice since the moment he had fallen asleep, and his mouth was as grainy as sandpaper. The light streamed in through the open curtains, and like a vampire in danger of self combustion he closed his eyes and covered his body protectively with the blanket, letting in snippets of light in the proceeding moments to allow his eyes to adjust.

"Some celebration," he whispered into the pillow. He sat forward a little and rolled himself towards the edge of the bed in a desperate hunt for water, his head as heavy as a cannonball. As he peered over the edge of the bed he saw a puddle of yellow looking fluid that looked suspiciously like vomit. He leaned in closer and his suspicions were confirmed by the cheesy smell. "Shit." He had no recollection of throwing up, but he knew that there was no way that Hannah wouldn't have seen it. Or smelt it. Either way she had chosen to leave it there, which meant that he was in trouble. He reached towards the bedside table, where there was always a carafe of water with a matching glass beaker. He took the beaker from the top, took hold of the carafe, and drank down the water. He had never felt such a thirst and no matter how much he drank, it didn't seem to satisfy his need. It was only then that he saw the red LED lights blinking back at him. Ten thirty. He was late.

Avoiding the puke puddle, he skirted up from the top of the bed and headed into the bathroom. Even the soft pile of the carpet seemed to grate against his skin like wire wool, such was the enormity of his hangover. Every footstep resonated through his body, striking his head as if it were the bell atop a tower. Underneath his eyes were two heavier than normal looking bags, puffed up and dehydrated all at the same time. He stood under the running water of the overhead rain shower, his face angled upwards and mouth wide open. He turned the water to cold, and as intolerable as the needle-like droplets felt on his tormented skin, a masochistic sense of relief ensued. He considered Hannah, who would by this time have already left for the day. Today she hadn't even bothered to wake him. No nudge, no coffee, no good morning. She had just left him where he was. Next to the vomit. As he dressed in his customary crisp white shirt and slim black tie, he looked back at the bed. Perhaps she had tried to wake him? On second thoughts, it didn't even look like her half had been slept in.

As he approached the top of the stairs he could see the broken picture frames, shattered fragments of chipped wood and smashed glass scattered about the steps. He remembered knocking them off the night before. Hannah hadn't even bothered to clean them up. He dodged past them, avoiding anything that twinkled as the light brushed over it, and headed into the kitchen. His congealed pasta dinner was still sitting there from the night before, and was starting to smell pretty ripe. He picked it up and tried to slide the leftovers into the bin, but it had congealed to the plate. It reminded him of a stylised version of Caesar's golden laurel headpiece.

"Screw it," he said to himself as he dropped the whole plate into the bin. He ripped off a few tissues from the wall mounted roll and placed them on top of the plate, concealing the evidence. The same odour that was emanating from the puddle at the side of his bed drifted from the bin, confirming his suspicions that the puddle on the floor came from him. He slammed the lid shut. He dropped a pod of coffee into the coffee machine and placed a small cup under the spout. Picking up the broom from the cupboard he approached the hallway in order to clear up the mess on the stairs whilst he waited. He swept the broken pieces into a pile, and retrieved his fallen certificates. One of them was from the Board of the Genetic Research Society. They had nominated him as an honorary member several years back, and it had been a particularly spectacular occasion. He had been invited to the head offices across the city. They were situated in a remarkably leafy part of the city centre and the building was a grand and ostentatious affair. There had been a presentation and champagne reception, but even the thought of alcohol now was enough to make him shudder.

He had been awarded a certificate and glass plaque for his research into the development of synthetic genes. He had accepted the praise gladly, and never once felt embarrassed by the constant stream of admiration and acclaim. In comparison to NEMREC, his previous findings were mediocre. But it was this very night when he had first been approached by Bionics, the owners of his current laboratory. This was the night that gave him the opportunity to change the world.

Smelling that his coffee was ready, he headed back into the kitchen, tucking his certificates under the small china dish on the hallway table on his way. Taking the freshly brewed espresso from the machine, he splashed in a few drops of cold water and knocked it straight back. It was good, and it was extra strong. God knows he needed it this morning. He was already going to be over three hours later than he should be.

The air was chilly outside despite the sun, and it bit at his nose and his cheeks as his breath formed vapour clouds in the air. He could feel the blood being pinched out of his face with each step he took into the oncoming wind. His head was thumping, and the current constriction of the small blood vessels on account of the chill in the air was doing little to help. It was only now, as his stomach gnarled away at him that he realised that he hadn't eaten anything. He remembered the small bakery that sold pastries inside the underground station. You could always smell it from outside as the wind from the passing trains whistled up through the corridors, picking up the aroma and enticing in the passersby. He would eat there.

It was late morning by now, and there was no queue for the entrance gate at the station. He took his identity card out from his inside pocket and savoured the smell of fresh pastry. He held out the card in front of the small scanning screen. Ben almost walked into the automatic door as it failed to open, his own automaticity too quick to spot the failure. The momentary confusion cleared and he stepped back to look at the screen. Instead of the usual green light and green letters greeting him with *Good morning Mr. Stone*, there was a simple grey X. He had never seen such a response displayed.

Only once before had his card not granted him access. On that occasion the green light had been replaced by a red stop sign and a courteous *Please attend the Central Government Office Mr. Stone*. That time, his pay check hadn't cleared after a breakdown with a particular server. There had been chaos that morning and there had been over one hundred people in line, all waiting for the same thing. It had been the governments fault, but there had been no apology. Ben had read an article in the national newspaper the very next morning about the success of the new identity card system and the ease at which people were now able to streamline their lives. One card for everything: it was your identity, your money, your underground access, your entrance ticket, your exit ticket. It was everything you were, loaded onto a piece of plastic. It stored biological data, a finger print, and retinal recognition data. You didn't get anywhere without it.

He swiped his card again in front of the screen and the same grey X appeared, but this time he noticed that underneath it in the place of the usual generic greeting another word was displayed:

Unregistered.

"What?" he said to himself. He swiped the card twice more, and each time he saw the same bewildering response. There was another gate to the left, and he walked over and held his card out in front of the screen, concealing it from the view of the people behind him. Same thing. He looked up to see a security guard standing in the main doorway, his interest pricked by the well-dressed individual struggling to get through the entrance gates. Ben was drawing attention to himself. He stood back, and let the woman who was waiting behind him pass. He thought about trying to sneak through behind her as the gate opened, but if he got too close to her and she caused a scene, that would be game over. The security guard would have him on the floor in seconds and that would be his day done. He would be hauled down to the Central Government Offices, and that was if he was lucky. If not, he'd get thrown in the cells of the central jail where all crime was dealt with now. There was no local police station anymore, and identity card crime was taken very seriously. Not dealing with an identity card fault could be enough to land you with a fine and a month in prison. They didn't rush to get you processed. It was no issue for them to let you languish in there for a month or so whilst you waited in turn amongst the real criminals.

Snatching at an idea, Ben took out his telephone and pretended to answer a call. He spoke in his loudest, most obnoxious voice, a tone which said *whatever I have to say is more important than what you have to say.* He made sure that everybody around him, including the security guard, heard him.

"Yes, I told you already that I would be there in court for midday. I am your lawyer and I will be there." Ben looked up and could see that the security guard had registered the telephone call. It was a good enough excuse not to carry on into the underground station where there would be questionable signal and a high chance of dropping the obviously important call. "I only stopped to answer your call." Ben looked up briefly, and spotting that the security guard was turning away from him he took his chance. This was one of the few stations where the security entrance gates still had low level walls either side of them. They hadn't been raised because Whitegate was considered a very desirable area in which to live. It was believed that high walls in such a station would have made the local passengers feel discriminated against, targeted.

As soon as the guards eyes had spun around Ben placed both hands onto the wall, and with as much force as he could, propelled his body weight over the wall in one giant hurdle. Arriving on the other side he scurried away, turning back only once to check whether the guard had noticed him. If he had, or if somebody else pointed out his misdemeanour he would know about it in seconds. If it had been two or three hours earlier the guard would have been standing closer to the doors, controlling the crowd where necessary, rendering Ben's top-of-the-head-plan useless. But the guard's attention was focussed towards the outside of the building, distracted by a fortunate altercation, and Ben was within minutes of boarding his train.

The lusty smell of pastry was ever present in the station. He rummaged in his pocket as he passed, and could feel a few stray coins. He thought about stopping, but he wanted to get on the train and get away as fast as he could. It would take only one person to mention that they had seen him skip over the wall. People who had problems with their identity cards made people nervous. It was the same for people who paid with money, if a shop would still permit it. If you weren't using your identity card there was a reason, and that reason usually meant trouble.

Ben could hear the train approaching and he could feel the gust of cold air as it filtered up through the tunnels. He quickened his pace, his footsteps resonating on the ground like a ticking clock counting down the last seconds before his escape. He risked a glance over his shoulder every now and again to ensure that he wasn't being followed. Ducking his head as he boarded the platform, he jumped straight onto the waiting train and sat down in a quiet corner.

What was wrong with his card? What the hell did unregistered mean?

As the train pulled out of the station he looked back at the platform to see nothing but silence. Nobody had followed him. Nobody had reported him. Nobody had seen his illegal jump, or, they had chosen to ignore it.

He slouched down in his seat, half trying to hide from the other people that were travelling in the same carriage, and half to continue his efforts to soothe his throbbing head. His brain felt like it had been on fire, charred and brittle, rubbing angrily against his skull. His stomach too felt like it had been pulled inside out. He was gripped in a hunger and thirst that he had never experienced before, and he needed something to counteract it fast. He was at least a twenty minute ride from the office. The effects of the earlier coffee hit had worn off, and he could feel the sensation of tiredness starting to wash over him again. He wanted desperately to close his eyes and take advantage of the next twenty minutes, but it was a stupid idea and he had to fight it.

When he had hopped over the wall he hadn't much contemplated what he was going to do at the other end of the line. You needed an identity card to get out of the station as well. There was no chance of hopping over the wall at a quiet moment at his next stop. That was *Central City*. There would be security guards on the gates, and the walls were high. The only way out of the station was through the gates, and the only way out through the gates was with an identity card. He had imprisoned himself on the train.

Ben looked around at the people in his carriage: an old lady carrying too much shopping, and one other guy like him, dressed smartly, carrying a briefcase. It was too quiet in this carriage. He stood up and moved through to the next, where he found a woman with a child and a young girl of no more than twelve years old wearing plaits and a pinafore dress. Ben moved methodically through the carriages until he found what he was looking for. The difficult element of his search was that he didn't know exactly what it was that he was searching for. Yet as he stumbled into the fourth carriage, busy and crowded, he saw it. A teenager, no more than eighteen. Alone. He was wearing headphones like the kid from the night before and remained oblivious to what was happening around him. He sat listening to his music, bopping and nodding his head in time with the electric beat. To Ben he looked like he might be a trouble maker. *Yes, got to be. Might even be in a gang,* he reasoned. He had him down as the type of teenager who would help a fallen pensioner only to snatch their purse. *Little bastard,* he said to himself, as if his thoughts had become reality. They passed *Western Two,* and then *Western One.* They rode through *Central Four, Three,* and *Two.* The boy with the headphones was still sitting there. He was young but he was big. This was important. Ben's plan was useless if he was just another kid. The train pulled up into *Central One.* Ben waited. The kid looked up at the screen. He stood up. If he got off the plan was ruined.

What should I do? Get off with him here? Walk the rest of the way?

Ben knew that his plan was only going to work in a busy station, and nobody used *Central One.* It was so close to *Central City* that everybody waited and got off there. He braced himself, ready to follow if he stepped off at the last minute.

Does he realise I have been watching him? Is he trying to lose me?

Just as the kid looked like he was going to disembark, the bell sounded and the doors closed in front of him. Ben eased back in his chair. His plan was still on.

Ben stood up as the train pulled into *Central City* station. The alarm sounded and the doors opened automatically. The kid slouched his way to the exit. There was a crowd; at least thirty people all getting off at the same time. Ben followed the kid, keeping back a few paces but staying close enough not to lose him as they negotiated the narrow corridors and neon theatrical advertisements. He could see the exit gates coming into view and there was already a small queue forming. Central City station was always mayhem, and if ever there was a problem it was dealt with. Quickly. With that many people coming through the gates decisions were made fast, and action was swift. Ben was counting on that today.

The kid was just in front of him, with only a few people between. They were about fifty meters or so away from the gate. It had to be perfectly timed so that any other variables were rendered void. As the crowd of people approached the gate, Ben darted his way through, stepping in front of other suited men and perfectly made up women.

Thirty meters to the gate.

Two people to pass. He darted in front of a particularly burly man, only just missing treading on his foot.

Fifteen meters.

A head of blond hair skipped along in front of Ben, her walk zigzagging in front of him, making it harder to get in front of her.

Ten meters.

He made one last push, almost knocking her down as his arms brushed past hers and suddenly the kid was in front of him, his hunched shoulders and headphone-covered ears oblivious to Ben's presence. One last move. Just before the gate Ben pushed past him and got in front, ensuring that as he filtered into the single file queue, the kid was behind him.

There were two people in front of Ben. A woman and a man. They didn't look like they were together. The woman scanned her identity card and Ben saw the flash of green light. The man in front was reaching inside his pocket and pulling out his identity card too. He held it towards the screen and Ben waited for the second flash of green.

Carpe diem, motherfucker.

Ben shoved the man in front of him with all of his force, sending them both flying forward and through the gateway. They landed on the floor, Ben directly on top of the man in front of him.

"What the!" the man yelled as he hit the floor.

"I know!" Ben bellowed, feigning disbelief and immediately pointing at the kid behind him. The security guards were at their side already. Ben was quick on his feet and already helping up the other man. "What the hell did you do that for?" Ben shouted back at the unsuspecting kid. All eyes were on the youth, who was thanks to his headphones, still unaware of what was happening and of the mounting guilt heaped at his feet. The man who Ben had landed on was still straightening out his suit and tie. He hadn't seen anything of what had happened but his instincts told him that the unfortunate and well dressed fellow who had landed on top of him couldn't possibly be to blame. Not with a suit that looked that expensive. The security guards were also staring at the kid, making the very same assumptions.

"What? What did I do?" the kid asked, pulling his headphones from his ears, realising that he was at the centre of the commotion. Ben had relied upon the fact that nobody behind them would have been able to see clearly enough to counter argue his claim.

"You pushed me right through there," Ben said as he pointed back at the plastic gate. Ben's other victim was angrily shaking his head, his cheeks blood-red, beetroot with rage, never once doubting Ben's story. "Right on top of this good man."

"Officers, did you not see what happened?" the burly chap asked as he inspected the knees of his trousers. Ben and his suited friend had formed an immediate alliance. The officers were standing either side of the plastic door, and the rest of the underground station remained perfectly quiet, save the shuffling of feet and the odd whisper, as it waited for the situation to resolve.

"Place your identity card against the screen now and walk slowly through this gate," the first officer ordered the kid.

"But I...."

"Do it!" The boy did so and walked through. The officers snatched his identity card from his shaky, sweat-drenched palm and held it against their card reader. This would tell them everything about him, and since the moment he hatched his plan Ben had been praying that they didn't do the same with his.

"Mr. James Priest. It seems that you have got quite the

record for causing trouble." Ben felt a twinge of guilt knot up inside of his stomach, temporarily rising over the hunger. His plan was working perfectly so far, but he hadn't counted on feeling so awful about it. He swallowed down hard and tried to suppress the guilt. The officers turned to Ben and the other suited man who had no idea what had really happened. "Thank you, gentlemen. You can be on your way." Behind him, Ben could already sense the other man leaving. He knew it would only arouse suspicion if he did not walk away with the same level of annoyance that he had so perfectly demonstrated as this situation began. Swiping a final, frustrated palm stroke down his sharp black suit he turned to walk away. He caught a final look at the eyes of the boy, whose age he had probably overestimated as he saw him now in daylight and without the hood or headphones. He felt the same guilt as only moments before rising up. The kid's venial face pleaded with him for help, for him to tell the truth, but instead Ben bowed his head and turned to walk away.

Ben walked towards the entrance and out into the daylight. He needed to breathe. He could hear the boy's feeble protest as he left the station, and it wrenched at his otherwise empty gut. He absolved his responsibility by reminding himself of the utmost importance of his work today, and the impact it would have for all mankind. He wondered if his thoughts were self indulgent, but concluded them to be reasonable in the grand scheme of things. One day he might get to save the kids life. That would make up for any trouble he caused him today.

The road was heaving with cars and buses and he couldn't see the entrance to the lab. He dodged the oncoming traffic as it glided past him, working his way across the road. It would take days of early summer sunshine to dry out the roads after last night's storm, and he skipped past the puddles, anxious not to ruin another pair of expensive leather-soled shoes.

Bionics Laboratories was on the first floor above another shop that sold sandwiches and salads. The first of the lunchtime traffic rush was already appearing, and there was a queue forming outside the shop door. Ben had eaten from here hundreds of times over the last four years. It was the best pastrami-mustard combo he had ever tasted. He didn't know if it was physical hunger putting thoughts in his brain, but he was certain that he could taste the peppered steak slices already.

He pushed the door that sat to the side of the sandwich shop, the entrance to the laboratory. He was expecting it to glide open as usual, but was surprised to meet resistance. He pushed the door harder, and put his weight behind it. Still nothing. He dug around in his pockets and found the set of keys that had both his home and office keys attached. He found the correct one and slid it into the lock. It was unusual for the door to be locked at this time, and on any other day it would have given him reasonable cause for anger that he couldn't get into his own laboratory with the ease he wanted. But he figured on a day when he was arriving four hours late, boss or not, any direction of his anger at those already at work would be unlikely to be well received. The door was heavy but he shoved it open with the weight of his body behind it. He took the steps one at a time, his head still pounding as he placed his feet, his eyes still dry and sleepy. He needed water, and coffee. Not necessarily in that order. Maybe Ami would offer to make it for him. That would make him feel better.

At the top of the stairs there was a small clearing that functioned as a staff room. There was a small fridge and a kettle, and a selection of chairs where people could sit to enjoy a caffeine enriched break. As he neared this clearing he paused, suspended in the void somewhere between expectation and reality. He stopped to take a longer look, thinking that his cloudy mind was trying to play a trick on him, like the satisfying delusion of a mirage in a desert of emptiness and dehydration. Only this mirage was the opposite.

In place of the chairs he saw nothing but floor space. In the corner where normally stood a fridge he saw a bare wall with a lighter imprint of clean, ice blue paint where the fridge had once been. There was no kettle. There was no.....anything. The room was empty.

Gone was the life that had been here for the past four years and instead in its place was a vacuum of empty space. He walked up the last few steps, his eyes wide and fixed in disbelief. He stood transfixed for a moment unable to comprehend the change in environment. He hesitated as he cleared the last couple of steps fearful of what he might see. He turned right to face the sliding door to the lab. Eyeing up the red button that would permit him entry, he gingerly pressed his finger against it. The door slid back as the pneumatics released a shot of air, and before him the extent of what he saw was almost impossible to register, so great was the horror of what lay before him.

Where there should be workbenches, there was dust. Where he expected to see laminar flow cabinets and hear the hum of the fluorescent lights there was empty space. There were no reagent-filled cupboards, no laboratory stools, and where he expected to see Ami, Alan, or Phil, there was simply nobody. He walked towards the back of the office, and pushed open the door. No files. No desk. No picture of his father. Nothing. He rubbed his hands across his face, his fingers probing at his heavy eyes like an udder, hoping to milk out the truth. He backed out of the room, his body turning in circles looking desperately for something solid to cling to. After a moment of bewilderment his body made contact with the nearest wall, and as his legs buckled beneath him, he slid down onto the floor, dropping the keys beside him.

When Ben was ten years old he got his first bike. It was June the second, nineteen eighty five. His birthday. He had woken up to the sound of his parents singing the happy birthday song as they danced along the crazy psychedelic swirls of the carpet of his bedroom, a remnant from the previous decade. They whisked him downstairs for a special pancake breakfast with extra sugar. It was a Wednesday, and he had been allowed an indulgent day of truancy from school. He played with the new Pac Man game for two hours solid, riding the sugar induced high until the shop installed batteries gave up. The disappointment was short lived as his father distracted him by wrapping a blindfold around his eyes, and led him outside. Without the benefit of sight, he held his parents hands as they guided him out towards the front garden. He could smell the overpowering bouquet of summer flowers filling the air, and the Honeysuckle that grew in an arch over the front door. He placed his feet carefully, treading with caution as he felt the movement of loose tarmac pebbles under his feet. They peeled back the blindfold and he saw the most wonderful red Spitfire bicycle, ribbons dangling from its curved handlebars. There were no words exchanged in that moment, and anything that his parents said to mark the occasion was lost in the haze of excitement. Ben walked towards the bicycle and sat down on the saddle, wrapping his hands around the hard rubber handles, getting a feel for them. They were perfect. He had learnt how to ride on his cousin's bike, and he knew that he would know how. With only the briefest of wobbles he was through the gate, making headway towards the centre of the village. At that point in his life, he had never been happier.

That night he returned home after covering more than ten miles of pavement and the odd field crossing, bruises on his behind and red chaffed palms. He sat in the bath with his father at his side listening as he told him what a wonderful day he had spent, and how not one of his fellow classmates had a bicycle as wonderful as his. But then Ben smelt the bleach, and his eyes began to sting. His screams brought his mother running into the bathroom to find his skin reddened and hair lightened from the bleach that his father had carelessly used to wash his hair. It was Ben's first memory of his father's demise. It was the first step in Ben's journey to the empty floor where he sat today, where only last night he had celebrated NEMREC's success.

Ben reached into his inside jacket pocket and pulled out the contents: the seemingly useless identity card, a few coins that would just about make up enough to buy one of those pastrami sandwiches, and his telephone. He scrolled through the menu to find Hannah's name. He hit the button with the green telephone symbol and waited, staring absently into the space before him. No answer. He dropped the telephone carelessly onto the floor, and threw his head backwards against the wall.

"I can't believe it," he whispered to himself airily. He racked his brain, trying to recall every face that had passed through the lab in the last few months. He knew who was responsible for this, but he couldn't understand their idiocy. "Another day! Another day and I would have called you!" He had two weeks of funding left, and had planned at the end of today to report to Bionics and tell them that it had worked. Instead, they hadn't waited and had simply closed him down.

Have they bought out the staff? Did they lose confidence in me? Has the whole thing been shut down and relocated without me?

Thoughts of them relocating the lab overnight were virtually impossible to comprehend, and too painful to consider.

One of my team been some sort of an informant? They knew we had done it? They cut the funding the.....wait, Saad. He wanted this work. Could he have stolen it? Overnight?

"In less than twelve hours?" he finally said out loud. Endless possibilities raced through his mind, and yet nothing quite seemed possible. How could a whole laboratory just disappear overnight? He was jerked back into reality by the sound of his telephone buzzing against the floor in a tune far too cheerful for his mood.

"Hello, Hannah?"

"No, it's me. What's up?"

"What?" He took the telephone away from his ear and glanced at the screen. "Mark," he said as he held the phone back up to speak. "I've got a problem."

"What's going on?" Ben explained how somebody had broken into the laboratory and stolen the equipment. Or how they had been shut down. Or how an insider had stolen the data. He explained how everything was gone and that he had no idea why. How a lifetime of research and personal aspirations had disappeared overnight. "I don't believe it, Ben. Listen, I'm coming over. Just stay there. Don't go anywhere, OK. I'll be there soon." With that, Mark hung up and Ben waited.

He had to eat something. He was beginning to feel queasy from the emptiness of his stomach, and he could feel it turning and pulling at his insides. He caught sight of the coins that sat on the floor to the side of him. Totalling them up they seemed to amount to about six pounds, and that would be enough to get him one of his beloved pastrami sandwiches. Mark wouldn't be here for another fifteen minutes. He grabbed the keys and fiddled up the coins. He left the telephone and the identity card where they were and headed down the stairs. The sunlight was streaming in through the windows as he approached the door, and he thought how unusual it seemed that there were no buses passing by to cast the door in shadow. He pushed the handle of the door down and after releasing the heavy door sufficiently, he started to move his body into the open space.

At first, the high pitched ping confused him, as did the small cloud of dust that swirled to the side of his face. He couldn't quite make out what had just happened. It took only a second to glance down, his eyes following the responsible object. He watched as the deformed slug of a spent bullet hit the ground and rolled away from him. Then a second hit the door. It flew past his head at a proximity that seemed like only millimetres away. It too hit the door leaving behind the same trail of dust and pain in his ears. He scrambled back inside, taking cover behind the door. He forced it shut, dropping the money that he had been clutching in his hand. Ben was stupefied and still, and watched as the third bullet hit the pane of glass. He jumped back in fright, falling and hitting his back against the tread of the first step. His first thought was that he was thankful not to be dead. The second was considerably more confusing.

Why had the glass not broken?

He stood up as two more bullets hit the glass at the level of his eyes. Both left nothing but a small cloud of dust and a crater in the glass as they ricocheted from the door, landing on the pavement.

"Bullet proof?" he asked rhetorically as he stroked his fingers against the pane of glass. Not a single palpable mark was present on the inside. "Why the fuck is that bullet proof?" The confusion of his survival had for a few seconds shielded him from the realisation that somebody had just made an attempt on his life. When the next bullet hit the glass panel it woke him from his daydream. He could hear screams coming from outside, as the crowd fluttered around like the feathers of a terrified bird, and he knew that there was no way out through these doors. He back-heeled his way up the stairs, climbing frantically on all fours, dragging himself to the top. Stopping briefly to catch his breath, he scrambled to his feet and raced into the empty laboratory.

"What the fuck is going on?" he screamed through panicked and desperate breaths, the room spinning around him. His mind switched to survival mode, and his eyes scanned the room for another exit. The only way out that didn't involve going down the stairs was through the windows. Then he heard somebody at the door downstairs. There was no time for consideration. Waiting here was certain to bring only one thing and he didn't want to think about that. His only choice was the window.

He opened the latch and slid back the mirrored glass and dust blew up from inside the frame. He wasn't even sure he had ever looked out here before, or if this window had been opened in the last four years. He moved his head and shoulders forwards to peer outside and he could feel the wind whipping past. The odour of food from the sandwich shop teased him from below, carried forth by the heat of a whirring extractor fan. He pulled his head back inside for a hesitative moment, but then he heard the door being shoved back and forth from the outside just meters away from him and it reminded him he had no choice. It had to be done.

He ran across the floor and snatched up his telephone and identity card and without a second thought he hauled his body up and over the window frame. He balanced his feet down onto the small ledge that was beneath him and slid the open window back into a closed position. His jacket billowed behind him, and the oncoming winds pushed him closer into the wall. He shimmied his feet along the ledge and gripped the wall to stop himself shaking, and by wrapping his body around the vertical columns he made progress along the ridge. He couldn't see through the mirrored glass properly, but could almost convince himself that he could see movement in his old laboratory. If he could see through, then maybe there was a chance that whoever was inside could see out. But there wasn't time to waste hanging around making assumptions and predictions. He had to find a way off this ledge fast.

As he approached the corner of the building he could see another building attached. The mood of the wind was as fickle as it was strong and as it blew around the corner he had to fight with all his strength to hang on. The attached building had a flat roof and he could almost taste its safety. It looked a damn sight safer than where he was currently. As he manoeuvred his body around the corner of the building he screamed as he felt the sharpest of pains searing through him, hot and acidic. He looked down at his right shoulder and he could see that there was a bloody looking opening in the top of his arm. It looked more like a graze than a hole, but nevertheless he shuffled around the corner and into the protection of the building. His arm hurt worse than when he had been shot in the foot by a stray arrow at outward bound camp during an archery session. It hurt all the more for knowing that he was balanced on the ledge of a first floor office building with somebody chasing him with a gun for reasons of which he had no idea.

Ben leapt towards the roof of the next building which was located only a foot or so below him. He landed on his right hip with a thump onto the roof. He sat round onto his backside, comforted in the embrace of a temporary reprieve, and he pressed his palm against the shoulder wound whilst hissing in a sharp breath through gritted teeth. He had only moments, and the previous sense of tiredness and lethargy that he felt had been ripped apart by the adrenaline that was pumping through his veins courtesy of his galloping heart. He heard nothing of the wind as it blew past the edge of the building, or the rapid chirrups of the city birds circling overhead. He was wired.

Where now?

He fled across the roof, no idea whether the gun toting maniac was following him or not. He moved at a good clip, past air conditioning pipes and vents. He bounded towards the edge of the roof and leapt forwards without thinking, jumping to clear the small space that separated the current building from the next. He landed on the next roof, never once considering the danger of a misplaced step or a misfortunate trip.

He found a door that would permit him entrance to the building below. It was the last building in the row. There was nowhere else to run. He tried the handle but found it to be locked. He wondered if his adrenaline levels had spiked sufficiently to break through the door, head-first like a raging bull, but assumed his conscious thought for the matter rendered it an unlikely possibility. Edging back around the corner of the wall, he could see the shooter, wearing nothing but black just climbing his way from the ledge onto the first flat roof.

"Fuck! Fuck!" Ben rolled his body back behind the security of the brick wall. He tried the handle, more desperately this time. The door moved ajar, and he could see that it was padlocked from the inside. He kicked it over and over, heaving his weight behind it and praying that the door would smash open. It budged, but stayed firm. He kicked the door one last time. It buckled under the pressure and the wooden door frame splintered away from the wall, leaving just enough space for him to slip through. He ducked inside, wedging the door back into place and crept down the first few stairs and into the shadow and safety of the building.

Through the small space that was left from the damage to the door he could see the black boots and trousers of the shooter stood just feet away. It sounded like the shooter tested the door, but there was no desperate pulling and smashing. No attempt to force it open. If there had have been it would surely have buckled inward like a flimsy garden gate. Instead Ben heard his voice. It was deep and gravelly, and belonged to nobody that he recognised. He spoke in a muffled tone, but Ben could hear his words. He was making a telephone call.

"Sir, he got away." Silence again. It seemed like an impossibly slow wait for him to speak again. "Certainly. We're moving into phase two? Yes Sir." And that was it. He saw the feet turn, walk purposefully away, the rooftop gravel crunching under his feet. For the first time in what felt like hours Ben breathed again, relishing the relief that he had achieved a stay of execution. But yet he couldn't understand it. There was nowhere for him to go. There was only one exit from that roof that didn't lead to the end of his life. Ben had been able to breach the door with only his foot, pushing his body weight against it. This guy had a gun. Ben knew this all too well. He could have shot through it in seconds, yet he had left him.

Why did he let me go?

Ben shuffled his left hand out through his jacket, then after peeling out his injured right arm, began to inspect the wound. His

crisp white shirt had a matching frayed hole at the level of his
shoulder, stained with the deep red of his blood which was seeping
down the fabric in irregularly scalloped waves. He clumsily
unbuttoned his shirt with his left hand to assess the damage
further. There was a cut, deep enough to cause a troubling amount
of bleeding. He loosened off his tie and wrapped it around the
wound, forming a makeshift bandage which he tightened with a
collaboration of his left hand and his teeth. He felt as if he was
currently somewhere between ridiculous and Rambo. He wiped his
bloody hands on the lining of his jacket and fixed his shirt the best
he could. Putting his jacket back on, he looked almost presentable.

He made his way through the dark and empty corridors
trying to recall what this building was. But he moved slowly, with a
new sense of caution that he had never felt before in his life.
Somebody wanted him dead. Right now everybody was a suspect.

FIVE

PASSING THROUGH THE STOCK ROOM was easier than he had anticipated. He had expected at least some resistance or confusion, but found none. The rooftop's lack of discernible architecture had disorientated him, and as he hid in the shadows staring at the boots of his would-be killer on the other side of a flimsy wooden door, he hadn't given any thought to what building he had concealed himself in. All he could think of was the proximity of his impending death and the wound that he had already sustained on his arm. As he inched his way through the stockroom containing rows of clothes and coats there had been a single thought running through his mind.

Why didn't the shooter break down the door and kill me?

He must have known where Ben was. There had been nowhere else for him to go. Yet the man who had chased him into the laboratory, shot at him, and risked his own life skirting around the edges of buildings simply gave up. And when he made that phone call there was a level of deference in that voice that made him nervous. He wasn't a random maniac that had mistakenly selected Ben. He was following orders.

Seeing that the stockroom was clear he tucked himself in a quiet corner and removed the sleeve of his jacket and shirt so that he could assess the wound on his arm further. The constant throbbing was driving him crazy. It was worse than the headache and the gnawing emptiness in his stomach combined, which he had at least for the time being forgotten.

The wound looked like it had been burnt around the edges and therefore conveniently cauterised. With closer inspection under the apparent safety and camouflage of the clothing store, he confirmed his earlier suspicion that it was indeed more like a graze . The bullet must have skimmed past him rather than travel through his arm. He thought of the times when he had sustained a paper cut, and how that always seemed to hurt more than any serious injury. Even when he had been accidentally shot in the foot as a child it didn't seem to hurt as much as this. He had after all been biologically anaesthetized at the time, high on endorphins surging through his brain as the adults had swarmed around him like bees to honey. Their buzz was electrifying. Some of them tried to comfort the crying children, others tried to establish how they would be able to get the arrow out of the ground and free Ben. Another teacher proceeded to stagger to the ground and throw up. Some of the vomit ricocheted back up and onto the legs of the surrounding children. He of all teachers had perhaps been the most successful in calming the otherwise agitated crowd, who after being vomited on by their teacher became much quieter, and much less interested in Ben.

The tight grip of his tie had stemmed the bleeding, and he adjusted it into a bandage style dressing, which even for a field soldier would have seemed makeshift and substandard. Ben rummaged through the rails, staying close to the ground in case his solitude was interrupted. He found a grey T-shirt and put it on, and then stuffed his old shirt behind one of the cabinets. There was also a selection of jackets and trousers. He reasoned that whoever it was that was trying to kill him seemed to be taking orders, and if there was some kind of order out for his death, it couldn't hurt to look different than when he came in. They were looking for a guy in a suit. With this in mind, he pulled off his trousers and found a casual looking pair of brown chinos and a blue jacket, the kind that you would throw on for a Saturday out in the park and that he would have undoubtedly worn himself this weekend. He ripped open the security stitching of his new pockets, the effort pulling at his wounded shoulder. He stuffed his identity card, keys, the few coins that he hadn't dropped, and his telephone inside. With anxiety-induced sweat pouring from every one of his pores, his hair flopped down onto his face and stuck to his forehead. He ran his hands through it in quick succession, trying to make himself look like he hadn't just been chased and shot at.

With his new casual attire, he broached his way towards the exit door. He tried the handle but it was locked. It didn't take long to find the exit button. It was the same type that he had in the lab. Virtually identical. It reminded him of all that he had just lost. All of his research, all of his effort, simply gone overnight. He searched for a way to comprehend how it could have been taken as it had, and who was responsible. He couldn't understand why Bionics would shut him down in this manner. As for his theory regarding Saad and his apparent appropriation of the data, it was difficult to make any definitive conclusions or convince himself that he was to blame. He had never even met the man, and had no logical reason to accuse him of the theft. Sure, he had a lot of money and that usually meant a lot of power, but how could he manage a theft on such a scale overnight? How *could anybody do this overnight?*

He felt the danger of his situation as he heard footsteps approaching and a voice on the other side of the exit door. Snatching his fingers from the button, he scanned around looking for somewhere to hide. A clothes rail lined one wall, but with a stroke of good fortune he realised that his legs would be visible from underneath, and that as a hiding place it was a poor choice. The nearest corner had several boxes stacked up on top of each other, and looked just about wide enough to crouch behind. He bolted for the boxes as he saw the red flashing button turn green.

A girl, no more than eighteen years old, walked through. As he peered out from the shadow of the boxes he could see that she was carrying about twenty coats under her arm, pulled directly from a rail, and still attached to the coat hangers. She was chewing gum, and her eyes were black under layers of heavy makeup. She paid him no attention, and the slow closing door gave him a chance to see out into the store. Immediately he recognised where he was. If he could get out of the doors unnoticed he could slip into the array of hanging rails that littered the shop floor.

The girl threw the coats onto a pile in the corner and sat down onto one of the unopened plastic boxes. She took a wad of gum from her mouth, pushing it underneath one of the finger grips of a close-by box. She pulled a chocolate bar from her pocket and peeled back the wrapper. The very sight of it was enough to reignite the agony of Ben's empty stomach and he felt it somersault, unleashing a gurgling cry. He gripped onto his stomach and clenched his muscles, hoping that she hadn't heard it.

The girl discarded the wrapper and stood up. Ben ducked as far into the wall of boxes as he could, concealing himself in the shadows, hoping that she would pass him by without detection. She headed for the clothes rail that sat against the opposite wall, and he praised his decision not to hide there. She selected a pair of dark trousers and used the inside edge of the cuff to wipe her hands, before pressing the red button to open the doors. This was his chance. He waited for her to pass through, and as soon as there were a few feet between them he slipped out behind her, light footed and surreptitious as a ghost. As he came out into the light she became acutely aware of his presence as he breezed past, and turned around to see him only feet behind her. She looked at him, her eyes scrunched up with confusion, her brow frowning and forming two deep vertical lines between her eyebrows. She glanced back at the doors to the store room to see them just closing. He had been quick to put distance between the store room and himself. He wanted to shake her suspicion, and he wanted to do it fast. He soon formed the opinion that the girl had an inappropriate level of self-interest considering the amount of time she must have spent applying the eye makeup. He shot her his best come-over-here-pretty-lady smile, the kind that forms only on the left side of his face and with a subtly raised eyebrow. He had perfected it whilst he was at university, and it had worked miracles. Today though, dressed in the cheap clothes that looked even worse in their starched just unfolded way, he looked like nothing but a forty year old man who was trying too hard. Her eye muscles contracted inwards, and her obvious distaste of the sight before her was clear to see, such was the antipathy of his advances. She began to walk away from him, all the while keeping a watchful eye that he didn't attempt to follow her. It had worked, and he knew that he should be grateful. But he also knew on some ludicrous and inexplicable level that he could not help but feel disappointed in his ability to repel a woman.

He slipped through the store without further hindrance and out into the street. He tucked his hands in his pockets and ducked his head down low as if bracing an oncoming wind. He wanted to look back towards his lab, but it was too risky. He had heard some sort of commotion as the bullets had hit the windows earlier, and wondered if a crowd had gathered, or if indeed the shooter was back out in the street initiating 'Phase Two', whatever that was. As he reached into his pocket and felt the plastic case of his telephone he suddenly remembered what he had arranged before the moment that somebody had attempted to extinguish his life. Mark. He was on his way to the lab. He had to warn him.

He ducked onto *Fifty First Street*, a quiet side street that ran away from the main *Central City station*. From here he could see back out onto the main *Fiftieth Street*, and it seemed to him that everything appeared to be carrying on as normal. There were mothers pushing pushchairs. Women carrying luxurious structured carrier bags which advertised their expensive tastes. There were men dressed like he was only half an hour ago in suits and ties, with hair slicked neatly into place. He scanned the crowd, not wanting Mark to be one of those guys approaching the lab. Who knew where the shooter had gone? He could be in the lab for all Ben knew waiting for anyone that turned up. He pulled out his telephone and scrolled through the list of recent calls until he saw Mark's name and then he hit the green call button. He heard it ring a couple of times, and then it sounded like it connected. He could hear some sort of static on the line and a click.

"Mark?" He spoke quietly, his finger held up to his ear to block out the humdrum of the background. He waited for an answer. He was sure that he could hear breathing. *Oh God!* He was too late. The panic rose in his throat.

Had they already got him? I have to go back.

Just as he was contemplating the first steps back towards the laboratory, he heard a voice speak on the other end.

"Yeah mate, what's up?"

"Listen, Mark. Don't go to the lab," he spluttered. "Don't whatever you do go to the lab." His words sounded as frantic as he felt.

"What's going on?" Mark still sounded calm. Alive. *Thank God.*

"Meet me at the café in the shopping mall. The one on the corner on the first floor."

"Ben, what's up? What's going on? Where are you?"

"I don't know what the hell is going on, but somebody just tried to kill me."

"What?" Mark shrieked.

"Listen, I have to go. Meet me there." With that Ben hung up, and stashed his telephone back in his pocket. He had backed into a disused door way, and wanted desperately to stay there, concealed and safe in this recess, obscured from view. He thought back to how secure the hideaway in the stock room had felt only minutes before, and wished now that he had just stayed there. He could have pretended that everything was okay and that there was nobody chasing him with a taste for his death. Every step that he took from this point on felt like it could be his last. He picked up his telephone again and dialled Hannah's number. He waited, but the call didn't connect. "Shit!" He had no choice but to press on.

Choice. He thought about that word for a moment. Did he really have no choice? If he could choose, what would he do now? If he hadn't just lost the last twenty years of a career overnight, if he hadn't just nearly been killed, if there wasn't an order to move into the unknown world of 'Phase Two', what was it that he would choose? Would he choose to go home and sit with his wife, pull up the covers on the bed like when they first met? Back then they would happily check out, let the world carry on without them. How long had that lasted, until he tired of her company and craved the sterile world of a laboratory? Would he choose Saturday afternoons in the park kicking a football? How long had it really been until he had sacrificed the first football session in place of an analysis run that just couldn't wait until Monday? How many times had he prioritised the lab and his research over anything else in his life? Mark had been right when he had questioned his happiness. His times at home felt like a countdown, a clock initiated when he put his key in the door, until the next time he could legitimately get out and back to his work life. All the time he had been focused on saving the future, he had forgotten what he had in the present.

He pushed himself out of the safety of his recess and took his first steps towards his next move. He didn't know if it was better to stay on the quiet streets, or head into the safety of the crowd. *Another choice.* The old adage 'safety in numbers' played out in his head, and he turned left into the main street and slipped the bustling crowd where he hoped that he would disappear. He thought how simple it was for these other people, going about their everyday lives without the knowledge of how easily it could all be snatched away. They were running backwards and forwards not paying any attention, living without thought in their carefree fantasies. To Ben, that's all they were now. Normal life seemed nothing more than a fantasy.

He walked the streets with his head down, glancing up every so often to see the direction in which he should walk. On one such occasion he noticed the magazine booth. It was one of the few places that you could still pay with cash, no questions asked. The newspapers were tucked into neat rows and secured underneath crisscrossing cords of elastic. When the weather was warm the ink would smudge off onto your fingers at the slightest touch, compliant under the strength of the sun, easily pushed out of place. Most people didn't bother with newspapers anymore, but there was something about this store that people clung to. There was a sense of nostalgia about it, and it reminded Ben of the past and childhood, and therefore of his father.

Every day the owner would stand a little A-frame notice board outside of his kiosk and write the main headline and the date on a sheet of cheap white paper. Today was no different. The little board was there. The headline informed him that interest rates would be falling in the next week. Ben had been waiting to reap the benefits of the reduction. But it wasn't this news story that grabbed his interest, pricking his attention with the same urgency as a pin to an inflated balloon. Interest rates have little to spike your curiosity when you have spent the last thirty minutes unsuccessfully dodging bullets. The details that interested him now were the day, and the date.

When he left Simpson's bar more than a little worse for wear, he had been more than certain that he was putting a wet and rainy Wednesday behind him. He had no doubt in his mind that when he returned home that night they had watched the soap opera that Hannah was obsessed with that is only shown on a Monday and a Wednesday night. Yet before him the news that was being advertised was for Friday. Friday the sixth of April. But what about Thursday?

"Hey, excuse me," Ben shouted up towards the news vender, temporarily forgetting his need for anonymity and his wish to keep a low profile. He looked at Ben as he picked at his fingernails, each finger poking through half gloves. He was scraping out traces of ink which had leeched onto his fingertips.

"Yeah?" he mumbled.

"Is this right? Are you sure you haven't made a mistake?" Ben pointed down at the board.

"What mistake?" he said, still only half paying attention.

"The date!" Ben could feel his voice becoming raised and frustrated. He consciously calmed himself down, pulling up the collar of his stolen jacket a little. "The day I mean. It's definitely Friday?"

"Well that's what these papers say." Ben looked down at the rows of newspapers tucked neatly inside their elasticated strings. He pulled at one, crimpling up the corner. He felt the familiar sensation of the cheap flimsy paper and the immediate residue of ink on his skin. He took no satisfaction in it today. He pulled out the paper and as it unfolded automatically before him he saw that sure enough the date was Friday, sixth of April. The vendor was already turning away, realising that Ben had no intention of buying anything. There was only one question on Ben's mind as he turned to walk away. It had nothing to do with interest rates or his uncertain future. Now he couldn't even be certain of the present. His question was simple.

What the hell had happened to Thursday?

SIX

THE REALIZATION THAT HE HAD slept for almost thirty six hours brought with it a whole new set of problems. The main one of which was his family. Realistically, he could accept that Hannah had left him in bed the first morning. She had probably woken up to the smell of fresh vomit, saw the pile of it on the carpet next to the bed. He could imagine her tiptoeing her way through his trail of drunken destruction on the stairway, privately and secretly savouring the fact that he would be late for his precious work. He could imagine her closing the door and smiling sweetly to herself at the prospect of his accidental placement of his feet into the expelled stomach contents as he swung them out of bed. If she had been feeling particularly malevolent she may even have enjoyed the idea of him accidentally stepping into the shards of glass on the stairs. The first morning was explicable in any way he chose to look at it. But later on that day when she had calmed down and succumbed to the inevitable guilt of her earlier thoughts, surely she would have questioned his whereabouts.

She would have found Ben still in bed that night. Would she not have attempted to wake him? Would she not be worried that he had slept for almost a day? Surely there wasn't a soul that could find sense in somebody sleeping for twenty four hours solid? Ben couldn't remember waking or stirring. He couldn't remember anything from that period of time. He could barely remember arriving home, if he thought about it. The only explanation for him remaining undisturbed in bed for that length of time was that Hannah hadn't been home.

If she hadn't been home, where the hell was she? Where the hell was Matthew?

Suddenly there was more at stake than a lifetime of research.

As he quickened his pace towards his meeting place with Mark he could feel the telephone buzzing in his pocket. He looked at the screen. It was Ami, his colleague from the laboratory and chosen subject for all manner of inappropriate thoughts.

"Ami?"

"Oh my God, thank God you're still alive." She knew what was happening to him and she sounded desperate, her voice quivering at an unnatural frequency. "I thought they had already got you. It took me so long to find you."

"Ami, what the hell is going on?" Ben found the entrance to a side street and slipped into another doorway to conceal himself as he spoke. He held his free hand up to cover his mouth as he spoke. "Who are they? Who is trying to kill me?" He couldn't believe he was asking Ami about this. "How the hell do you know anything about it?"

"I can't explain now. I need you to meet me. You're in danger, Ben."

"Ami, I think they might have taken my wife and son." Ben's mind was working double time, impulses firing off with the fervidity of new lovers, fumbling and grappling around for sense that doesn't exist. "I don't have time to meet you. Tell me what's going on."

"Forget Hannah. Meet me at….."

"Forget Hannah? I can't forget Hannah. How do I even know I can trust you? How do you know all this?" He was sure he had never told Ami his wife's name. He had made a point of not talking about Hannah with Ami.

"I'll explain when I'm with you. Meet me at the park behind Seventy Fourth Street. Stay out of sight. They're looking for you."

"No way! Why should I trust you? Where is everybody from the lab Ami? Huh? How do you know all this? You know too much. I can't trust you."

"Ben you can't trust anybody. Whatever you do don't trust anybody." After this all he could hear was the empty hum of a dropped call. She had hung up.

For a moment he stood in the doorway watching the nearby crowds as they passed him on the main street. He began walking towards them in a daydream, a state of mental paralysis. The people knocked him left and right, while his telephone hung in his limp hand. His mind was overloaded by the lack of a logical explanation. He lived by logical explanations, and when there was doubt he would retrace his steps and find the fault, the mistake, the unexplained variable until he understood. He felt like his body was being pulled in a million directions by every random synaptic response charging around in his brain. But Ami was wrong about one thing. He still had somebody that he could trust. He had known Mark his entire life. He had stood at his side in the line-up for football practice. He had stood at his side when they graduated from university. He had stood by his side throughout his father's illness and death. If ever there was anyone he could trust, it was him.

Lacking the advantage of a functional identity and the freedom to use the underground train system to travel around the city he was confined to moving around on foot. He had selected the shopping mall knowing that it was close to the centre of the city and therefore not too far. Mentally it felt close, but the city was crammed full of people, and his progress was hindered.

But he was propelled onwards by a developing sense of responsibility for what had happened. He had no idea what he had unwittingly involved himself in, but whoever it was that was after him, they were serious. They had tried to kill him, and there was a good chance they had taken Hannah and Matthew. If he hadn't drunk himself into such a stupor on Wednesday night maybe it would have been different. Maybe then he wouldn't have slept for a whole day and he could have been around to protect her.

Slept for a whole day?

No, that just didn't make sense. Even in the muddle of his thoughts he couldn't see how it was possible for him to have slept for such a long time. He had been drunk many times before his celebratory night of inebriation, and yet had never suffered the same inexplicable after effects. It just wasn't possible.

Could they have drugged me?

He trawled through his brain, trying to remember all the people he had come into contact with that Wednesday. He had spent the day at the lab, drunk the Champagne from the flimsy plastic cups. But he had bought that himself and he had opened it himself. He had watched Phil pour a measure into each of the other cups before he had got his own share, and he remembered it being less in his cup than any of the others. He wondered if somebody could have drugged him at the bar, but even thinking about these scenarios made him feel like he was losing his mind.

Ben was aware of every movement and every person around him as he passed from the main street into one of the quieter side streets. He called Hannah three times, but the calls didn't connect. The side streets were filled with small cafes and little shops, the kind that Hannah liked to nose around in on trips to the coastal villages in the early days of their marriage. Before the research had taken over their lives. Without any conscious thought he was following Ami's advice and staying out of sight. Her other instruction, *don't trust anybody*, had positioned itself uncomfortably at the forefront of his mind. She hadn't even requested that he extend any trust to her. She virtually begged him to meet her and then told him not to trust anybody. She even knew his wife's name. He knew he had never told her that.

He knew this because Mark had been right. Ami did have feelings for him, and he knew it. He could see it in every single thing that she did in the laboratory. When he was discussing results with Phil, he would see her staring through the glass partition watching him. Watching his lips as they handled each word. She would tap her beautiful hands against the glass of his office door, hands which never seemed to be inflicted with a scratch or blemish. She would offer coffee or to collect his pastrami sandwich from the shop below. She would ask for help with procedures that he knew she understood. She listened as he spoke about his dedication to his research, kicking off her shoes to tuck her feet up underneath her legs when there was nobody else there. He had courted her attentions and had given her every reason to believe that her flirtations were far from foolish. He had allowed her to massage his ego. She was a carer who tended to him, offering attention in ways that he had forgotten that he needed. By asking for nothing, she gave him everything, and in doing so made him feel like a king. She never argued her point. She accepted. She never demand his time. Instead, she gave hers. When Ben told Mark that his work came first it was the truth. But he knew that on a handful of occasions when work was over he had still found himself sat in the office with Ami long after everybody else had returned to their lives. He had never dismissed her then. Was it so easy to dismiss her now?

Ben decided not to approach the mall from the main entrance. He knew there was a side entrance and that it led directly to the lifts where he would be able to approach the first floor without being seen in the corridors. Even though nobody but Mark knew he was coming here he had to be careful. He slipped in quietly where the side corridor was virtually empty, the only exception a few weekday shoppers. He watched from the shadows as the lift arrived. He waited for the doors to open and made a quick dash inside. The elderly woman next to him eyed him suspiciously as he snuck inside, and she clung to her shopping bag. He realised from her reaction that he must be starting to look strange and act suspiciously, so he reminded himself of the need to go unnoticed and to blend in. He smiled at the old woman, and she smiled back because she was polite and that's what a woman of her generation was supposed to do. He pressed the button for the first floor and waited, and when the doors opened he slipped out first.

The first floor cafe was visible from his vantage point just behind the lift shaft. He stood with his back to the wall, concealed within the green foliage of the abundant planters. He scanned the cafe, and found Mark sitting at a table just outside. The cafe was surrounded by ornate and oversized planters, the same as the one he was stooping behind, and that was another reason that he had considered this to be a good place to meet. He had correctly anticipated that it would be quiet on a weekday, and with the greenery blocking the view it would give them plenty of space to speak privately. Mark was too visible though. They would have to change seats. He scanned the room for anything suspicious, although he knew he had no idea what that might actually be, and after deciding that everything seemed to be safe he took the first step out from behind his cover when the telephone that he was still clutching in his pocket began to buzz. He snatched it out and with urgent, fumbling fingers, answered the call. It was Ami.

"Ben, stay behind the lift." Ben looked over his left shoulder, and then his right. He felt as if he had been touched by a ghost, there one minute, gone the next.

"Ami, are you..." She didn't let him finish.

"Shut up, there's no time for this. They are tracking this call. Look behind the plants on Mark's left. Recognise him?" Ben looked out from behind the lift and took a second glance. This time he saw what Ami was referring to. A man, blond hair, wearing nothing but black. He was sitting motionless with his legs crossed, his feet weighed down by heavy black boots. It was the same set of boots from the rooftops earlier on that morning. His stare was fixed ahead at the entrance to the cafe, but tucked behind the foliage to camouflage his presence. Just the sight of him made Ben's arm throb again, and he pressed at it with the palm of his hand. "He won't kill you here, but they will take you."

"Does he have Hannah?"

"Sshh, listen. Do exactly as I say. Call Mark. Tell him there is a change of plan and you are across the city. Tell him to meet you at Twenty Second Street. Then hang up. I told you once, trust nobody. But do this, and then trust yourself. The next move is up to you." She hung up the telephone, not leaving him time to answer.

She spoke at such a rate that the words slipped from her tongue as if oil-coated, and he could barely comprehend all that she had said. But he was sure that Ami was trying to warn them, and she knew things he couldn't explain. Like how she knew where he was. He had to take her advice. He held up his telephone and tried to tuck himself deeper into the foliage of the leaves, and then dialled Mark's number. His palm was sweaty and damp as he stayed behind the cover like a soldier peering out through the bushes, just keeping Mark's table in view. He did as Ami had told him to do and kept the call short. He gave Mark the exact instructions as Ami had relayed to him, and cut the call without explanation. With any luck Mark would walk away and lead the other man away with him.

Beads of salty sweat trickled into Ben's mouth as he watched the man dressed all in black. The shooters interest had been spiked, that was for sure. Ben watched as Mark put his telephone back down on the table. He looked confused and angry as he rested his forehead into his hands. He looked to be breathing heavily and seemed frustrated, momentarily bubbling over into a flash of anger as he struck his fist against the cold plastic of the cafe table. A few people witnessed his outburst, and they turned to look his way. One of them was the shooter. He was watching Mark and waiting for him to make a move.

Mark stood up, but he didn't leave. Instead he clicked his fingers, and the shooter stood up and walked over to him, obedient as a pup to the call of his master. They stood together talking for a moment, and Mark picked up his phone again. Ben could feel his phone buzzing in his hand. It was Mark.

Ben silenced the telephone and stared at the screen. Had he really just seen Mark talk to the shooter? Mark had been his friend for years. It had been Mark who Ben had called on the night when the doctors explained to his mother that they should not expect his father to survive the night. The pneumonia was severe, and he was weak. It was only a month before Ben's eighteenth birthday. Mark had waited in the corridor, surrounded by the pungent smell of perfume that his mother sprayed to mask the smell of human waste. Losing his father had been a long, slow lesson for Ben, and Mark had lived it with him. It was the first time that they both had tangible proof that life never stays the same, and that nothing and nobody lasts forever.

Ben wanted to answer the call and tell him that he knew he had double crossed him, but he was no fool. He knew that if he answered that call Mark would know he was here. So Ben slid the telephone back into his pocket, and folded his body into the shadow of the lift. He watched as Mark, followed by the would-be killer, left the café. They walked towards the lift, and Ben felt his pulse quicken. They came within a metre of Ben, a concrete wall the only thing between them. He could hear their mumbled voices from where he crouched.

"I'm going to go to Twenty Second Street. Did you find her yet?" Mark spoke to his killing machine with venomous words, spitting them out like a bad taste. Ben had never heard this hateful tone in Mark's voice. Mark was the one in control here. He wasn't scared at all.

"No, Sir. We are still looking."

"She'll find him. Find her, and follow her. That's how we'll find him."

"Yes, Sir. What about Catherine?" Ben pressed his hands against the solid concrete panel that separated them from him.

Who is Catherine?

"She wasn't to know. Leave her to do her job." With that, Ben heard the ping of the lift as the doors opened. The two men walked inside, and their words became muffled. Ben heard the doors close and his legs buckled beneath him as the immediate danger passed, and for the second time today he found himself sat on a cold concrete floor contemplating what the hell was going on. Ami was right, he really couldn't trust anybody. The only person that had helped him so far was Ami. He had no choice but to call her.

"Yes?" She waited for him to speak.

"Ami, I'm ready to meet you." He already understood that he would receive no explanation over the telephone.

"Good. Meet me at the park behind Seventy Fourth. I'm waiting."

SEVEN

BEN HAD NEVER BEEN TO Seventy Fourth Street before, or the park behind it. A narrow side street lined with coach houses led to the park. It was a dead end, surrounded by an old regal building that had been left to its own devices. It had once been a grand old place, but after a period without attention and much like love, it became less than precious, riddled with cracks, and had now been forgotten about altogether. He didn't much care for being here, and couldn't for the life of him think why Ami would arrange to meet him in this place. The thought that this dead end could be a trap rose poisonously in his mind, inserting doubt upon doubt, cairns set to lead him in the wrong direction. He quashed his hesitation because he had no other option, and so despite his fears, steeled himself for the moments ahead.

He turned from Seventy Fourth Street into the narrow lane. Above him were rows of poorly constructed coach houses, abandoned and no longer in use. Old newspapers covered the windows in several layers, the deepest of which were peeling and yellow from the heat of the sun. Before him he saw the beautiful regal building, decorated with ornate iron balustrades. Underneath rows of purple Paulownia trees there was a series of benches, all rickety and rotten. The park opened out to the left and right, a *T* shape with the narrow lane that led up to it.

On his first look he couldn't see anybody. He was standing

beneath the trees, heavily laden with early flowers. There was no wind here, and it felt warmer surrounded by the height of the buildings. He was hit by an overwhelming desire to bring Hannah here, and to sit with her on the benches beneath the blossoming trees. In his vision they wouldn't speak, only sit, needing nothing more than each other's company and the sight of Matthew playing at their feet. In his visions Matthew remained an eternal toddler, short of words and rich in love and awe for his father. He realised his reflections were always from the past, every vision born of a time before Bionics.

He was snatched back into reality as he heard Ami whisper his name. As he turned in the direction of the voice he saw her standing in the corner of the square. She was tucked into the shadow of the great building, and she motioned for him to sit. He sat as instructed onto a bench, but his eyes never once left her face.

Ami waited hesitantly for a moment, seconds ticking by at a pace which felt as if time had become stationary. He could see her indecision in her first cautious steps, and in the way that her eyes darted left and right, occasionally looking back over her shoulder. For a moment Ben was sure that he had seen a man dart back into the shadows of the building behind Ami. But as she approached he focussed on her presence, remembering why he was here, pushing everything else aside. Just before she sat down next to him she took a deep and fortifying breath, and he wondered why it was that she looked so apprehensive. Surely it should be him that was nervous.

Her long casual hair that he had admired on so many occasions was wrapped neatly into a bun behind her head, and she was wearing a long Macintosh that swung open freely. For the first time that he could remember she was wearing trousers. She appeared different from his memory, beautiful still, but rather than the softly painted vision that he kept close in his mind, it was a harder edged reality in which she appeared focused and dangerous.

"Ben, there isn't much time. You have to listen to me carefully."

"Hang on, Ami." This was his first chance to try to find out what the hell was going on, and if there wasn't much time he sure as hell wasn't going to hand it straight over to her. "Before you start, I need to ask you something."

"No, Ben. You need to listen." This woman looked like Ami, but now he could detect a slight accent in her voice that had never been there before. It reminded him of Mr. Saad, the man who was trying to fund his continued research programme.

"No, Ami, wait. I have to ask *you* some things."

"There will be a time for your questions but it isn't now. At the moment your questions will get us both killed." He didn't interrupt her again and he sat with his hands in his lap, his muscles limp and helpless. "Ben, everything that has happened to you over the last few hours was not supposed to happen. It should already be over. We are only lucky that it is not." Ben's mouth dropped open in shock. *Lucky?* He didn't feel too damn lucky. "You should already be dead."

"I know that. Somebody tried to shoot me at the lab."

"I'm not referring to the lab. You were never supposed to wake up today. They started it much quicker than I anticipated. If I had known I would have found a way to tell you at the bar."

"What bar? What did they start? Who are *they*?" Ami wasn't making much sense to him. "Is this about Mark?"

"Ben, who do you think you work for?"

"Bionics."

"You work for the government. Bionics is just the public face of the Office of Scientific Weaponry Development. OSWED."

"The government?"

"Yes, but not the one you see on the television, or in the newspaper. It's the same one, but it's the side of it that nobody knows about."

"Ami there is only one government," Ben scoffed nervously.

"That's what I just said. There is the government that you see, the one that stands up and leads the country with clean hands. They can deny everything without ever having to lie because not even they know the truth. They are public puppets." She took a long swallow and then met his eyes with hers. "Then there are the rest of us. The people that nobody knows about. The people that do what you might call *dirty work*."

"Ami, you're a scientist."

"Correct. But I don't work for you. I work for OSWED. They are supposed to be the people that keep you safe. It's supposed to be about intelligence and development. They believe it is what makes your *Great Country* so great." Ben could hear a certain level of sarcasm coming through in her newly accented voice. "We work outside of standard military intelligence. We don't exist, at least as far as the rest of the world knows. That counts for the rest of the staff at Bionics."

"You're telling me that I work for a secret government agency, and that all of the staff I work with knew nothing about it except for you? What have you done with them? What happened to my research, Ami?"

"Start paying attention Ben. *You're* the only one that doesn't know anything about it. Why do you think the lab and all of the staff have disappeared? The mission was complete. Your theory had been proven and NEMREC worked." She saw the surprise on his face, the inability to understand as his mouth hung open. She wished that she could spare him the details, but she had to be honest. If ever there was a time it was now. "You were already supposed to be dead."

"What the hell?"

"They knew how good you were. They targeted you. They knew you would succeed so they started to control everything about you. They wanted your brilliance in the palm of their hand, and they did everything they could to get it. Your friends, your wife, your whole life. It's a set up Ben. It was all about getting NEMREC. Now you have achieved that, they don't need you anymore."

"You're saying my whole life is a fake? That's bullshit, Ami!" He was up and off the bench now, arms flailing like compliant branches in the wind without any control over their own movement. "I have a wife. A son."

"It's not bullshit. It's the truth. It's the first truthful thing you have heard in years. You discovered how to change people's DNA, Ben. You know what they can do with that kind of knowledge." She was up on her feet now too, trying to make contact with him reaching out for his arms as he span around, propelled by the inertia of disbelief.

"I'm trying to cure disease, Ami. Not make weapons for your government."

"Your government, Ben. You might not be trying to make weapons, but OSWED are. They want the ability to change DNA, to build a stronger army. An elite force. They don't want to manufacture pharmaceuticals to cure Huntington's disease like you do. They want to make a stronger army and build weapons. They want people to be their weapons, and you have given them everything they need."

"And you?" He was stood still staring straight at her. "Why are you helping me if you work for them?" She sat down onto the bench, her head bowed. For a moment he thought he could see tears forming in her dark almond eyes.

"I want what you want, Ben." She turned her head up to look at him, and her eyes looked swollen and set to burst. "My father is dying. So am I. I want a chance to live to grow old." The pain in her face, in her blurry eyes and crumpled brow was a feeling that he recognised. He understood those feelings, and he felt them every day in every one of his mutated cells. Her words could have been his own, his own feelings, his own hopes, his own aspirations. Any fears he had, any caution for the woman before him had passed. He saw his own reflection in her glassy eyes as he contemplated her sadness and regret. It softened him and he sensed the need for truth and trust, believing in the freedom and strength that it offered.

"Ami, why am I not dead already?"

"I don't know. You should be. What she gave you should have been enough to kill you?"

"What who gave me?" He saw that same sense of pity on her face, as she wiped away a tear from her cheek. He traced his thoughts back to when he passed out on his settee, how he assumed he had merely been drunk, and how he had been dragged up the stairs, and how he had slept for thirty six hours, and how he had been sick, and how it was still there the next morning, and the next morning, and how Hannah hadn't been home. Suddenly he had visions of her as a spy carrying a gun and speaking in Russian on a foreign mission and seducing people to steal data chips. Again, he reminded himself that such an explanation was utterly ridiculous. Yet still he said it. "You think Hannah tried to kill me?"

"No, Ben. I know she tried to kill you. She poured you champagne, right? It was drugged. That's why you feel so awful now." She sat down on the bench, steadying herself, attempting also to steady Ben with a hand on his arm, a real connection. She knew they had felt that connection before, and she hoped he felt it now.

"I threw up," said Ben. He thought back to the pile of sick on the floor and couldn't remember ever being so pleased that he had been ill. He tried again to remind himself of the absurdity of her accusations, but found that the more time that passed and the more he listened to himself, the dismissal of her theory didn't seem quite so easy. He didn't have any other explanations to work from.

"Then that's why you're still here."

"Ami. What do they want from me?"

"They want you dead, Ben. It's their only aim. To them," she paused apologetically before she finished her sentence, "you already are. There is no record of your life anymore. It's not like you died, it's like you never existed."

"Unregistered," he whispered as he looked away. He bit his lip and tried to think what to do. He looked to Ami. "Will you help me?" She nodded reassuringly. After everything that had happened this morning he had only one other question. "Ami, where have they taken my son?"

EIGHT

"AMI, COME ON. WHERE HAVE they taken him?"

"Ben, I don't think you understand. It's not going to be as simple as walking up to the door and asking for him back." She could barely look him in the eye. Instead she looked around at the broken buildings in search of absolution for her involvement.

"Ami." Ben bent down in front of her and took her face in his cupped palms as he had with Hannah only days before. Her cheeks were frozen, and in spite of her olive skin appeared pink and wind battered. At first she had looked so tough walking across the square in her Macintosh and heels, his only source of help. Now he found himself wanting to comfort her, as he saw the softer Ami that he had grown so fond of in the laboratory. He knew how he felt about her ever since the first day when she walked in, introducing herself as she threw her bag under the nearest chair in a nonchalant manner. The rest of his team were uptight and focussed, with no space for fun in their structured and orderly lives. But Ami breezed in without a care in the world. He fell for her in an instant, but he suppressed and stifled his passion for the love of his work and his son. "Ami, it doesn't matter how difficult it is. Where have they taken him? Nothing else is important anymore. Where is he?"

"There is so much that you don't understand yet." She

70

looked over to her right hand side. Ben followed her eye movement to see what had alerted her attention but saw nothing.

"Start by telling me where they have taken him." As he finished speaking he saw Ami look over her shoulder again. Ben heard a high pitched whistling sound above their heads. He instinctively ducked, recognising the sound from earlier on in the day. It was moving too fast, like an asteroid through the atmosphere, there one moment and gone the next. Ami heard it too, and she knew what it was. Immediately he heard her scream, fright and panic straining through her voice.

"NO!" She set off, running towards her right, grabbing Ben as she took off. He saw a man dressed in casual grey trousers and a winter jumper slump to the ground just inside a doorway. Ami was running towards him, her head ducked down and her shoulders hunched over, all the while pulling Ben with her.

The bullet had caused a cavernous red hole in the centre of the man's forehead. Ami stumbled to the pavement in front of the man, ignoring the bloody gloop oozing from his head as she cradled him. She pulled Ben down to join her, pushing him underneath the cover of the ornate porch. She gripped Ben's arm with her free hand and opened her mouth to speak, but then came that air-splitting sound again. It was the whistle of the bullet piercing a channel through the air as it thundered towards them. Ami's head shot back as if she had been punched in the face, before falling flaccidly, collapsing into Ben's arms. The weight of her body pushed him behind the wall of the porch, protecting him even in her death. Blood and fragments of her flesh and bone sprayed over his face. Her head flopped forwards and hit him in the chest. He began to fidget and shout in revulsion as her body slumped lifelessly on top of him. He fumbled his hands up through her hair and grabbed her by the face, holding her as he had done only moments ago. He calmed himself by taking some deep breaths and then rolled her head back to reveal the full force of the impact. Scarlet blood and lumps of matter oozed from the hole in the side of her skull. His fingers slipped around in the warm silken fluid as he brushed her hair back from her blood streaked face. The horror of what he saw before him wasn't just death. Death had visited his life before. He knew death. What he saw today was incomparable.

His father's passing was peaceful. A relief to the agony. But there was no peace here. He thought how only minutes ago she had told him that she wanted the chance to grow old, and he began to cry. The tears streaked through the crimson droplets that had settled on his face, before falling onto Ami's cheeks and doing the same.

"What do you want from me!" he screamed as hard as he could, his words stumbling over the lump of pain that sat in his throat. He sobbed as he said the words over and over, quietly and with no particular audience. He was paralysed by what he had seen. He sat there for several moments, cradling Ami in his embrace. But then he saw a dust cloud whip up in front of him as another bullet hit the ground. His leg was in full view, and whoever was responsible for the death of Ami and her friend had a new primary target. He dragged his foot towards him, wriggling his whole body about underneath Ami's in order to break free. He held her face up towards his lips, his fingers weaving in and out of her slick black hair. He kissed her on the unblemished half of her forehead and silently offered an apology for her death.

He couldn't stay here, and so far he knew he had ridden a wave of good fortune to still be alive, but he couldn't shake the thought that his luck was about to run out. He tried the door handle. It was locked. He pushed harder and harder. The door gave way a little but it didn't budge. He rammed it again with his intact shoulder, harder still this time. It hurt terribly, but he kept jamming his weight behind it. He could feel the skin on his arm breaking and bruising underneath the repetition of each impact, but there was no other option. Eventually the door burst open in a cloud of wooden shrapnel, and his body fell into the empty room into a cloud of kicked up dust. He coughed as he stood up, before spotting that the man who was lying under Ami was still holding a gun. He didn't know what type it was. He barely knew anything about guns. He dragged the body towards him wiping, his bloody hands on the man's torso before picking up the black handle of the gun. His hand was still weak from where he had been shot earlier, but he mustered the strength to grip the weapon. He had never fired a gun before, but he had seen them fired hundreds of times on the television. He tucked the gun into the waistband of his stolen trousers. His mind raced fortuitously ahead, and his hands delved into the pockets of the dead man. Inside he found what looked like an identity card, immediately recognising the green plastic token. He shoved the card into his pocket and headed into the derelict building.

The inside was a striking contrast to the ornate facade of the old buildings. The covered windows concealed a rundown interior. The floor was scattered with old paperwork. His eyes darted around, taking in the peeling paintwork and doors which were hanging from their frames by nothing but the odd screw. The rooms formed an interconnected labyrinth with no discernible exit to freedom. He looked towards the windows, single paned and easy enough to break, especially with the butt of the gun resting inside his trousers. But the thought of the noise and commotion seemed like a prime reason to try to avoid that idea.

He knew that he was getting close to the opposite end of the building which would open out onto *Seventieth Street*. That meant that he was getting closer to some sort of public place, which he presumed must be safer. To his right, he could see a door on the far side. It was the first door that sat in the place where it should, secured by a frame, and from the look of the window lined wall which it intersected, led to the outside. He headed towards it, the inertia of his run broken as his body hit the thick wooden door. He tried the handle, never really expecting it to budge. Gripping it tight with both hands, he crouched a little, straightened his arms in line with the level of the handle. He braced his feet apart and placed the sole of one foot against the door frame and pulled and twisted the handle as hard as he could. He prayed that with time the mechanism of the lock, or even the door itself would have degraded sufficiently for him to be able to disturb its position, but it stood firm, barring his escape. The windows to either side were also sealed shut by several layers of paint.

He began to pace around in small circles, his hands running through his sweat-drenched hair as he muttered words of desperation. He remembered the gun as his arm brushed past the handle sticking out from his waistband. He took hold of it and his hand slid into position, his finger slipping onto the trigger as he had seen thousands of times in movies. His breathing was hard and shaky, and the sense of power that he had seen so many characters exhibit as they held the cold black metal in their hands was lost to him. He felt at risk with the weapon capable of both protecting him and ending his life, depending on whose hand controlled its power. He didn't know if it was loaded or ready, but despite all of his other concerns an overwhelming sense of necessity crept upon him. In his life he never had the need for such an accomplice, and had no desire to own or fire a gun. But today, every rule by which he had lived his life so far had been subverted into a position where they no longer held any weight, and whatever position it was that he had found himself in, this weapon suddenly seemed like his best, if not his only option.

Gripping the handle tighter, he held the gun shakily in front of him. Remembering every Hollywood lesson, he popped the button to the front of the handle and the magazine slid out of the gun, hitting the floor. Instinctively he jumped back, his fear of its power betrayed. Snatching the magazine back up from amongst the scattered papers he could see that there were more than a handful of bullets, and looked just short of being full. He slid it back into position, ramming it hard with the base of his hand. He pointed the business end towards the handle of the door and squeezed the trigger. The bullet left the gun at a force that he had never experienced before. The muscles in his arm shuddered at the impact, shooting upwards as his shoulder buckled from the shot. The bullet flew upwards, tearing into the plaster of the wall, and a small cascade of crumbling lime plaster work feathered to the ground. Ben held his breath, realising that a different strategy was required.

He stuck the nose of the gun directly into the locking point between the door and the frame. Bracing not only his hand, but also his stance, arms, and shoulders, he fired again. This time, although his arms jolted back, his shoulder painful and acid hot, he stood firm. Shards of wood sprayed backwards and the door wobbled out from its position and he saw the safety of daylight stream inside. He dragged the door open, its swollen underside catching on the floorboards. Realising the gun was still in his hand, he stowed it back into his trousers and covered it with his stolen jacket. He stood for a moment on the steps of the old building, looking both left and right. He could see the entrance to where he had just come from. Just in view was the back end of a black van, the kind that until today didn't automatically look to him like the kind that people get bundled into. But now, knowing that this van had not been there only ten minutes before, and was stationary with the engine running, it looked like exactly that. He didn't doubt that this was for him.

He pulled up his jacket collar and slipped down from the steps making his way right. He knew that only two streets away from here there must be an underground line. If he could make it there, he would be able to get away easily enough, as long as the identity card worked. After that, he had to find Hannah. He had to find his son. And with Ami dead he only really had one option. Mark. He had to get to Twenty Second Street, even though every single thing about that decision felt wrong.

PART TWO

NINE

HE DIDN'T LOOK OVER HIS shoulder as he left the steps and headed along the pavement. He didn't want to look back until he had put some distance between him and the black van. This was a quiet part of town, often the birthplace of trouble, and he didn't want to draw attention to himself. He figured that whoever it was that shot Ami and her accomplice, and who had tried to shoot him too, would surely by now have realised that he had got out. They would have found the broken door. He listened closely for the grunt of an erratic engine in pursuit. He imagined the terrifying scenarios in his head, and the image of his own demise played out in myriad fashions, first being manhandled into the van, followed by the inevitable interrogation that somehow seemed more terrifying than a quick bullet to the side of the head.

As he reached the first corner, he risked a glance back towards his escape route from behind the edge of the building. He gripped the corner of the wall, his knuckles so white they looked like the bones were coming through the skin. But the black van was still visible in the same place as before. Besides plumes of vapour pouring out from the rear exhaust, there was no other movement, and no man dressed in black chasing him. He reached inside his pocket and retrieved the identity card that he had taken from Ami's accomplice. It looked like a regular identity card, green, with a small photograph and a metal chip that carried your details and financial status. The photograph was of a young blond man, maybe no more than thirty years old, and bore no resemblance to the man from whose pocket he had retrieved it. The man with Ami was no younger than fifty, and he had dark hair and brown sun-kissed skin. Ben stowed it safely back into his pocket and took another one eyed glance back around the building. Still nobody chasing him. He was overwhelmed by an unbelievable sense of luck, and then remembered that he still had Ami's blood on his face and a pool of semi-congealed blood on his chest. He wiped his cheeks with the sleeve of his jacket, before zipping it up to cover his chest.

After concealing the patchwork of blood that Ami's crudely anatomized head had left on his grey T-shirt, Ben kept up his pace as he cut into the busier *Sixtieth Street*. There were crowds of people here and the street was lined with small shops and cafes. It seemed to Ben after witnessing Ami's death, safer to stay enveloped within the crowd than it did to stay in isolation, so he slipped amongst the people and bustled his way towards the underground station. He remembered coming here with Hannah. She loved to visit the smaller districts of the city, where people courted art and culture rather than power and money. She always told him that it was those things that enriched their lives, and that made the world a better place. They would sip coffee and eat bagels for breakfast in one of the cafes, or when the weather was fine outside on small patio tables on the pavement. He passed the flower shop where he would buy her tulips in the spring and roses in the winter, and wondered if it was possible for everything to be a lie.

He hung back on the opposite side of the road to the station, observing the entrance and its passing traffic. From his vantage point he observed nothing more than an ordinary scene as people dashed about during stolen time from work. As he scanned the changing array of faces, he found no trace of the shooter. There was no crowd of people on his tail, not least that he could see. There was no sign of the black van. He snatched up every ounce of his courage, knowing full well that staying where he was, was not an option. He took purposeful and determined steps. Hanging close to the wall, his eyes darted about the entrance foyer, scanning the room for signs of possible attack whilst trying not to alert the guards to his apprehension. He stood with his back up against the side wall of the newspaper kiosk. There was no sign of anybody that posed a known threat, and so he slipped into the queue, clutching his stolen identity card in his hand.

His heart thumped in his chest, every beat reinforcing his anxiety as he held the identity card up to the small scanner screen. Each pulsation pleading *Stop*. The two seconds that it took to register the details seemed like a lifetime as he waited for the red or green letters to either permit him entry. The small red light flashed to green and the usual greeting message flashed up, greeting one Mr. Smith, and bidding him a good morning. There was no grey X, and the doors swung open in front of him. He breezed through, momentarily comforted by the brief realisation of success, before once again feeling the return of his overenthusiastic heart beat as he concluded that as of yet he had achieved nothing.

As he rounded the corner towards the east-bound lines he immediately saw a small group of people crowded in the corridor, no more than twenty meters ahead. There were five of them, each wearing a grey suit or beige jacket, long and sweeping and contrasting to the usual attire of this area. If he had been at *Central City* they would have gone unnoticed, blending in perfectly with the rest of the crowd. But this was an artistic area, where people wore colour, and changed their style according to their beliefs and theories on life. They saw their bodies, clothes, and hair as a canvas on which to display themselves to the world. Here, a well fitted suit or run of the mill office clothes had no place. Ben backed up and ducked into one of the telephone booths. He hid with his back towards the group, his torso and head shrouded by a small plastic canopy. Too far away to hear what they were saying, he picked up the receiver of the payphone and held it to his ear, pulling the handset across his face to obscure himself from view. He peered back over his shoulder towards the group. They had disbanded, flanking both the left and right sides of the corridor. As he could see it, there were two people on the left and two on the right, and a sole person, whose face was alien to him stood alert in the centre of the corridor looking his way. Ben had no way of knowing if these people were waiting for him, but there was no denying that their behaviour and attire were strange and out of place. He decided that his best option was to assume that he was their target and that his capture was their aim.

He had only two options. Westbound trains or the entrance from where he had just arrived. If the security guards recognised him, taking the entrance would alert their suspicions. They may ask to see his identity card, and showing it would under no circumstances go smoothly, and would almost certainly lead to his arrest. Using false documentation and using the identity of another person was heavily punished. It left his only other option the westbound trains, for which the entrance as far as he could see looked clear. He hung up the receiver and stepped out from the plastic canopy and began walking away from those blocking the eastbound entrance tunnel. He took steady steps towards the westbound entrance.

On his right he passed the walkway that would lead him to the main entrance. He turned his head just a fraction to look towards the main entrance. At first he saw nothing but a multitude of colourful clothes, a mixture of races and unnatural hair colours. But in the very corner of his eye he caught a glimpse of the same cropped, blond hair that had pursued him that morning. Ben quickened his pace, his steps gathering speed until eventually he stumbled his way into a run. But the shooter had seen him and Ben could hear the commotion of discontent behind him as he barged his way through the crowd. The corridor wound left and right, and Ben hoped that its tight winding path would prove a bottle neck, trapping the shooter behind crowds of people, giving him a chance to catch the next train. But as Ben arrived at the platform there was no more than a handful of people waiting, and no crowd into which he could disappear. The signs stated the next train wouldn't be there for another five minutes. His eyes skimmed about as he ran towards the other end of the platform, putting as much distance as he could between him and his assailant but desperately aware that there was no obstruction between him and the imminent arrival of the shooter.

He heard a chorus of screams emerging from the mouth of the corridor, and as Ben turned back he saw the shooter emerge with his gun held in his hand. With not a second lost he extended his arm in Ben's direction and squeezed the trigger. Ben ducked down as the bullet skipped past him and hit the ceramic tiles behind where his head had been. As the sound of the impact rang out like a bell through the hollow of the tunnel the handful of people on the platform threw themselves to the ground, letting out a chorus of screams. On his knees, and therefore considerably less mobile, Ben hauled himself towards the tracks, and in one heave managed to drag his body down behind the temporary safety of the wall just before he felt another bullet impact on the floor above him. He hit his head as he fell onto the tracks, but he pushed his body in as tight to the wall as possible and blessed the presence of a recess in which he could hide.

He was almost out of options. The shooter would be coming up closer to him with each passing second and in no time at all would be above him without any chance of missing his target. Ben tentatively pulled the gun out from his waistband. He gripped it as tightly as he could, his arm shaking. He pointed its nose just over the wall. Squeezing off two rounds in the general direction of the shooter. He prayed that one of them would hit. With no time between his shots and the subsequent shots from the shooter, he heard the impact as bullets struck close to his own head and he ducked again for safety. Ben fired off one more shot, and then as fast as he could, he shuffled his body along under the cover of the platform towards the other end. He moved like a ghost, gentle steps so not to disturb the loose gravel beneath him.

Two minutes, left on the clock.

He kept his body in the recess of the wall until he was sure that he must have passed the location of the shooter. Fuelled by the rising levels of adrenaline and the drumming in his chest he dared a look above the level of the platform. He prayed as he raised his head that the shooter had passed him, and sure enough as the platform came into view he saw that he was behind the shooter.

One minute.

With the shooters back to him, Ben aimed the gun at what he thought was the centre of his back and fired. The bullet hit the shooter in the right arm, delivering recompense and satisfaction on Ben's part for the equivalent wound on his own arm. Ben couldn't feel his own pain or his heartbeat, even though it thundered along with the fast paced gallop of a racehorse. The shooter swung

81

round, startled by the shot, almost falling to his knees. Clutching his wounded arm in his opposite hand he raised the gun at Ben.

For Ben there was only silence, and it seemed that time stood still. He pulled off two more shots in the direction of the shooter, both making an impact in his stomach. As the shooter's body swung wide open, a forth shot rang out through the tunnel. The well aimed shot did exactly as was intended, and rocketed into the centre of the shooters chest, flooring him in an instant. It was the only shot that Ben had been aware of.

Ben began to hear the rumble of the train in the background, and the lights which were close enough to illuminate his position on the tracks came precariously close. The driver was still sounding his horn as Ben hauled his body up and over the wall. Once on his feet he staggered towards the body of the shooter as it lay before him. The commuters who lay crouched on the ground buried their heads further into their shoulders as the train rattled on through. In a single moment Ben realised that he had become the feared. He could hear people crying and begging for safety. Ben stood beside the shooter as the train rumbled past, the driver already informed that under no circumstances should he stop.

Ben watched the body as it quivered during its last moments of life like a bird caught in a set of locked feline jaws. Dropping to his knees at the side of his victim he felt a bewildering sense of guilt mixed with the paradoxical sensation of satisfaction. The shooter coughed up a mouthful of blood. But the gurgle of fluids at the back of his throat stopped bubbling, and the blood pooled into his lungs. As he took his last breath, Ben felt the burden of guilt at having taken a life, where before he had dedicated his own to saving the lives of others.

He thought he had seen both sides of death after he had watched it violently take Ami's life and also soothe his father's agony. But now he realised there was a third face to it, the most evil of all; death brought by your own hand. He fought back his tears and wiped his face, smudging the dirt from the tracks across his cheeks. Ben forced himself to rifle through the shooter's pockets looking for clues of his identity. In the bloody inside pocket of the shooter's coat, Ben uncovered something that bore a resemblance to an identity card. It was not like any card that he recognised. There was no picture or name, and instead just a small metal chip and a number. He reached his hand down to pick up his gun, but before he could touch it he heard a voice distinguishable from any other.

"Ben, leave that where it is." Still on his knees, he turned to face the direction from where the voice came.

"Hannah?" He could barely believe his ears, or his eyes, as the image of his wife formed before him. She wore a long beige jacket and was flanked by two men either side of her. "What..."

"Ben, there is no time for us to discuss this here. On your feet." She spoke in a way that was so direct and decisive that he obeyed her without question.

"I killed a man." His voice trembled as his stare alternated between his victim and his wife. She looked for a moment as if she felt sorry for him.

"Don't feel bad for it. He would have put a bullet in your head gladly, had you not killed him first."

Ben waited before he spoke again, unable to focus on anything but the burgundy pool of blood forming underneath the waist of the dead shooter. "Why did he want to kill me?"

"Because you are already dead, Ben. There are no options left for you. They will kill you. They will not stop until they do. They have hundreds of these men, and each one of them will die before they give up their duty," Hannah said, looking at the body on the floor. "Four of those men are standing next to me right now." Ben looked up at the men to his wife's side and contemplated in what possible reality his wife would be flanked by four assassins. "You are going to walk out of this station with me, and you will get into the van parked outside."

"If I don't?"

"Then we will kill you here and now. I will do it because you will leave me with no other choice. If you come with me, if you trust me, I will protect you."

"Hannah, you wouldn't kill me. You couldn't."

"Your choice, Ben. Come with us."

"Hannah," he said as he began to raise his voice, "what about our son?"

"Ma'am, we need to move, one way or another." The man to Hannah's left hand side had his hand on his gun and was pushing her to take action. He paid Ben no attention, as if he were as insignificant as a crushed ant under his shoe. He tried to tell himself that they were controlling her, forcing her into something, and that he had to find a way to save her. Yet the more he tried to convince himself, the more unlikely the story seemed, until the point where it became utterly unbelievable. She was the one in control.

"Ben," she shouted, "they are coming. "With me, or against me?" He thought about his options which seemed slight in any stretch of the imagination. He thought about the loaded gun on the floor beside him, but knew that there was no chance of him being able to take down all four of them. A radio buzzed on her waist band and through the crackle of static he heard a voice announce what to him sounded only like a threatening confirmation of what Hannah was saying.

"They're approaching."

"Last chance, Ben," she said, pulling at his jacket. One of the men on Hannah's left whipped out his gun and pointed it at Ben, as if to confirm her offer. He noticed Hannah swallowing hard as her eyes begged him to accept her offer.

"With you." She was his only hope. She held all the cards. The gun held out towards him dropped to the side of the man who held it, and the other two men on her right stepped towards him. One of them held up a small device, similar to a gun but smaller. The agent pushed it against Ben's neck and pulled the trigger. It felt sharp, as if something scratched at him.

"Don't struggle Ben." After a sharp prick to his neck that felt like an insect bite, instantly warm and swollen, he felt his eye lids heavy and his head woozy. "Go with them," he heard her say.

Half walking and half dragged, Ben disappeared into the shadows of the tunnel. In a medicated delirium, he questioned if he should even trust Hannah considering that she appeared to be the only thing that stood between his life and death only moments before, but she was for now his only option.

He became aware that his feet were failing him, and he felt the bump as his effort became increasingly passive. Then with a pull from above and a push from below, he was hauled from a tunnel and into the street through an inconspicuous works entrance. They bundled him into a waiting van.

Only meters away from the van, Hannah was explaining to another colleague how two of her men had chased him into the tunnel. She would meet them back at her base because the former Mr. Stone had once again evaded capture.

She stepped back into her own car and began the journey towards her base. She soon found herself trailing the back of a black van inside which lay Ben, her husband and father of her son. It would only be a few hours until he woke up, and she hoped desperately by that time she would have worked out what the hell she was going to do.

TEN

BEN AWOKE JUST OVER TWO hours later on a bed of cold concrete. As he had become accustomed, he had a global headache. It felt like his brain was swollen, pushed up against his skull. He was badly dehydrated from the effects of whatever it was that Hannah had administered in the side of his neck. He raised his fingers towards his neck and he felt the swelling from the injection. He had a tight nervous feeling in the bottom of his stomach, which he thought likely to be the consequences of the perpetual hormonal surges that had helped keep him alive. But he had been drugged at least once, most likely twice. Could be that too. And the lack of food.

Pushing himself to his feet he rubbed his head, trying to shift some of the haziness that he felt. He propped himself up, first onto his knees and then reluctantly back down onto his backside when he realised that movement was less comfortable than he had anticipated. He realised that he was wearing a donated shirt, much like hospital wear. He was grateful for the absence of the blood-covered T shirt.

He was enclosed in a room no larger than two meters square, with a ceiling low enough that he might not be able to fully stand up. It didn't help much with the sense of entrapment and claustrophobia. The floor was grey concrete, the same as the walls. There were no windows, and the only source of light was a tatty old strip above his head that trailed exposed and damaged wires, tacked onto the ceiling and which buzzed constantly. Just below the point where the wires exited through the corner of the room where the walls met the ceiling, there was a small video camera. He didn't know much about closed circuit television recording equipment, but to him that's what it looked like. He was strangely reassured that somebody must be watching him.

With no stimulation from inside his bleak prison-like cell his relived everything that he could remember from the past day. In the space of only a few hours there had been an attempt on his life, Ami had been killed in front of him, and he had become a murderer. On top of that, as if that wasn't already enough, Ami had told him that every element of the life that he knew was a lie. That idea had gained good ground when Hannah turned up in the underground station. Up until that point, the precariousness of his situation had been equalled only by his desire to seek the safety of his wife and child. Even thoughts of his research, which until that point he had assumed meant more to him than anything else, waned in the very real prospect of never seeing his family again. Now Hannah was just another face not to be trusted. He could have never imagined raising his hand to her, but he found himself entertaining thoughts of striking her, blacking her eye, or cutting her lip. He imagined how it might feel to be that person, the one that does harm, that belittles and denies another person a normal healthy life. Then he reminded himself that he was now a murderer, and so he should know how that feels very well already.

On the other side of the door he could hear the thud of footsteps. They were not gentle, and didn't sound like Hannah's high-heeled footsteps. Rather, they sounded like the dull thud of a male boot, heavy and murderous like the shooters from earlier on that day.

The footsteps stopped at what sounded like just outside the door without a handle. He had no idea who or what lay behind it. He had no recollection of what had happened to him since he had been with Hannah at the underground station when he had allowed himself be drugged. What a fool he really was. No wonder they had managed to deceive him so impressively. It could be anyone on the other side of that door. Maybe Hannah never even got him back after he had been dragged away. Maybe her intentions were good and she too has been fooled. He didn't leave with Hannah, after all.

Oh God, let Hannah be here. Let her be the one who has imprisoned me.

"Let me out!" Ben yelled, as somebody pushed a tray of mediocre looking food through a small inward opening portal at the bottom of the door. He clambered over it, tipping over a glass of orange juice. "I want to talk to Hannah! Let me out!" He banged against the door with a clenched fist, encouraged by the knowledge that there was at least somebody on the other side of it. His demands went unanswered, and as the hopelessness of his situation hit, knowing that he was fully under their control, he realised that it was pointless to waste his energy. He stumbled back into a seated position on the floor, propping his back up against the wall of the door. He dragged the tray of food towards him with his fingertips. He devoured the dry edged cheese and ham sandwich and banana as if it were a succulent and juicy fillet steak. It did little to soothe the headache, but it did settle the emptiness in his stomach. He rubbed in small circular motions at his temples to try to find some relief for his pain. He became aware of something pulling at his arm, and as he rotated it inwards for a closer inspection he saw that the wound on his arm had been rather expertly dressed. He sipped at the spilt orange juice and began to feel better.

After what felt like an hour he heard more footsteps, but this time they were softer and lighter. They stopped on the outside of the door, and after a short electronic buzz the door popped open. Hannah appeared. She walked through and closed the door behind her. For a moment husband and wife simply stared at each other, paralysed by the void of truth that lay between them.

"We're being watched, so don't try anything. Okay?" He nodded in agreement as he got up onto his feet. He regarded his wife with fresh eyes. Physically she looked the same, with her blond hair fixed in a twist behind her head. Her imposingly beautiful face somehow always appeared as if it was shrouded in silk, the only imperfections the palest blue eyes, the same colour as the oceans of Bali. There was a part of him that wanted to hold her and be held by her in the familiarity of an embrace. Yet there was something tangibly different about her today, and he felt the sharp corners of an edge that he had never detected before. There was something colder and focussed about her approach as she stood in front of him with her arms folded across her breasts.

"Hannah, what is going on? What the hell is happening to me?" She motioned for him to sit down on the raised block of concrete lining the back wall, and he did so without question, never once taking his eyes off her. She stood in front of him, arms folded, pacing back and forth.

"Ben, there are things going on that you have no idea about." The sure as death hilarity of that statement made him want to grab her by the strained tendons in her neck, scream down her ear, and ask her if she thought he was stupid. He found the idea blended very well with his previous violent thoughts. *How quickly a person can change,* he thought, *given the right stimuli.* He sat patiently instead, staring at her and waiting for her to speak. "What do you remember last?"

"We were at the underground station on Sixtieth."

"No, no", she waved her arms in dismissal which for some reason settled him more than when she stood with them crossed. "Before today. You came home on Wednesday night. We drank some champagne. What next? Before that?"

He scoured his mind for the minutiae of detail, the smallest recollection that may help him to understand. "I remember going to bed, you dragged me up the stairs. We were celebrating."

"You remember NEMREC?"

"Yes, NEMREC." He was quite surprised that she had remembered the name of the formula. She couldn't usually. "After that I woke up today with no identity, Mark is trying to kill me, Ami is dead, and you," he paused as he looked away from his wife, unable to hold her gaze. Had he looked at her, he would have seen a hint of guilt on her face. "I don't even know what to say to you, because I have no idea what you are doing here, or what you want with me."

"What did Ami tell you?"

"She told me that nothing is real. That you are not real. That you are not really my wife." As soon as he said it, he wondered how she knew he had met Ami. Panic rose inside of him, bubbling up as if his blood had reached boiling point. *Could it be that she knew Ami?* More importantly, could she know that he had feelings for her? He decided it was best not to say anything in the interests of not incriminating himself further. Simultaneously he found himself clinging to the hope that she was not responsible for Ami's death and the brutal acts that he had witnessed earlier.

"I am your wife."

"But you don't work as a secretary like I thought you did. I don't know the truth about you, do I?"

Hannah placed her hands on her hips and looked towards the ceiling of the small prison cell as she searched within the flat grey concrete for a way to explain the facts about a reality that she had hoped she would never have to face up to.

"No, I am not a secretary, Ben. I work for the same branch of the government as Ami."

"You mean the OS, something," and he trailed off unable to remember the name that Ami had told him.

"You mean OSWED. Office of Scientific Weaponry Development." He nodded in agreement. "Yes, that is where I work. I am your wife, but that is also part of my job."

"What do you mean, part of your job?" His offence was tangible, and its burden sat heavily on both of their shoulders.

"My assignment was to marry you. My job was to shadow your life and know everything about you and do everything I had to do in order to ensure you were never far away from The Agency's control. You worked for them too, you just didn't realise it." She knew what she was saying stung him. He couldn't look at her.

"That's what Ami told me," he whispered.

"You were targeted, Ben. They believed that you were the only scientist that would make the theory work. They hijacked your life. The day you met me, that was just the beginning."

"You're telling me that everything since I met you has been a lie?"

"Not a lie. Engineered." Gripped in a masochistic moment of silence, he recalled his memories for the last seven years of his life. He thought about their earliest days when they would while away time with no other company but their own, restaurants and bars, holidays and lazy days, all racing before his eyes like a movie playing on rewind. They felt real, and he thought of moments they had shared together when it was just them, and wondered if it was possible that everything about their lives was as fake as it was supposed to be.

"All of the times that you said you loved me. All of the times that I held you in my arms. They meant nothing to you?" His words seemed frail, and came out heaped with shame and hurt at the depth of her deception. "Nothing at all?"

Aware of the camera behind her, and of the eyes and ears that would surely be privy to their discussion, she was careful not to leave her personal feelings exposed. "It was my job to make you feel that we had a real life. It was how it had to be." She didn't want to confirm his beliefs, but she couldn't find it in her heart to lie to him anymore either.

"Every time we made love?" He was angry at her as she dragged their shared history through the mire and discredited his memories. It was hurtful and unfair. He couldn't believe her. It couldn't be true. "When we made our son?"

Hannah looked away desperate for any detail in the otherwise monotonous grey of the wall to focus on, unable to look her husband in the eye. She wanted to tell him that she was sorry, that she didn't want for it to be this way, and that's why she was there, to help him. But nothing that she thought of seemed good enough or suitably poignant to express the profundity of her regret.

"You have to focus on what is actually happening, Ben. We do not have the luxury of time." Her refusal to discuss his pain felt as raw as the bullet wound to his arm. He wanted to rip the dressing off just to spite her, just in case she had been the one to dress his wound. He knew that they had their issues, and that their relationship had been under strain. But he could barely believe that there was nothing left between them, or indeed that perhaps there had never really been anything there at all.

She couldn't be that good at lying, could she?

The love he felt for her was real, but with every passing moment of her refusal to acknowledge his hurt, shards of anger crept between every feeling he had ever felt.

"Ami said that you tried to kill me. Is that true?"

"Her real name was Amena. Yes, I drugged you." She turned and looked at him straight in the eye, hoping that her words would seem truthful and would help make him see the gravity of his situation. She watched as his muscles tightened from his jaw through to his fingertips. She hoped that her own pain was hidden, and that it would fail to break through her thin veil of strength.

"You drugged me with the champagne."

"Yes."

"And Mark? What has he got to do with it?"

"He is my boss. He was Ami's boss too. He gave the orders. He wants you dead, like you are supposed to be, and he will not stop until you are." Two hours ago this would have seemed a ridiculous joke, but he had no doubts anymore that she was telling the truth.

"Then why am I still alive?" She stood silently for a moment, as if contemplating her answer. There was so much that she could say, and that she wished to say, and yet the complexity of the situation prevented the revelation of truth. For a split second her lips parted and Ben expected her to answer. Her initial strength and authority had been weakened by his repeated questioning, and he could sense it. But suddenly her jaw locked shut, her lips closed and her shoulders backed up like the hooves of a stubborn mule.

"Enough with the questions. I told you already there is no time for this. You have a choice Ben, but only one. As far as the world is concerned, you are already dead. Your bank accounts are closed, your identity card is void. There is no trace of the life that you lived anymore, you are now what we call *Identity X*. Don't think that you are the first. You are just the first to survive. It's over, Ben." He sat motionless, his mind thinking back to the grey *X* that flashed up at the underground station when he used his identity card that morning. "I am your only chance, and I'm giving you only one option. I will say that you were shot. The men on my team, they will back me up. We will say that you were lost in the river."

"And where will I go?"

"Initially to a safe house, and then in a couple of weeks I will move you."

"To where?"

"That's not important because you don't have a choice. The only other option for you is to be turned in."

"Your job was to kill me. Why would you help me?" She walked towards the door, aware of the contradictory nature of her story. She held what looked like her identity card in her hand, and he noticed that it looked identical to the card that he had pulled from the pocket of the shooter. She swiped the card against the wall, where until now he had not noticed a small card reader like those in the underground station. The door buzzed and opened just a crack.

"Don't play me, Ben. One hour. Your choice."

"Hannah," he pleaded as she half walked through the door, turning just before her body disappeared into the shadows of a world that he had already lost.

"My name isn't Hannah." She turned and pulled the door shut behind her. He sat listening to the sound of her footsteps as they diminished into silence. He felt an overwhelming sense of regret for every stupid notion he had ever entertained for Ami. Because now, the woman that he truly loved, had been lost to him forever.

ELEVEN

HER FINAL WORDS TO BEN as she left him behind in the cell were playing over and over in her mind, like the stylus of the tone arm stuck in a groove of an old long play record.

My name is not Hannah.

As she had listened to Ben regale his exuberant story on that miserable Wednesday night she had felt enlivened by every bit of his enthusiasm. She drank in his enthusiasm over the smell of his cologne, that somehow managed to stay sweet from morning until night. She had hoped that he wouldn't hear the telephone ringing at their sides as he explained their success. As she answered and heard the simple instructions, *Phase One is activate*, she knew that she didn't have much time. She cracked open the bottle of champagne and poured him a glass. She hadn't been expecting it that night, but she was ready. She knew the moment he told her that he had done it that the telephone call was coming.

She was certain that he hadn't seen the white powder as she tipped it into the flute, and she swirled it around with the smallest of her fingers, blending it into the bubbles. It was a time for celebration and pride in her wonderfully capable husband, and yet his exultant mood was matched only by her own desperation. Desperation that it would go to plan. She had scooped up Matthew as soon as Ben was asleep. As she passed the last step, she heard

Ben wretch, and she took heart knowing that he had at least already been sick. She promised herself that she would deal with her guilt, that there would be a way for him to understand. He had to, because there was no other way.

She left the house that night and reported to her base and her waiting team. She set Matthew down to sleep in a makeshift bed formed from several layers of blankets on the cold floor. Unable to sleep, she sat up drinking coffee throughout the night, watching the steady rise and fall of Matthews's chest as he dreamt about the adventure that she had described to him, his legs twitching as he imagined the lies and mistruths he had believed. She should have slept but she couldn't, such was her anticipation of the next twenty four hours.

When she was given the assignment, Mark had made it seem so easy. He was the new Head of Operations of OSWED, and he was keen to make his position strong. He knew about Ben's research and knew its value. Following his progress had been Mark's first proposal to the board, and they had accepted the idea, such vultures that they were. Mark was smart, but his weakness in character left him susceptible to corruption, and as history would demonstrate, without loyalty.

His first task was to prepare for Ben's future employment. The acquisition of Bionics materialised with such simplicity, and his early victory left quite an impression on the board. Acquiring the right company in order to employ and control Ben had been easy, but the real challenge, Mark had decided, was to control Ben's whole life. To select a woman for him to fall in love with. The first two attempts had proven fruitless. They had equally demonstrated its necessity in the reactive emotional disturbance that had ensued when both relationships failed. Ben did not cope well with loss, each time reliving the death of his father and the painful betrayal of the disease in the years before he died. For weeks after Ben debated the relevance of his research and will to continue. The more Mark had heard about the possibility of Ben taking time out, it had only served to reignite his determination to find him a partner with which he could balance his life. If Ben had chosen to quit, forsaking his dreams and ambitions, how would Mark ever find the opportunity to recruit him into Bionics. *It would really complicate things.* This he had said would be the decisive factor. *Hannah* was the third attempt. From their first meeting it was obvious that Mark's new recruit was perfect for the role. Ben was smitten.

She arrived at the end of the cell corridor and looked to her team for an update.

"Smith, where is he?" A champagne haired man who had the appearance of Scandinavian descent, looked up from his desk. His face was cast in shadow from the dimmed light of his computer screen.

"He went back to headquarters after he found nothing at Twenty Second Street."

"Good. What about the bodies?" She wanted to know what had happened to Amena's body, and that of Agent Adamson, the shooter who had been following Ben.

"Everything is clean, Ma'am."

She had been surprised to feel a faint rumbling of pride as she had approached Ben hovering over the lifeless body of an agent with a gun at his side. In fact, she wished she had got there moments earlier to witness it for herself. Phase One had been an all round disaster as far as the Agency was concerned, and a resounding success in her eyes, even though it had never been her plan for it to get that far. Ben was proving himself to be quite capable, and she wondered if subconsciously any of her influence had somehow been contagious. She liked to think so, but she doubted it. Her only regret was that he woke up too damn soon, and she told herself that she should have waited longer, especially after she heard him vomit before she had even left the house. She should have waited and given him the laced champagne later.

It was an unfamiliar feeling, and not one that she found easy to admit to, but she had panicked a little after taking that call and had rushed to administer an antidote that would regurgitate any drug that Mark must have already given him. She had expected a day or so between the success of NEMREC and the activation of

Phase One, but there had been little more than hours. He should have been lying 'dead' in his bed until the cleanup operation went in on the Friday, and this would have given her plenty of time to get him out. But when she took the call from Mark to say that 'Phase Two' had been activated, she knew something had gone wrong.

Selling the idea of trying to save Ben to her team had been a risk. Going against the will of the Agency was a danger to them all, which she knew could result in the loss of all of their lives. If her plan failed she could try to take the blame, but they would all pay a price. Each of them carried a gun and the knowledge to use it. They too would have had to explain why their weapons had remained in their holsters. They had backed her, though, through loyalty or stupidity she wasn't sure, but together they had agreed to find him and provide him with an escape route.

She sat down in front of the monitors and viewed the map of the city before her. There were five red lights blinking in the region of Twenty Second Street, and several others spread across the city as she zoomed out to get a full view. Their presence, one dot for each agent in the field told her that they were still looking for him.

"Did you transfer his phone signal?" She looked to another of her agents working at a computer in front of her.

"We have hooked it up to skip to different numbers. His signal will hijack different lines as people make calls. They won't be able to track it. Not yet. But they will, if given enough time, and they will know where the hack came from. We don't have long."

"How long?"

"It skips to a new line every fifteen minutes. That should throw them off for a couple of hours. But I need to shut it down before then. They will see that it's not real activity."

She sat back in her chair and sipped on a cup of sweet coffee whilst watching the stationary red lights as they blinked at her on the screen, every one of them baying for Ben's blood. "I have given him an hour. It's enough time."

She looked at the agents around her, each working against their given mission at her request. She wondered how it was that four people with their own lives would accept their new instructions so readily. Perhaps it was loyalty that made them agree to their new instruction. They were trained to be loyal and unquestioning, and to surrender all other aims than that of the company, and to them at least that's what she represented. She always dictated their actions when on an assignment and when Mark remained at a distance.

Why should today be so different?

But today was the first time that she had exercised her own will. Today was the first time that she had really taken a decision. It was the riskiest day so far.

Her thoughts were broken by the sound of the telephone ringing across the other side of the desk. She stood up, and reaching across she grabbed the receiver. There was only one person that called on this line.

"Sir?" She listened as Mark began to speak.

"I need an explanation for what happened earlier at the station on Sixtieth." She felt her pulse quicken, progressing from a walk to a trot. She fiddled with the bottom button on her shirt, just as she always did when she wanted to focus but yet simultaneously wanted to flee.

"Sir, we picked up a signal from his phone and we followed him to the station. We got ahead of him…." Mark didn't let her finish.

"Where did you get this signal? Why were you not at your base? You had played your part in the operation. You were told to stand down."

"Yes, I know, Sir. But we picked up a weak signal and knew we were close. Closer than anybody else could have been. You were on your way to Twenty Second. There was no time to inform you. I knew Phase Two was already active."

"You should have called it in regardless. I have two dead agents now and still no Ben. I take it you know about Ami."

"Yes, Sir." She knew alright.

"I haven't established exactly who she was working for yet, but it's lucky for her she was shot in action. It makes the cessation of her service sound a little more glorious than being exposed as an informant."

"Yes, Sir."

"I want you back at The Shop for immediate debriefing." He hung up the telephone leaving no option for her to answer, argue, or barter her position. She placed the receiver back onto the base and felt four sets of eyes resting upon her, waiting to know what was coming next. She tapped her fingernails along the side of the coffee cup. The whole agency was searching for a dead man, who was already safely accosted in one of their own cells. She had the whole of the Agency against her, and the only thing in her favour was that they were yet to realise it. She looked up at the agents at her side.

"Time's up. Get him in the van."

TWELVE

SHE HAD NOT BEEN ABLE to listen as she heard her agents shouting at Ben to get his own clothes back on, and she had taken herself outside on account of it. He had been screaming, demanding to talk to Hannah. They tried not to be too rough as they forced his stolen jacket back on. After shackling his hands and feet like a slave, they forced a pair of goggles over his eyes, blacked out with duct tape. It heightened his sense of smell, a fact for which he was most ungrateful. The splatters of once hot blood on his jacket had now congealed into damp cold patches that smelt stale and rusty, forcing him to suck his chest away from it by arching his shoulders forwards. They dragged him by the armpits towards the door. He heard the buzz as it popped open and they marched him up the corridor and towards the central work room.

"Ben, listen to me," Hannah said as she greeted him at the door. His head jittered left and right in search of her voice. "We have no time left. You have about five minutes to make your decision. We will have to kill you if you don't agree to the plan." He listened as she spoke in front of him, his ears his only guide to her position. "Get him in the van," she demanded of the others.

The four agents trawled past her and pushed him into the same black van in which he had left the underground station. She went back to the building to close down the computers and tracking systems at her desk. She waited for them to exit the room through the large sliding door, and then she collected the telephone, wallet, and fake identity card that Ben had been carrying with him. There could be no trace of him left here. They would find it. As she picked up the wallet she was stunned by the sight before her as it fell open in her hand. Inside the wallet was a photograph of Ben, Matthew, and her cuddled up together. She remembered it being taken one Sunday morning as they had lounged around in bed, all three of them. Ben had held the camera up in front of them, and they had all squashed their heads in together in order to fit in the frame. Now as she held the wallet in her hands she realised that neither Hannah Stone nor Ben Stone existed anymore. Both identities had been wiped at the onset of *Phase One*, and she would have to go back to being who she had been before she met Ben. Matthew was effectively an orphan, and the family that she saw before her was dead.

"Ma'am, we are ready to go." The voice from behind her requested her attention. She turned to face the agent, closing the wallet as she did so.

"I'm ready." She walked out into the gentle April sunlight, the air cool whipping against her skin. She wondered how cold Ben might be in the light clothes that he was wearing; ripped, damaged, and bloody from his time in the underground station. She took the handle of the heavy sliding door and dragged it into place. The automatic locking code activated, and with the last and longest beep, her base was officially shut down. She pulled the second, original wooden door shut and flicked the latch before securing the padlock, leaving no visible trace of what this building actually was. Once again it looked just like an average cabin in the woods.

Ben was placed in the back of the van with three agents, and Agent Smith sat in the front. She found the small black device that was located on the underside of the van and she leant down closely, pushing her weight behind it with her foot. It dislodged from its position, dropping to the ground. With a cautious eye on the door of the van she fiddled her hand around in the mud until she located the box and picked it up. She smashed it against the side of the van and stuffed the remains in her pocket.

"Let's go." She prompted Smith, who nodded his

agreement. After a quick look back to his fellow agents through the small window to the back of the van, he started the engine. She too took a glance through, but she paid no attention to the agents. Instead she watched Ben, whose head was tilted upwards. She heard him say her name, muffled as it was through the thickset glass, and she stifled her feelings of guilt with the intention to remain focused on the task in hand.

They drove away from the disused wood yard following a poorly trodden dirt track that formed the only road to and from her base. There was a small gate that granted access which she activated from a button inside the van. The white barrier rose, and as they passed through she pressed another button which resulted in the closure of the gate. They rattled over the lumps of the road to a chorus of requests from Ben. She could hear him shouting, demanding to know where they were taking him, as he banged his feet repeatedly against the floor of the vehicle with all the insolence of a school boy. She held onto the dashboard with her right hand to steady herself as Smith negotiated the unpredictable surface of the road, whilst in her left hand she fingered the soft leather of her husband's wallet. She hoped so much that when presented with the only option available to him, he would take it without question or incident. She could hear him in the back, shouting at his three companions, and she hoped that he would manage to calm down by the time they drew to a halt. It would be a difficult task for any person to control him should he choose to encumber the necessary steps of her plan. His repeated demands to be unshackled and released fell onto ignorance, and trained as they were, she knew that her team's patience would only stretch so far.

She remembered her training, when unexpectedly one night she was taken in this way, terrified and bound in the dark with no clue who it was that held her captive, or where they were taking her. She was interrogated for hours in an effort to assess her strength and commitment to the Agency. She had passed the test easily, never once giving any indication to her captors of her level of fright and terror. Not when they punched her. Not when they pulled the wrist straps tighter. Not when they burnt her with their cigarettes. Not even when they threatened to take so much more, slipping their filth-covered hands into the waistband of her pyjamas. Ben had received no such training. How was he supposed to be calm? She slapped her sweaty palm on the metal wall between her and her husband leaving a visible wet patch. She wondered what it was that was making her sweat, the memories of the past, the uncertainty of the present, or her fear for the future. But then she heard a break in Ben's demands.

"Ben, stay calm. We are nearly there," she called.

Smith, the most senior of her agents, drove towards their destination. They exited the forest, proceeding along a narrow country lane which meandered towards what looked like a lake. But this body of water led directly to the sea. It was her planned escape route for Ben. The road was good, and they began to cover ground much faster.

"Smith, keep moving along this road for another two hundred meters and then pull into the parking area." She pointed to her left, indicating a small gravel clearing alongside a boat house that wasn't visible from the road. The tyres skidded on the loose surface as the van ground to a halt. She pulled her telephone from her pocket and held it up to her ear to make a call. There were no sounds, not even from Ben, and the silence of his uncertainty and anticipation felt almost as smothering as his dissidence.

"We're here," she said into her telephone. Her words were like a quick slap, delivered, rhetorical, no response needed. She hung up, and nodded to Smith to exit the van.

A man appeared to meet her at the entrance to the boathouse. He was small in stature with a full beard. He was wearing a thick jumper and burgundy corduroy trousers that seemed too heavy for the April weather, even with the chill that hung in the air. Agent Smith stood by his closed door, watching the couple as they embraced. The bearded man regarded her as a grandfather might regard a grownup granddaughter, proudly, but with perhaps a hint of sadness that the easy days of childhood had passed her by. She turned back and nodded to Smith, a signal that he should bring Ben forth. He hit the side of his fist against the van three times, and then heard the footsteps of those inside as they moved towards the door.

The smell of the fresh countryside air and the breeze on his face was a welcome relief to Ben. It was claustrophobic under his blacked-out goggles and the clean, salt-tinged air helped. He felt two sets of hands either side of him pushing him forwards, and he was certain that he could sense footsteps behind him too. The sound of trees rustling overhead made him think they were still in the forest, and the background lull of the water as it lapped against the shore gave him an inappropriate sense of peace.

"Bring him here." Ben heard his wife's familiar voice as she shouted instructions. The agents pushed him forward, and the sound of the shore intensified as he was led in her direction. She pulled the goggles from his face. The overpowering daylight forced him to squint and cower away. His focus came back into view and he saw his wife standing alongside an unfamiliar man.

"What are we doing here, Hannah? Who is this?" Ben held up his shackled hands in the direction of the bearded boatman, only a couple of arms length away.

She didn't answer. Instead she instructed Agent Smith. "Take these off now," she said, pointing to Ben's ankles. Ben stared at the back of Smith's head as he leaned down to remove the shackles. He considered the strength of two clenched fists against the soft bone at the base of the agent's skull. With enough force he could likely snap the delicate spinal cord it he caught it just right. He could at least knock him out. But then Ben glanced around and saw the other agents, each of them with their eyes trained on him. It was a stupid idea, and wouldn't help. He looked up and found Hannah staring straight at him.

"Your choice is very simple. You go with this man, or you go with us. Going with us only leads in one direction. Remember, in our world, Ben, you are already dead. Killing you isn't a crime if you don't exist."

"Hannah, I haven't done anything. I haven't done anything wrong. I'm Matthew's father. Have you forgotten that?" She reached her hand in her pocket and delicately stroked the soft leather of the wallet as if it were their actual faces on the photograph inside. "What will you tell him?"

"What I have to. The fact that you are Matthew's father is the only reason I am risking my own life now. You have to go with this man." Ben could feel the lump of hurt forming in the back of his throat, and he tried to swallow it down so that he could continue to plead for a chance to see his son again. A chance to save his old life.

"But I love you, Hannah." A solitary tear broke free from his eye and trickled over his cheek before falling to the ground. He reached forward, striking her arms with his shackled hands. His movement caught the attention of the agents, each taking an assertive step forward, the pack moving in to strike, before she called off the hunt with a single shake of her head. Smith stepped away and stood to the side. "I love Matthew. Don't take everything away from me." She knew when he referred to everything that he didn't just mean the two of them. He was referring to his work, his other baby which never ceased to require attention and time. It was the child that never grew up, and he was the parent that never tired of feeding and nappy changes. "The people I could have saved. I could have saved Matthew."

"You don't need to save him, Ben." She looked at his reddened face, his eyes puffy as the leaves of the towering Ash trees danced about above him. "He doesn't have Huntington's disease like your father did."

"But we had him tested, he carries the gene faults just like I do. He had enough glutamine repeats in his genes to cause the disease. That means he will get ill, Hannah. I'm just a carrier, but he will become ill. I'll be able to cure him. Give me a chance to do that." He raised his hands to her face, wanting to touch her. Perhaps something would transfer between them and make her see sense.

She shook her head and averted her gaze, pulling herself away. "He won't get ill. He's clear. He doesn't have Huntington's like you think he does." Ben looked at Hannah as if he may have met her once and vaguely recognised her. "You were lied to."

"Why?"

"So you wouldn't stop."

Ben felt a simultaneous sense of relief and anger as he heard that Matthew was healthy. In a single moment he had won back his son, and lost him all over again. How she could allow their son to be used like that was beyond his ability for comprehension, but the relief was so great that the single tear that had already fallen was followed by a torrent as he brought his hands up to his face to shield himself from view.

She placed her hand on his shoulder. "Get on the boat, Ben." Her words were soft and warm, and it reminded him of the thousands of times that she had whispered three enchanting words in his ears. Now she was offering him something back. Another chance. All he had ever wanted was to cure Matthew, and now he knew he didn't have to his concerns seemed to fade faster than fog on a summer's morning.

She had risked everything to offer him safety. In a cruel twist of fate, by stepping on that boat, he was offering Matthew a future with his mother. She, at least, would return safely. She took out the wallet and placed it against his chest and he took it in his hand. For a moment their skin connected and he felt her warm soft fingers against his own. He glanced at the photograph inside and gulped down another lump in his throat. He nodded his head solemnly as he wiped the tears away and allowed himself to be guided by her hand, still resting on his shoulder.

As she turned to walk with Ben to the boat she heard an almost inaudible sound that her trained ear would never miss. She swung round, pulling her gun from its holster, aiming it upwards to meet her fellow agents. The agent's gun was ready, his arm outstretched, pointing at Ben.

"Smith, what are you doing? Lower your weapon!" She spoke with the urgency of somebody who had no time to stop and think, her words bursting out from her subconscious.

"Ma'am, I can't let you go through with this." Smith spoke on the behalf of his henchmen. "If he gets away and the part this team played in it is discovered, it's our lives that are over. I can't let you risk that, Ma'am. I can't let you risk our lives for his."

"Nobody will find out if everybody keeps their mouths shut. How could they find out?"

He ignored her pleas. "We have to turn him in. None of us will say a word about your part in this. But we can't let him get away."

"Smith, you don't understand. We can't kill him. We can't..." Smith didn't let her finish.

"We respect you, Ma'am. We do. We have given you every chance to rein this in. To do the right thing. But now we have to take over. I promise that your part in this will stay with us."

"Smith," she said with definite and purposeful words, "you will not kill this man." Ben was looking frantically between Smith and Hannah, realising that suddenly he had more than one option. Hannah couldn't let them kill him.

She had pulled her gun on her own team in his defence. All of the things she had told him, she couldn't carry them out. *She wouldn't let them be carried out.* The bearded boatman took tentative steps around Ben's other side, and as he moved forwards Ben saw the gun strapped to his back. Ben remembered the power that he had felt in the underground station and wished that it had been a weapon rather than a wallet that Hannah had placed in his hand moments ago.

"I will, Ma'am."

Her eyes darted between Smith and the other men, analysing each of them and waiting for their next move. She silently pulled her finger back on the trigger, squeezing it a little, and braced her arms.

"Ben, get on the boat." Smith's eyes were on him, boring a hole into his forehead as deep as a bullet. Hannah repeated her words again, never taking her eyes from the gunman.

"Get on the boat, Ben."

"Don't move, Mr. Stone." Smith didn't care about putting a bullet into Ben's chest, but he genuinely hoped to avoid putting one into his boss's. "Stay where you are."

"Hannah," Ben cried, even though he now knew it wasn't her real name. "What should I do?"

"Get on the boat!" she shouted.

"Stay where you are, Stone."

Hannah's eyes were fixed on Smith's trigger finger. She watched as he strengthened the position of his finger and braced for a shot. He was well trained and there was very little chance of failure from this distance. Without a second thought she unloaded a single shot into the centre of his forehead, sending a fountain of blood and bone spraying into the air. She didn't hear Ben scream behind her as she trained her sights on the next agent, and as smooth and seamless as the passage of light she delivered the same fatal blow into the side of Agent Roberts' head. The third agent had enough time to get his hand on his gun, but not enough to remove it from the holster before the boatman unloaded a double round into his face, hitting him in the right eye and levelling him to the ground to meet his team. She turned and pointed her gun directly at the forth agent. She was joined by the boatman, putting a line of weaponry between the agent and Ben.

"He's getting on that boat." The agent looked at her as she spoke, knowing that he had no chance to arm himself, and no way out of the situation that allowed him to secure his prisoner.

"You're making a mistake, Catherine," the final agent said. Instead of reaching for his gun, he took a step forwards towards her. He raised his hands in half-surrender. "If you leave on that boat, I will have to turn you in. I'll give you some time, but I have to do it."

"I know you would have to." Only a second passed after she had finished speaking before she unloaded a final round into his forehead, dropping the last of the agents. She felt the spray of blood on her skin from the close range hit. The body landed at her feet with a thud, and she turned to see Ben staggering to the ground, his arms raised up in a protective arc around his body. He watched as a pool of bright red blood, the purity of which was tainted only by lumps of flesh, formed underneath his head.

"It's time to move, Ben. Get yourself on the boat and wait for us."

"You shot them," he said as she leaned down and pulled the keys from the top of Agent Smith's bloody torso. It was the final kill that had surprised Ben. The agent had spoken to her as a friend, had offered her time to get away. He had known that there was no chance to control the situation, and instead had conceded his defeat to save his life, but she took it anyway. Ben knew she had done it for him.

He watched his wife and the boatman as they pulled the first of the bodies along the ground towards the black van. "You shot them all," he repeated in disbelief staring at the heaped up bodies which had fallen onto each other like a pile of old coats.

She looked up at his stunned face as she grabbed a second body. "They would have killed you, Ben. As soon as I knew they weren't with me, it meant they were against me. That changes a lot of things." She horsed the first of the bodies into the back of the van and pushed it in like a butcher would manhandle a carcass of a pig ready for sale. "I had to kill them," she justified, sensing his distrust. He stood back and surveyed as the man and woman team worked to drag the remaining three bodies across the ground, leaving tracks of blood and debris in their path.

Ben watched as the duo spoke before looking back towards him. Then she walked over to him, wiping her hands on a rag that she had recovered from the back of the van, transferring red streaks as she moved it across her blood stained hands. He felt his muscles tighten as she approached. He thought about running, but where would he go? She stopped a few feet before him, hanging her head. She looked like a child whose delinquency had been exposed.

"I'm sorry, Ben. I'm so very sorry." He stood motionless,

wondering how he could possibly find the words to answer. He wasn't sure that the words he needed even existed. Not even the greatest of poets had ever managed to mould words to express such depth of feeling. He didn't even know what her apology leaned towards: the lies, the capture, the drugging, the shooting, or the loss of his life and child?

Take your pick, Ben, he thought to himself.

"Hannah..." he said again, before realising his mistake. "Or should I say Catherine?"

She raised a hand to stop him. She wanted to speak. In her mind she had everything ready that she wanted to say and to tell him. But everything was so well compartmentalised and secured, her secrets so deeply hidden, it was virtually impossible to find the key to unlock them. She barely knew herself what the truth was anymore.

"Ben, I don't even know where to begin, or how to explain everything to you. What I told you back at my old base, most of it was true. But I also kept things from you. I had to."

"You kept things from me? Just today? You mean like the fact you kill people. That you work for people who want me dead. The fact that Matthew isn't ill." There was more than a hint of sarcasm in his voice, and he looked away, ashamed of just how he had been duped. How easy it had been to pull the wool over his eyes. How easy it had been to lie to him for all these years. He suddenly felt very stupid as he stood there with his limbs shackled and splattered in blood. He wanted to spit at her, just to make her feel some of the shame that raged through him. Instead, he bit his lip and locked his fingers together.

"I kept things from you because I wanted to save you. I wanted to avoid this."

"Avoid it?" He was momentarily distracted by the boatman who had by now finished shoving the last of the dead bodies into the van. She used the distraction to get closer to him. By the time he looked back was standing so close that he could feel her breath on his cheeks, see her hairs fluttering in the breeze. "You have been part of this whole thing. Since before we met you were part of this. You've been planning to kill me for years."

"No, I haven't. The beginning is true. I work for them, and you began as an assignment. But I fell in love with you, Ben. You're the most amazing man I have ever met." She began to cry and he felt the urge to hold her and comfort her. But as soon as he moved his arms closer the image of her holding up the gun and firing at the agents pulled him back. She wiped her tears and smudged the blood splatters across her face. "For years now I knew that I wouldn't go through with the operation. I was willing your work to take years and years, but you're so brilliant you achieved where everybody had failed."

"I was trying to save people's lives, Hannah." It was all he could do to stop himself from crying, as he gulped down the painful lump that obstructed the back of his throat. "You were trying to destroy mine. You tried to kill me."

"No, I didn't."

"You drugged me! You admitted it, remember?"

"But not to kill you. It was Mark that drugged you at the bar. I lied to you back at my old base because I knew that they were watching us, and listening. Mark drugged you. I gave you champagne that I spiked with something that would make you throw up, and something to make you sleep. My plan was to pick you up at our house after the effects wore off. I thought I had more time."

"You expect me to believe that?"

"You can believe me or not. It's the truth. I never wanted to kill you. You're Matthew's father. How could I have ever looked him in the eye? I would never have turned you in, and I would kill them all over again if it meant getting you on that boat. It was my only chance to save you."

"But you didn't save me. I don't exist anymore, Hannah. I'm dead already."

"In case you haven't noticed, I just killed my whole team. That pretty much means that I am dead too. Hannah Stone doesn't exist anymore either." She walked away towards the shore where she began to remove her clothes. She washed away the blood by splashing the cold water on her face. Then the boatman walked towards Ben, stopping just long enough to deliver his verdict.

"She loves you, Ben." He rested his hand onto Ben's shoulder, cupping it affectionately. "She is telling you the truth, and she has just caused herself a whole world of problems to save your life."

"What am I supposed to believe?" Ben found himself confiding in the cordially faced stranger, searching for help from an unknown source. Perhaps that was the only thing that he could really trust after the events of the past two days.

"Believe what you feel. She could have killed you already. More than once from what I understand. She didn't, and she just floored four men in order to protect you. You know I am right."

"I don't even know who you are. Why the hell should I believe you?"

"I'm her father, Ben." His father-in-law, a total stranger, offered him a warm smile, in which Ben found an unexpected level of comfort. He patted Ben's shoulder before he walked off in Hannah's direction. That's when Ben caught a glimpse of his reflection in a window of the boat house. It revealed several spots of blood across his cheeks and forehead. He spat on his fingers, imagined that the spots were his wife's face, and proceeded to rub frantically and angrily at Ami's blood.

THIRTEEN

AFTER A PERIOD OF IMMOBILITY and disbelief, he looked back at the shore towards father and daughter as the boatman held out fresh clothes for her to wear. She dressed into a fresh clean polo neck sweater and readjusted her hair which had been disturbed in the process. After loading her handgun with a fresh magazine she stowed it back into its holster on the back of her hip. She loaded two bags into the boat and then walked back towards Ben. He was sitting on the rear steps of the boathouse.

"Can I sit with you?" She pointed to the empty space on the step next. He continued to fiddle with the loose rocks that were resting at his feet. He shrugged his shoulders in a display of indifference, and she sat down, curling her knees up in front of her chest. To Ben it seemed to function only to put another barrier between them. Whilst he flat out refused to look at her, as obstinate as a teenager, he could feel that she was watching him. She held out a key for the shackles, and it was the token she needed to soften him up. He held out his hands and feet and she removed his restraints. He rubbed his wrists, angrily at first, a protest at the injustice of it all. But he couldn't hide his gratitude for their removal, and eventually he cracked a light smile.

"My name is Catherine Mulligan," she began. "I was born in Cork, Ireland, and moved here when I was three years old for my father to work. He was an agent like me, but I grew up believing that he was an engineer, building bridges all over the world. I was sixteen years old when I discovered the truth, and it broke my heart. I wrote a school assignment on paper which I had taken from his desk and he went crazy, telling me that I couldn't use the paper that he kept in his drawers. He made me rewrite it there and then, and afterwards he put the original in water and I watched the letters disappear. That's when I first realised there were things in our life that I didn't understand, and that didn't make sense.

"He sat me down afterwards, explained what he really did for a living. At first I was angry that he had lied to me. But then I decided I wanted to be like him." Ben continued to wriggle his hands and feet about in a circular fashion, reigniting the flow of blood to his fingers and toes.

"So what? You enrolled in a school for assassins?"

"I joined a training programme, yes. You sign yourself over. No going back. Only one way out. You were my second assignment. I was twenty three, young, and naive. I thought that I could do it. I thought I could live with you and pretend to love you. But that was before I knew you. It was before I actually loved you." Her eyes darted away. She twiddled with the button of her trousers, something she accepted as a pathetically comforting distraction.

"And then what?" he asked in a calm moment.

"I knew it was over, as far as the initial plan went. I couldn't kill you. Then we had Matthew. I kept the pregnancy from them for the first five months. I only told them when I thought that they wouldn't make me abort the baby. That's why I never wanted us to tell anybody about the pregnancy."

"I believed you when you told me that it was hard for you because your mother died when you were young. I tried to support you and all the time you were lying." He closed his eyes for a moment turning his head away, thinking of all the times that he had wanted to celebrate the imminent arrival of his child, and how he had worried so much for his expectant wife and her emotional state as she had wrestled with the memories of the loss of a parent. He thought of his father, and it reminded him of his research. When he opened his eyes she was looking at him again, and he felt the waves of hatred roll in, hating her more in that moment than he had ever before as he thought about the many lies she had spun him. He felt like such a fool.

"I know you supported me. But it's not all lies. My mother really did die when I was young. It was hard for me. I was scared for our baby. In the end I told the Agency that I got pregnant on purpose because you wanted to leave me."

"I never wanted to leave you."

"I know, but it was a way to make them accept it, because secretly I was so happy we were going to have Matthew." She reached out for his hands but she realised as soon as her skin touched his that she couldn't feel the same familiar spark that was always there before. Even in the bad times when they drove each other nuts and when she wished he would just disappear for a while, she still felt it. Now he felt like a stranger, that first date awkwardness when nobody knows if touching is allowed. There was no response, no minute muscle twitch or movement towards the stimuli of her skin. She pulled away, terrified to feel the nothingness between them. She took some breaths and counted in her head. She got to five and then carried on. "After that, I formed links with people. People that could help me. People I found who thought the same way that I did."

"Which is what?"

"That sometimes their way," she paused as if only to add time for confirmation, "isn't necessarily the right way." They looked at each other, searching each other's faces for a sign; Ben for truth, Hannah for forgiveness.

"Hannah, where is our son?"

"He's at Headquarters. I was really hoping that you would have got on that boat." She smiled, half heartedly. "You kind of messed up the plan."

"I would have got on the boat. It was your own men that

messed up your plan." She nodded in solemn agreement. He was surprised to feel sympathetic towards her as he began to believe in her explanation. "Fortunately for me, it seems that I married a woman who is pretty sharp with a gun. My father-in-law seems pretty handy, too," he joked as he nudged her shoulder with his own. "Thanks for saving my life."

"I didn't save it yet. You're still here. You're still dead, remember?" She looked at him, her face stone cold serious, with a determination that he had never seen before as she reached up to place her hand against his cheek. He didn't stop her. "But I will."

As they walked towards the boat that was moored on the opposite side of the boathouse, Hannah's father handed her a set of keys, and pressed her hand shut. They stared at each other, telepathic words exchanged with nothing more than a look. She nodded and tucked them into her trouser pocket before she turned back to Ben. Ben felt like a stranger, somebody who didn't belong, as if he had been eavesdropping and now had to promise never to tell their secrets.

"Ben, it might be a bit late for this, but this is my father." Ben automatically held out his hand, and the boatman took it with wholehearted warmth that gave Ben a sense of reassurance. His handshake was firm and laconic.

"Ben, she's a good girl. She did what she had to. Now it's your turn to do the same. She has risked her own life and that of Matthew in order to get you out. Trust her. She won't fail you."

"Yes, sir," Ben said, feeling eighteen years old again. "Aren't you supposed to tell me to look after her?"

"Son, you've seen her handle this piece," he said as he tapped the gun that sat on her hip. "She can take care of herself alright. Just back her up by doing as she says." The boatman reached down and produced another identical gun, placing it into Ben's palm. "I heard you're not too bad a shot yourself." Ben wondered in how many situations the first time you meet the father of your wife an exchange regarding the positive nature of how you had killed a man earlier on in the day would be deemed acceptable.

Positive even. The boatman reached a strap around Ben's waist, and helped him adjust the firearm into the newly positioned holster. "Best just to sit it here," he said as he shuffled it into the same rear facing position that mirrored Hannah's. "It'll be more comfortable if you have to run."

Ben stepped onto the boat, a small white vessel no longer than a few meters in length and with rounded sides that made it look like an inflatable dinghy. In the middle of the boat stood a small pillar which housed the throttle and steering wheel, and an array of gauges that he had no idea how to read or handle. He waited as Hannah held her father in her embrace, before she too stepped onto the boat, rocking its balance as she did so. Ben should have realised that it would be the last time that she would ever see him, but the thought didn't even cross his mind.

"Ben, take those bags from there," she said, and she pointed to the two rucksacks that she had thrown in a few moments before. He picked up the first, which was light. The flap was open slightly, and inside he could see pieces of fruit abutted up against a flask of something he desperately hoped was hot and caffeine rich. The second bag was heavy, and as he moved it the contents inside fell around, ringing out the sound of metal on top of metal. "Careful with that one. Place them both in the compartment over there. We don't want them wet." He lifted the lid of the box that she pointed to and did as he was told. Placing the lid back onto the box, he sat down and waited for her next instruction.

He was surprised by her expert control of the boat, manoeuvring it out onto the still water, which until disturbed bore a resemblance to the finest silk imprinted with the reflection of trees from above. She pulled a small black box from her pocket and threw it overboard. He didn't ask what it was.

He wondered how it was that he had made such a mistake when it came to his impression of his wife. How could it have transpired that their relationship was so complex? How could she have fooled him for as many years as she did? In the recent years he had come to regard her difficult, even whiney at times, desperately on occasion seeking his attention and approval. This woman that stood before him with the boat steering wheel in one hand and the throttle in the other was anything but needy. In fact, it was only because of her, her courage and her quick fingered willingness when it came to a trigger of a gun that he was still alive. She didn't once look back to her father, who was already walking away from the water's edge and back to the black van which held four dead bodies. Ben didn't know what he was planning to do with them. *Bury them? Burn them?* Whatever it was, it had been arranged. On the spur of the moment when it had come to killing four people Hannah had thought nothing of it, and four dead bodies in the back of a van appeared to prove nothing more than an inconvenience. He had no idea which side Hannah was really on, or her father. But for now he had to assume that whatever side it was, they were on it together.

FOURTEEN

MARK SAT WITH HIS ARM resting against the heavy set door as the car snaked through the roads towards Headquarters. It was almost as thick as the door of an aircraft. The reflection of his face in the inch thick glass rippled in and out of view, yet he barely recognised it as his own. He saw dark eye sockets and ruffled hair. He looked smaller somehow, disarrayed like his plans. He felt weaker, a man cut down by a virus, consumed as a host, unable to function.

The vehicle draw to a halt, and the sound of both front doors opening prompted him to ready himself for his exit. He had loosened his tie on account of his throat feeling constricted, so he straightened himself and his clothing up. In the centre of his head he felt a familiar pressure. It was a tight knot that had positioned itself between his eyes and fed off his stress. The patch of eczema on the palm of his hand was itching, and it had got worse this last week. Coincidental, he had told himself. There was a new patch on his foot too, and he could feel it itching in an inaccessible location. He crunched up his toes and rubbed the side of his foot against the other as if trying to stimulate a spark between two dry sticks in the search for a snippet of relief.

The heavy door opened, and he slipped out his feet in one steady motion. He heard the raindrops drumming on the waiting umbrella as he stood up underneath it.

"Sir." He was greeted by a faceless agent, somebody that he didn't know. He said nothing in reply and walked at his usual quick pace. The agent quickened his pace in order to keep up with Mark as he climbed the steps to Headquarters. Above him the rows of identical windows offered no view in. They appeared reflective like mirrors, and yet as black as the raven that he could hear cawing in the trees that encircled the building.

The rain began to fall heavily as he approached the front doors, and the flanking agents at Mark's side stepped up their pace to move ahead. They stood with their hands on the covered keypad, and as they simultaneously entered their private key codes. The doors opened, and with second perfect timing Mark approached the thick, mirrored-glass doors. His reflection rippled away and he stepped into the belly of Headquarters.

The heels of the agents resonated as they walked through the foyer, each step vibrating up to the high level ceiling. Captain White greeted them as they neared the rear door, his arms laden with papers. His usually coiffed hair appeared tousled, scruffed up, like he'd had a really rough night's sleep. He looked spent.

"Sir, all of the arrangements for Agent Sadler were made, and Seventy Fourth Street has been cleaned." His words came spluttering from his lips, all breathy and eager like he was talking to a really hot woman. Nerves. He fidgeted the papers about in his arms waiting for a response, hoping he had impressed.

Mark stood in front of his subordinate, his crowd of underlings waiting anxiously for his reaction to Agent Sadler's name. Sets of eyes twitched left and right, looking for comfort in another man's gaze at the uncomfortable mention of Ami. They had all heard by now what had happened. The news had filtered through like Chinese whispers, bringing with it sorrow and disbelief. Then the second wave of gossip had spread, she was a foreign agent, a double agent, working for both sides. *Oh in that case, good job. It was for the best.* Even the ones who didn't really mean it kept their grief to themselves.

"It is quite clear to me now that Agent Sadler was not at all what she seemed. Amena Saad was in fact the daughter of Abdel

Salam Saad, a well know buyer of weapons who feeds not only the east, but the west, the north, and the south. Had they have successfully stolen the data that we have tried for many years to acquire he would have undoubtedly made a fortune from the nearest buyer. In the near future we would have been the victim of our own success, and subsequent failure.

"It is your department that manages recruitment and dissolution of contract, is it not, Captain White?" The whole crowd knew the meaning of dissolution of contract. It was a phrase that made even the most secure of agents fearful. There was not a single agent who would have wished for 'dissolution of their contract.' The discomfort rippled through the ten pairs of feet as they shuffled about.

"Yes, Sir. It is indeed."

"Then you were, as I understand it, solely responsible for her recruitment."

"Yes, Sir. That is correct."

"Then you and I have much to discus regarding Amena Saad. But right now I want to know the location of Ben Stone. That is our priority. What do you have?" Mark began to walk towards his office, through the corridors and hordes of eyes that gazed upon him. The rumour of the operational failure had began its diffusion throughout the department. Captain White glanced repeatedly at the papers, reading as they moved through the crowds, sidestepping the other agents in order to get close to Mark.

"Sir, Agent Mulligan tracked him to the underground station on Sixtieth. He shot an agent and disappeared into the tunnels. Her team followed him but came up with nothing. We picked up a signal from his phone line briefly, and we have sent agents in that direction, but it was a very brief signal, and has subsequently not been identified again."

"You mean you haven't got anything on him since he left the underground station?"

"For half an hour it looked as if he was heading in an

easterly direction, but the last activity we recorded was over forty minutes ago."

"Tell me, Captain White, how can a man with no identity, no financial resources, and approximately one hundred agents on his tail, manage to evade our grip? We have tracked this man successfully for many years and controlled his life to the point that I could even decide what he was eating for breakfast. What holiday destination he may visit. Short of controlling when he goes to the toilet we knew everything about him. Yet suddenly we know absolutely nothing. How is this possible?"

"Sir, we have every agent out looking for him. We have every underground station sealed. There is no exit he could take that doesn't go through us."

"But yet he is still loose. Find him." They had reached Mark's office door and he held up his access card. He turned to look at Captain White for the first time since they had started walking together. "Find him, and kill him." He turned to another agent on his right just before he closed the door behind him. "Mulligan is on her way in. When she gets here, send her directly to me."

Mark didn't wait for a response. He didn't need the confirmation from his staff that his instructions would be followed. There wasn't a single person working in his department that would dare go against his will. Yet there had been many whisperings that his appointment had been misguided, a gentle nod from most of the staff with military experience that his lack of exactly that had made his position untenable. They had all been professional to his face, of course. But he knew that they were talking about him now that things had gone awry. This one mistake could be the very thing that justified their beliefs. He couldn't let that happen.

To fail in Ben's elimination at the final hurdle had the potential to show weakness, and therefore undermine everything he had ever achieved. It would render years of work worthless. He knew people were wondering if his friendship with Ben had prevented him from delivering the fatal drug. They thought he was trying to help Ben. The only proof of his dedication to the agency now was Ben's body, cold and dead and on a slab. It was his only option.

He gazed at the computer screens around him. He saw the multitude of red lights, each representing an agent in the field. It corroborated Captain White's account that there was indeed no underground exit left uncovered. The red lights blinked in uniform straight lines following the course of the train system, equally spaced and in pairs as his team sat guard at the stations. There was also a small collection of dots forming an arc around the eastbound perimeter of the city, a backup team in case Ben's travel east had in some inexplicable way been successful. He rested his heavy head on the palm of his hand, as if his muscles couldn't cope with the weight of it, which served only to make his painful headache feel worse. He took several deep cleansing breaths, safe from view of his team on the other side of the reinforced wall where such a display of tension he had forbidden himself long ago.

His private office was a fortress within a fortress. The walls were reinforced against radiation and built with an aluminium and steel layer. He had his own passageway towards an underground bunker. It was an emergency shelter for the face of the government that not even they knew existed. That was the best way of keeping its existence secret. If ever that secret was compromised it would be the end of the system as Mark knew it. For his Agency to survive, first it had not to exist.

He pulled the top file from the pile on his desk. After pushing aside the large glass paperweight he placed the beige cardboard folder in front of him. It was marked three of ten, which meant that the pile had become irritatingly disarranged. Mark had ensured that the documents from Ben's lab be entrusted to his own safe keeping. In truth, he wanted to read through them. He wanted the words to lift from the page and transfer into his own mind, reawaken his scientific abilities. Eventually he intended for them to become his own words, his own work. That way he could replace the one thing that until then had been irreplaceable. Ben.

He knew that he wouldn't understand the majority of what was written immediately. It would take time. These were after all, Ben's handwritten notes from years of research. The date on the top of this file was from three years previously. He leafed through the contents, the notes and diagrams a foreign language to him. He brushed his thumb against the spines of the other files. He found the latest file, marked *ten of ten.*

Opening the folder he saw that the latest page was dated only two days before, the final day of Ben's existence. It was unimaginable how Ben had failed to maintain computer records. He scanned through the results before closing the file, telling himself he had all the time in the future to read it.

Taking one final look at the red lights blinking on the screen, he stood from his desk, leaving the office behind him as he stepped out into the corridor. The only sounds around him were the tapping of computer keyboards or the occasional scratch of the lead of a pencil against paper. *Which one of you was talking about me before I came out of my office,* he asked himself rhetorically, fearing that the answer could be all of them.

He knew they were thinking him to be a weak leader, or worse, a traitor. He ignored his desire to question them, to ask if they had any idea what it was that he had given up in order to get this operation off the ground. If they had any idea of what personal cost he had paid in the pursuit of success, the thought wouldn't even cross their minds. He held his head up, and pushed all memories of his youth to one side. *There is no shame in what I have done,* he told himself. *Anybody would have done it. It's normal to want the best for yourself.* He focussed his mind on the metronomic beat of his shoes as they struck the stone floor of the corridor. *It's true, nothing and nobody lasts forever.*

As he approached another door he swiped his access card against the screen of the card reader. The red light at the side of the door changed to green and he slipped into the room beyond.

"Where is he?" The nearest agent stood to attention as the door opened and his boss walked through. Mark's words were cannonball-blunt.

"Just through here, Sir." The guard led him towards another doorway which had no locking mechanism or card reader to grant access. Mark pushed the door open to see the little boy playing on the floor with a popup book. A female agent, who looked less than excited with her appointment to this latest assignment, stood to attention. Mark brushed her away, ushering her to resume her disinterested position in her seat as if he knew this assignment was beyond boring.

"Hey Matthew," Mark said, as he got close enough to crouch down next to the boy and ruffle his hair. His sudden change of tone, a full about turn, sounded alien to the other agents. They shared their surprise in a quick glance at each other behind the safety of Mark's back.

"Uncle Mark!" A smile spread across Matthew's face and he threw his arms around Mark's body. His hands gripped onto Mark's clothes, and Mark naturally and softly slipped his hands around the small boy. In a genuinely warm embrace Mark scooped him up. "Did you bring it?" Matthew asked.

"Did I say I would bring it?" The boy nodded, unsure if the response was in his favour or against him. "If I said I would bring it, then I must have brought it." Mark pulled out a rolled up book from his inside pocket, no thicker or smaller than a magazine. Matthew's eyes grew wide as he saw the blue of the book appear.

"Wow!" exclaimed Matthew, unfolding the football sticker album onto the grey tiled floor as Mark placed him back down. Matthew pushed away his popup book and comics. "And the stickers?"

"I got ten packs." Mark pulled the packets from his inside pocket and scattered them onto the floor. He crouched down next to Matthew.

"Shall we do it now?" Matthew asked, as he tore open the first pack and scattered the contents to the floor. Faces of football players tumbled to the ground. "No, we should wait. We should do it with Daddy when he gets here." Mark slipped his hand underneath Matthew's chin, and pulled it towards his. He leaned down so that their faces met. Matthew's smile drained away, just as if somebody had pulled the plug on his excitement and dreams.

Mark saw the shift of the female agent next to him, and wondered if she too thought him to be the libertine that he knew he had become.

"You remember what I told you yesterday, Matthew? You remember what I told you about Daddy when you got here?" Had he not been holding Matthew's head so tightly it would have dropped like a fallen ice cream, splat into his chest. Instead Mark pulled on his chin, dragging his eyes back up to meet his own. "Do you remember what I told you, Matthew?"

"Yes. You said he had to go away," Matthew muttered.

"That's right."

"But he promised me that we would go and play football on Saturday. He never breaks his promises. You promised too."

"And we will, Matthew. But not this Saturday." Mark stood up, ruffling his fingers through Matthew's curly blond locks which looked so much like Ben's. But Mark felt him pull away. He added in, "Mummy will be back soon," hoping that would ease his distress.

Matthew pulled the comics towards him, discarding the sticker album in an act of childish defiance. He allowed his dreams of one day becoming Wolverine or Cyclops to replace the idea of his father. His fantasies drowned out the last words to leave Mark's lips before he left the room.

"Don't let anybody else in here," he said to the agent that stood guard against the door.

"What about Agent Mulligan, Sir?" the guard of the main exit door asked. Mark glared at him through cold eyes, glass eyes, glistening like polished crystal.

"I said nobody." Mark pulled his jacket neatly back into place, before once again swiping his card and passing through the door. As he walked back up the corridor, he saw Captain White approaching. He looked even more harassed, his hair having a party atop his head, crazed like it was on a bad trip. He hurried towards his superior.

"Sir, we need to talk." Mark had seen this look before. It was the type of clenched-jaw tension that never proffered good news. Add into that 'we need to talk', and you virtually guarantee disappointment.

"Tell me you have found him." Mark clung onto the last unrealistic hope.

"We lost Mulligan." In an instant, hundreds of half formed ideas raced through his mind, uncertain if any of them could represent the truth. He looked back to the door behind which Matthew was hidden, and then back to Captain White.

"What do you mean you lost her? You can't just lose an agent." He could feel his throat drying and pulse quicken as his muscles tensed across his body, like an electric shock they tightened in waves.

"Sir, it's not just her," he paused, as if saying it would somehow make it worse. "We just lost her whole team."

FIFTEEN

As Hannah steadied the boat into the small mooring station hidden by bush and shrubbery, she motioned for Ben to stand up. Raising her hand, she waved him out and pointed to the rope that was curled up at the bow of the small vessel.

"Take that and tie it to the jetty. Not the first post though, it's a bit wobbly. Be careful where you put your feet, too." Ben pressed his hands against the wooden slats until he found a stable section which didn't shift under his weight. He pushed a few dangling Willow branches to the side, and with a bit of a wobble as the boat became unsteady, he hauled himself out. he secured the rope with a simple knot and she checked that it was taut. Noticing his lack of confidence in his effort she smiled and said, "It's fine."

She lifted up the seat cover and removed the bag with the flask and fruit inside. She threw it down onto the jetty. She pulled up the other bag and offered it out to Ben.

"Take this one. It's too heavy to throw down." She passed him the bag and he felt the weight of it as he slung it over his shoulder. She jumped from the boat and snatched up the second bag. As they moved through the canopy of trees the first drops of rain began to fall. It was open and uphill, and the ground was slippery underfoot. Hannah was still wearing heels, and progress was slow, her feet as steady as the legs of a new born deer. He instinctively took hold of her arm to help.

She didn't speak as they broached the house. It was a small bungalow, constructed from white wood panelling that had weathered gradually through the years. It looked like a large version of the jetty, and he imagined that in the right conditions it would have been quite beautiful. The windows were small and dark. Ben peered through but he saw nothing but his own reflection staring back at him.

Inside the cottage smelt musty, like damp wood, as if it had been closed up for years. He heard a series of beeps as she punched in a code for an alarm system. The low light through the windows illuminated the dust motes floating through the house. She dumped the bag onto a couch. Ben could feel the dust at the back of his throat, and watched his wife suspiciously as she pulled back the curtains to light the room. She turned to look at him as he stood aimlessly in the doorway, no idea what to do or say.

"We have to wait here for a while," she said. "We need a car and a few other things. They will be delivered for us." She could see his discomfort at the prospect of waiting longer in this temporary base. "Matthew is safe for now, as long as nobody knows where we are, and what has happened." She stopped a few feet away from him, uncertain of the welcome that she might receive should she attempt to shorten the distance any further. Ben had considered her silence on the boat as a display of strength, but in reality it was born out of fear. What would he say if she spoke to him?

"And if they do work it out?" Ben dared.

"They won't," she said. "You need some rest too. You look dreadful, and you're starting to get the shakes." Ben held up his hands palm-down in front of him. His fingers jittered back and forth just as she had proclaimed, scoring one or two on the Richter scale. She approached him, her arms outstretched and submissive, trying to look as reassuring as she could, her aim to do anything but intimidate. She helped him to remove the heavy load of the bag and placed it on the floor next to the couch. She reached for the other bag nearby.

"Come on, take a seat," she said, as she closed the door behind them. He allowed her to guide him to the nearest seat, a small armchair with wooden armrests, a cushion worn and threadbare. More dust motes circled above him. She unfastened the holster of the gun that her father had attached to his waist and slipped it out from around him, placing it on the table behind her. She saw his blue tinged fingertips, and took both hands into her own. "You're cold." She rubbed her hands across the top of his, trying to restore some blood flow. Afterwards she placed his hands into his lap, and pulled out the flask from the rucksack. She poured him a cup of tea, taking one of his hands and placing the plastic beaker into his cupped palm. She felt the hesitation in his wrist as she pushed it towards his lips. "I promise, it's just tea."

She stood up and grabbed a woollen blanket from the settee and shook it open. She draped it over him, tucking it underneath his knees, and raised it up towards his chest. "You need to get some rest. Try to sleep. You have time." She stood up and side stepped the chair. As she did so, he looked up towards her, arching his neck backwards.

"Hannah," he called, his eyelids heavy. He raised a hand upwards, and his finger tips brushed the exposed skin of her wrist. To hold her hand seemed so alien to him now, yet to not touch her was even worse.

"Yes?" she looked down at Ben as she stood at his side.

"If it wasn't for you, I'd be dead. Right?"

She nodded her head before shamefully muttering, "Yes."

She feared that even her willingness to save him might never make up for what she had done beforehand.

"Thank you." He pulled his arm back under the woollen throw, and allowed his eye lids to close. Before she left he was already drifting into sleep. She rested the palm of her hand onto his face, stroking his cheek, whilst praying that there would again be a time when she could do so again, when the risk of death for either of them was a distant and terrible memory.

She threw her jacket onto the settee exposing the holster and gun resting on her hip. She left that in place and picked up the heavier of the two bags, transporting it to the small kitchen table. She unzipped the bag, which opened from corner to corner unfolding like a blanket. She took comfort from the familiar sound of Ben's breathing as his chest rose and fell, and the patter of raindrops as they dripped onto the tiled roof above her. She let herself dream for a moment that they were just an average couple on a weekend retreat. *Yes, that was where they were, a rented cottage somewhere. Later she would cook and Matthew would come out from his bedroom and eat. After, when he fell asleep, Ben would turn and kiss her and they would have fumbled half naked sex.* Then she saw the weapons in front of her and the image passed.

She inspected each of the weapons as they lay before her; a selection of hand pistols, and an Uzi submachine gun with its shoulder stock wrapped around the bulk of the gun making it look short and squat. She zipped the bag up and left it on the table.

Grabbing a chocolate bar from the rucksack at Ben's feet, she peeled it open and took a large bite. The air felt cold so she picked up another throw from the settee and draped the thick woollen pile across her shoulders. Walking towards the window, which she knew offered no visibility to the outside world, she traced the line of the driveway from the house as it meandered towards the forest. The road was shielded by the cover of trees for over five hundred meters before you hit a main arterial road.

Nothing would come down the track to the house that didn't intend to. Taking her telephone from her back pocket, she looked at the screen in search of a message but as of yet, it was still blank. She wanted the car here already, and didn't want to linger wasting time. Her son was at Headquarters, and every moment that slipped by was a moment closer to Mark finding out what she had done.

She knew at some point he would discover her betrayal. He wouldn't care about the agents that she had killed. But to foil his plan, to take Ben's life back, that was going too far. With Matthew still at Mark's side, he had more power over her actions than she ever wanted to imagine possible. There is nothing that she wouldn't risk for his safety. She had known that from the moment he was born. But with his birth the same protectiveness extended to Ben. As he shifted uncomfortably in his chair, his sleep disturbed by the drugs and memories of the past day she promised herself that there is nothing that she wouldn't give to keep both of her boys safe.

Moving through to the kitchen, her muddy heels leaving a trail of triangular footprints on the wooden floor, she could hear Ben stirring. She hoped that he would be able to sleep for a while longer until the message arrived from her father to say that the car was on the way. She opened the kitchen cupboards, more out of curiosity than necessity, wondering if somewhere inside her memories were waiting for, hidden in the dusty corners of this cottage. The smell that had first hit them could be explained twice over by the decomposing bag of potatoes that she found in the kitchen, and another of onions that were in a similar state of putrescence. She shut the door again, hoping that as little as possible of the odour had escaped.

She opened the adjacent cupboard door and saw a few old cans of paint, remnants of string, and dirty rags. The man that lived here had welcomed her and her father into their home when they had needed sanctuary. When one of his missions had proven unsuccessful they had spent a summer here in hiding. It had been a difficult few months, watching her father stand relentlessly at the window monitoring the driveway, night and day as immobile as a mannequin. But there were happy memories of those times too. It was only now that she realised that she appreciated the bizarre life she had lived. Why else would she have chosen the same reality and a life of detachment for herself?

It was as she was closing the cupboard door that she saw the large white pot hiding in a back corner. She remembered how there had been a pot just like it many years ago, and how Mr. Johnson, the man that had sheltered them, had tried to show her how much fun she could have without having any toys around. They had mixed the contents with sugar, thrown in some baking powder and watched as a soft glue formed. At the last minute they had thrown in some old red paint powder from the shed and left the mixture to dry in little pots. Once they added a fuse and a bit of tape he had given her a box, and into it he made her place the three black cylinders. She took little disappointment as he sealed up the box with more black plastic tape. He had made her promise not to open it until he took her somewhere where she could play with it.

True to his word, one day he woke her early, before first light had broken. He had already made them a flask of hot tea, and gave her a rucksack to carry that was almost too big for her eight year old shoulders. After they had driven for just over an hour through a snake box of winding roads, he parked the car at the edge of the forest. He tightened the rucksack on her shoulders, and they set out along a small path. It wound through moorland where the Heather grew wild and required their careful footing. The light was just coming up as they reached the top of the rocky ridge. They sat high above the fields of wild plants below, sharing a cup of sweet tea as they dangled their feet over the ledge. He fastened a small rope around her waist, and secured it to a stable boulder behind her. He pulled it tight and wagged his finger mockingly in front of her face. He said *that son of mine will never forgive me if anything happens to you.* It had never made sense at the time. She had no idea who Mr. Johnson's son was.

After they had eaten a breakfast of jam sandwiches he asked her if they should open the box. She hadn't realised that he had been carrying it in his bag. As he handed her the first black cylinder and struck a match, he told her as soon as he lit it to drop it over the edge of the cliff. At first, as she dropped the little black cartridge she didn't know what to expect, but then the first swarms of princess pink smoke filtered up through the sky. The silence of the man beside her only enhanced her sense of wonderment. As she turned to look at him he was smiling at her, not a Cheshire cat *I'll get you* type smile, but rather soft and gentle, a hug waiting on his face. It was one of a handful of memories of her grandfather, and one she treasured as preciously as she did the memories that she created with her own child.

Pulling the other cupboards open she found some sugar, baking powder, and a cigarette lighter. The sugar bag was hosting several lodgers, and a small colony of ants had found their way into the cupboard, marching regimentally in and regimentally out. Brushing the insects aside she took a large pot and threw in the sugar and the contents of the white pot, cooking up the memorable sticky brown paste. She threw in some baking powder and took the pot away from the cooker. She picked up the lighter and stowed it safely in her pocket.

Braving the heavier rain she ducked back outside, lowering her head forwards to avoid the drops as they descended from the sky. The clouds had swung in low, and as she pushed open the door, she smelt the same balm of that summer; the damp, the peat, the dusty remnants of terracotta pottery. She had forgotten to bring a torch with her, and the diminishing light from outside made it difficult to see into the darkest corners of the small shed. She checked her wrist watch. It was a quarter past three. *The car should be here by now,* she thought to herself.

She spotted the dusty old box in the corner on the floor. It was the probably the same box that she had used all those years ago with her grandfather. As she pulled up the box and opened the lid, she saw how it had been sealed with an old piece of string, the paint itself in several layers of plastic bag, each a little less worn as she pulled the first degraded layers away. Giving it a shake, she could hear the contents skirting around inside, like sand grains in an hourglass. Grabbing the black tape that she never doubted would be in the old toolbox on the floor, she darted back over the grass, slipping as she did so. She pushed the front door open, slamming it shut behind her.

The sound of the door closing woke Ben. "What are you doing?" he asked. He startled her, and as she gasped the roll of tape in her teeth made a thud as it dropped and rolled along the floor. He leant over and picked it up as it arrived at his feet.

"You scared me!" she exclaimed, as she held her hand up to her chest. "Help me with this, quickly."

"What are you doing?"

She shed her woollen throw, tossing it to the floor. She held up the bag containing the paint and began tipping it into the pot of brown goo.

"Bring me all the toilet rolls from the bathroom cupboard," she demanded.

"Why, what do you…."

"Ben, please, just bring them here." He did as she asked. He dropped them onto the table in the kitchen, next to the bag full of weaponry, and she brought over the pot from the cooker, now transformed into a red, glue like substance.

"What is that?"

"It's our cover, Ben. We don't have anybody on our team.

136

Everybody is against us, even if they don't know it yet. Anything I can think of that might help us get Matthew out, I'll try. Here," she said as she took the first toilet roll. "Take off all the paper, we want the cardboard tubes."

After covering the wooden floor in a fanciful swathe of tissue, he lined up four cardboard tubes on the table. She covered one of their open ends with black insulating tape. Turning them closed side down she instructed Ben to fill up the tubes with the red paste. By the time he had done so, she had returned with two pens and two pencils, and stuck them into the sticky pots one by one. She also threw a box of matches onto the table, which she had found by the fireplace.

"Cut the heads off these."

"How many?" he asked, as he opened the box of matches.

"As many as there are." His heart sank as he saw an almost full box. His disappointment was interrupted by the buzz of a telephone. It reminded him of the outside world and the threat that it posed. She picked up the telephone, read the screen and then placed it back down on the counter.

"Car will be here soon. It's late, but at least it gives us time to finish this."

As they sat waiting for the smoke bombs to dry out, making match head fuses, it was virtually impossible for Ben to concentrate on the task that she had set for him. All he could think about was Matthew, imprisoned in a building that she referred to as *Headquarters*, or, *The Shop*. Neither place sounded acceptable for a six year old boy.

"What do you think Matthew is doing now? Where is he?" She looked up from her match head fuse and eyed up her husband coolly.

"He'll be where I left him."

"Which is where? Where did you take him?"

"It was agreed that he remain at Headquarters on Thursday. That gave us time to complete a full debriefing. But Mark was so over excited by your research. He couldn't stop celebrating, and everything got put back. Debriefing was moved to Friday morning. That's why I never got to you in time before you woke up, because I should have moved you on Thursday night. Matthew is safe there, until I collect him." She offered up the idea of his safety convincingly enough, but she wasn't sure who she was trying to convince.

"And what about me? You told me that I was supposed to get on that boat. Where was I going?"

"Here," as she raised her head and motioned to the room before her. "My father would have brought you here. I didn't expect them to turn on me."

"I don't think they expected you to kill them."

"Nobody expects to be killed, Ben." She looked towards him. "You of all people should know that." They sat in silence for a few moments, until Ben spoke again.

"What is this place?"

"It's my grandfather's home. My real grandfather. I came here as a child. I didn't know at the time he was my grandfather, but we came here when my father had to stay off the grid."

"What was he? A spy?"

"No, and neither am I. Our job is not to spy. It's to do the things that are necessary, but that a nation cannot be seen to do publically. We do the work that the public don't need or want to know about, and make the politicians look clean. They look clean because they are. They don't know anything about us."

"And what now? What happens when you turn up with no agents, no van, and no prisoner? Do you think that they'll let you just turn up, pick up our son and walk out like nothing has happened? I don't know these people, but that sounds a bit naïve to me." He set the first smoke bomb down and assessed it. It looked okay to him, but what did he know? He looked to Hannah and she gave him a nod.

"I only need ten minutes. I have access to almost everywhere in that building. When I am almost there I will call Mark. I'll report a car accident, and say that we have stayed with the van. That's protocol. You are going to stay at the car, just out of view. They are looking for you, but not right outside their own front door.

"I have to go through the main entrance. Once I am in, I can go directly to the room where they are holding Matthew." The words cut Ben deeply. The very thought that Matthew was being held against his will, against Ben's will, was enough to shatter his hope, but it also strengthened his sense of purpose. "I will have to move fast, but from the main door to being back to the car I can do it in ten minutes. I'll be out before Mark knew I was there."

"And you guarantee that this will work?"

"There is no other choice, Ben. They have no reason to suspect me until they realise that there was no accident. By that time I'll be back in the car with you and Matthew." She set the last smoke bomb on the table. They both stopped talking and raised their heads towards the front door as they heard the sound of gravel crunching under the weight of a vehicle.

"It's the car," she said as she rose to her feet. Get your stuff together, including your gun. Get these bags, and get ready to go."

SIXTEEN

"ARE YOU READY?" SHE ASKED Ben, as he craned his neck to get a better view of the figure walking away from the car. "It's time to leave." She picked up the first of the bags from where he had readied them on the floor by the door as if they were preparing to go on holiday, and walked towards the boot of the black saloon car. The delivery man was walking towards the boat, his grey hood just visible as he ducked underneath the low lying tree branches. He grabbed his stolen jacket as Hannah stepped back into the hallway of the house. She placed a small black box onto the coffee table in front of her. Lifting up a tiny antenna, she flicked a switch, activating a tiny, red flickering light.

"What's that?" he asked, as slid his arms into the jacket sleeves.

"It's you, kind of. This is your phone signal." She grabbed her coat and flicked it around her shoulders to the sound of the engine of the boat firing up. She checked her wrist watch again. Only a few minutes until four in the afternoon. "I want them to track you here. It won't be long until they pick up the signal. It will be enough time for us to get there, and it will divert their attention. If they think you are here, they sure as hell won't be looking for you outside their own building." She ushered him towards the door. "We will be there in half an hour, and they will be here not long after that. That will provide me enough time to get in and get

140

out with our son." For the first time he saw apprehension in her face, and he knew that she felt nervous. He wanted so much to hate her for what she had done to them. But the thought of what she had done since to save his life, and at least to give him a chance, prevented him. "Let's get moving. The clock is ticking."

He adjusting the gun on his hip as he sat in the car. He heard her open the boot, and the once alien sound of the gun barrel as she loaded her hips with two new handguns rang out from behind the car. With the guns concealed by her jacket, she looked just like his wife, and yet still seemed like such a stranger. She dumped a rucksack onto his lap and handed him the roll of black tape and the homemade fuses.

"Put the fuse into this hole," she explained, as she picked one up and demonstrated placing the fuse in the hole from where she had removed the pens. "Then stuff a bit of this tissue inside and tape up the top. Just leave a bit of a hole in the middle. Got it?" Even if he hadn't followed well, the 'got it' sounded so terminal that he would not have dared say no. So he nodded and set to work on the second smoke bomb. She nodded a series of positive affirmations as he completed the task before she said, "Good. Now do the others."

"What are you going to use them for? What do you mean, cover?"

"Creating confusion. They might help, and we need all the help we can get."

They drove through the forest away from the cottage, and when they reached the end of the dirt track they picked up the first main road. As the density of the forest lessened, in place of trees there was real life, pedestrians, other cars, the general hustle and bustle of normal everyday existence. They passed restaurants and cafes, and places that he had been to before. As he travelled through the backdrop of his memories, they seemed to him now like nothing more than a theatre stage, full of props and imagery designed to create the illusion of real life. He regarded the people as they went about their busy lives; crowds waiting at pedestrian crossings, business men working from laptops on coffee shop tables, street sellers offering newspapers and food. He thought about how each of them would have an identity card tucked safely inside their pockets. But as he watched life carrying on around him, nothing about what he observed seemed real to him anymore.

"What is it?" she said, as she caught him staring sentimentally from the window. "Are you nervous?"

"Everything out there, Hannah. That's what's wrong. None of it is real anymore. I have all these memories, but none of them mean anything because none of them were ever real."

"They were real."

"Not the best memories," he snapped. "You married me because you had to. I met your father today, so I don't know whose hand it was that I was shaking on the wedding day, and who I thanked for such a wonderful wife. Who was it that I promised that I would take care of you?" He didn't wait for an answer, even if she was about to offer one. He knew the answer; it was nobody. "Here for example," as he pointed up to the small French restaurant that they used to visit. "We used to come here. This is one of the first places we ever came together, and I loved it there. Now that memory is lost. It's all lost. Everything. My life. My family. My memories. Every piece of research that I ever did. All the work that I did to try and make people's lives better, disease free. It's gone. Gone in order to be used for weapons. Everything was just a big ploy. A cover up. I was just a tool in the whole thing. A tool for warfare. I will be the man who created a monster, rather than the man that saved people from them."

"That's not true. I loved you. I still love you."

"Love me?" Being back in reality made it all the harder to believe that she could really have learned to love him when he started off as nothing more than an assignment. "You can't love me."

"I saved your life," she pleaded, half-heartedly, knowing that she was also responsible for almost destroying it. "If I didn't love you, why would I do that?"

"Guilt. You did it for Matthew. If you wanted to save me, you could have done it ages ago."

"I was coming back for you."

"You could have taken me from the moment I got home that night. You could have told me anytime. What about last week? You could have said, '*hey guess what, my love*,'" he began. "'*Next week your best friend will try and kill you. I know all about it because I'm in on it too. Fancy doing a runner?*' Yet never once did you try. There was nothing from you until the guilt set in and it was almost too late. You have destroyed my life, Matthew's life, and the lives of everybody that my research would have saved."

"I didn't…"

"You didn't what? I can't believe a word that you have ever said to me anymore. All the stories that you told me about your family. All the lies. You told me that your mother wasn't at our wedding because she died when you were young. How could you lie about such a thing when you knew what drove me to work was the death of my own father?"

"Ben, I…"

He didn't let her finish. "I don't want to hear it. Don't talk to me. I have heard enough."

The rest of the car journey fell under a veil of silence as the black saloon meandered through the streets towards Headquarters. She drove as if under the scrutiny of a driving instructor, her eyes always alert for any sign of hazard. More than once she allowed herself a glimpse of Ben as he sat staring dead ahead at the dashboard, his eyes watery and tear filled. She knew that he was right. She had wasted endless chances to tell him how she really felt. To tell him the truth. Once she had even considered it. They had been arguing one Sunday morning. She was shouting at him about the mess in the bathroom and the crumbs on the floor from where he had dropped his toast. She was screaming at him as he sat behind his laptop, text books, and endless piles of handwritten notes. She had complained and complained at him, until finally he rose to his feet, his cheeks ruddy from anger. *What do you want from me*, he had screamed as he slammed down his sweaty palms onto the tabletop, accidentally knocking over a glass of orange juice. The juice spilt over the notes, soaking the pages. She had grabbed a towel to mop it up, which he snatched out of her hands faster than she could take a grip on it. She tried to help him, but instead he body blocked her, forcing her out of the situation. As she watched him mopping up the spilt juice, she thought about how it might sound if she tried to tell him why she was really so angry. She mouthed the words over in her head, sounding them out internally. *There is a plan to kill you. I want to save you. Please listen to me. I want to save you. I love you.* But he looked at her with such harsh eyes, his breath streaming through his nostrils in punctuated jets, quivering with anger. It was the last time she wanted to feel his judgment. His hatred of her was too much a burden for her to bear.

Pulling the car into the side of the road, she pulled on the handbrake and shut down the engine. She turned the key and sat back in her seat, the only sound in the car that of the material of her coat as it crimpled under her shifting weight. She turned to look at Ben. He was still staring at the dashboard in front of him. She placed her hands down onto her knees to steady herself, but what she really wanted to do was to rest them onto his leg and try to comfort him.

"Ben, I know it's hard to believe me. I have made so many mistakes when it comes to you." He remained motionless, as if he hadn't even heard her words. "But you have to try to believe me. I had to let them believe they had succeeded. I was scared for Matthew, and for you. If the operation failed, they would have killed you anyway. If they discovered that it was because of me, they would have killed me too. What would he have done then? I tried to manage the situation. I just didn't do it very well."

"The situation?" he asked, turning to look first ahead, and then at her. "Matthew and I were a situation that needed managing?" He shook his head in disbelief. "This just keeps getting better."

"You're mixing my words Ben, and you know it. I tried to save you. I did it badly. I was coming back to the house, but you woke up faster than expected when I was delayed."

"Hannah, honestly. Listen to yourself. You left me in our house for over twenty four hours! They could have come and got me at anytime. You had no intention of *saving me.*"

"It was part of my plan. I didn't leave that night like you think I did. You threw up at about half past midnight. I gave you a slow release sedative to make sure that you wouldn't wake up. The branch of the Agency which organises recovery and clean up isn't based at Headquarters. I have a contact there. He helped me make it look like you had already been picked up. Mark assumed that I had done it when he checked the status of your recovery on the system."

"So then what?"

"My debriefing should have happened on Friday morning after being put back from Thursday afternoon. It would have meant that the operation had been closed. Deemed successful. Ben, Hannah, and Matthew Stone would have been erased from ever existing, and Matthew and I would have gone on to live a new life, with different identities."

"Without me." He locked his jaw and looked away.

"Yes, at first. But I have a lot of contacts, Ben. People to help me. I was planning to come back and get you on Thursday afternoon, but when things got changed I had to put it back to Friday morning. The same man that delivered the car to us was going to help me. I know him through my father. They are good people. Honest people. But when your identity card was detected in the underground it was as much a surprise to me as it was to Mark, and it threw the whole plan into chaos.

"There have been all sorts of people in trouble over what has happened, and I have lost good people over this. So far, they haven't made the connection back to me, but they will, and that's why they want me back at Headquarters. They want to know how I could have made such a mistake and thought you dead when you weren't. If they knew already about my involvement, I'd already be dead." She reached over with her left hand. She wanted to feel him, a connection to the man that she still loved, and who she hoped still loved her. She let her hand rest onto his leg, and whilst she felt his knee tense a little, he didn't brush her away.

"So what now? What are you planning to do?" he asked. She reached across him to open the glove box. He watched as she pulled out three burgundy red passports, but they looked different to what he recognised. The lettering was different, and in a language that he didn't understand.

"We run. Together. These are our new names. Our new lives. Ben Stone is dead. So is Hannah. Matthew too. But our new lives are here. You just have to trust me to get him out, and trust me to love you. This kind of thing cannot be organised in a couple of hours Ben. This was my plan all along. Please believe me." She reached into her pocket to retrieve her telephone as Ben thumbed the passports, staring at his new photo and new name. "I have to call Mark. Keep quiet."

Even the name made him angrier. "What will you tell him?"

"Like I explained. That there has been an accident and that we are with the van. He will expect that. That should give me enough time to get in, get Matthew, and get back out. By the time he realises, we will be long gone." She waited before sharing her next thought, immeasurably scared to hear the answer. "That's if you will come with me."

His arms hung flaccidly in his lap, his hands cupped like a choir boy, and yet still somehow his stance appeared defiant and obstructive. He was motionless and it only worked to reinforce his untouchable facade, like a bronze statue, lifelike and beautiful, yet cold and unresponsive to her touch. His eyes flickered downwards to see her hand resting on his leg. He thought about his options, and how narrow they really were. Her words seemed genuine, and as much as he wanted to bolster his anger, he was in no position to be difficult. It was hard to argue with the arrangements that she had made, and harder still to deny his feelings. His mind was at war, wanting to hate her, but yet utterly incapable of ignoring her plea. He reached out his hand, just his finger tips at first which brushed against the side of hers. It was the signal she needed, and immediately took his hand in hers, relishing the warmth of his touch and the life in his veins.

"I still have no idea how you could do this," he began, "but I believe in you." He took a big breath in. She motioned to speak, but he shook his head and continued with what he had to say. "I know this has been difficult, and you have risked a lot. But more important than anything else is that you are Matthew's only chance. Only you can save him. Let's focus on that, and anything else we can work out later." Her head dropped as she started to cry.

"I love you, Ben." He took her face in his hand in the way that made her skin pucker and her heart flutter in her chest. He held her cheek, and her tears trickled over his finger tips. He brought her in closer to him and he allowed their foreheads to rest together. He felt her breath tickling his eye lashes. "Ben, I'm so, so, sorry." Her body started to shake as the built up tears and fragility of their situation weighed upon her shoulders. He pulled her face up, their eyes never as close, as he looked to find strength enough for them both from somewhere in his soul.

"Stop it now. Focus. It's only you that can save Matthew, remember?" He saw a wave of composure creeping in and she released his hand to wipe the salty streaks away from her face. She nodded her head agreeably, understanding the enormity of his words, which replayed over and over in her head. *It's only you that can save Matthew. Only you.*

"I need to call Mark. I will let him know about the accident, and that I and the team are at the van. I will tell him that I am on my way in as soon as possible, as he requested." She stuffed the smoke bombs into her inside pockets, and pulled out her holstered gun to check the magazine. "You will be in the driver's seat. We will only be a few minutes from the entrance. When I call you, start driving in the direction of Headquarters, I'll show you where. It means that I am on my way."

"Then where are we going?"

She paused, knowing that for the first time he meant they would be together. "We will be following Second Street straight and turning into Fourth. We will be heading towards the old docks. We need to swap seats. Shuffle over here. Don't get out of the car." He shuffled across the seat as she lifted her weight up on clenched fists and stretched out arms. As he brushed past her, their bodies crossing midair, he felt the two guns poke at him from underneath her coat. It was hard to accept this new version of his wife.

She asked Ben to park the car as far away from any camera location that she could remember. But in truth it had been many years since she had worked in a position where she had to remember all of the cameras in the centre of the city. She just hoped that the unnamed side street just off *Twelfth* was a good option.

"There is so much about you that I don't know," he said as the car idled. His words were soft, non-judgemental, with sadness rather than anger. He shuffled uncomfortably in his seat, scratching at his face, his nose, brushing nonexistent strands of hair away from his eyes. "I don't even know what to call you."

"Hannah. Hannah Stone." She said it without a second for thought between his words and hers. She looked hopeful, desperately willing the name to not repulse him. "That's my name. It's the only one I want."

"Not Catherine Mulligan?"

"She died a long time ago, Ben. The Catherine Mulligan that signed up for this job, that wanted to be an agent, that was happy to sell her life away to them," she paused as she considered the passage of her life and the loss of who she was, "she is gone. Even if I wanted to be her anymore, I couldn't. They destroy who you are, Ben."

"If they destroyed who you were, who are you now?"

"Your wife. Matthew's mum. Hannah Stone. At least for the next few hours," she said as she picked up the new passports and handed them to him, "but after that we all have to start again." He smiled at her sweetly as the idea of Matthew's laughter filling the empty space in the car filled his head. It made him wish that they already had him so that they could just get out of here.

"I wish there was something that I could do to help Matthew. I feel so useless."

"Being ready in the car is all you need to do. You'll get us out of here." She took a long hard breath before picking up her telephone from inside her pocket. "Are we ready?" He nodded, and this time it was Ben who rested his hand onto her leg. He squeezed her skin between his fingers and she knew he was with her. Everything that had gone before hurt like hell, but she could take the pain. She had always told herself that the people capable of hurting you the most are the people worth caring about. She had made it a mantra, making herself believe it. She had no clue if Ben felt the same. She hoped so. She wanted him around. She needed him around. There was nobody else she would rather have on her side.

SEVENTEEN

THE TELEPHONE RANG EIGHT TIMES, seven more than she expected as she counted each ring. Just as she convinced herself that something was wrong, and that somehow they had traced her location, Mark answered the telephone in his usual abrupt way.

"Yes?"

"Sir, Agent Mulligan calling in." The sound of the name made Ben feel uneasy as she sat next to him in the car, talking to Mark, his best friend and worst enemy. He still couldn't believe Mark to be fully responsible. *There must have been pressure from the Agency. There must have been for him to do that. They must have forced his hand.* "We have an issue."

"What issue? Are you at Headquarters yet?" Mark asked.

"There has been a car accident involving our vehicle. It was compromised and our GPS is down. Sir, I am..." He didn't let her finish. His voice sounded edgy on the telephone and she was trying to read it as he spoke. To her, he almost sounded excitable.

"Yeah we know about your little accident." Panic immediately set in. *How could he know? There was no accident?* She felt her heart racing. She remembered her training and began counting in her head to slow her heart rate in order to relax and shield any anxiety in her voice that may betray her. But knowing he held her

150

son captive didn't make that easy. She fiddled with her trouser button. It didn't help. "We realised that we lost your signal. Thought you had slipped off the grid for a while. But it doesn't matter. Just get in here. We've got him." She swung round to look at Ben, and he felt an immediate injection of anxiety.

"You've got him? Where?"

"East of the city. He got a long way. Don't worry about it though. It's over Catherine. Come in. You've earned your freedom."

"Yes, Sir." She looked at Ben, knowing that it must be her intended plan falling into place, the transmitter back at the cottage emitting its signal. If they were tracking this it would mean all resources would be out of Headquarters, if she knew Mark as well as she thought she did. He would have them all heading east to claim their bounty. There was no chance Mark would take the stationary target lightly, or the prospect of letting Ben go free again. If she had judged Mark correctly, he would send every agent, every hit man, and any set of hands that stood a chance of catching Ben to bring him in. He would have gone himself if he didn't know he was so useless. This time, there would be no faith in the system. There would be no trust in a junior officer. He would want that body on his doorstep, head on a stick or over a barrel. He would want to see his body to believe they had captured Ben. But the fact that Mark had detected the signal meant that they were on a countdown. The clock was ticking. It was time to move. Time for delay, for consideration, or for anything other than setting her foot back into Headquarters and executing her only chance to save their son, had passed them by.

As Ben drove the car away in the direction she indicated they remained silent with the only interjections her instructions as she guided him. Ben wanted to ask questions. He wanted to know timings and locations. Where should he park the car? What should he do if somebody came to him? Would she let him keep the gun he was wearing? Should he use it? Ideas raced through his mind like the whirling and swirling cars of the Waltzers at the local fair. Nausea washed over him as he drove along the road, and more than once he wanted to stop the car to throw up. Instead he kept a steady pace and with a tightly clenched fist across his mouth, stifled that feeling. There was no way in the world he would stop now.

But Hannah looked calm. She held her hands delicately in her lap, almost as if she were meditating. Every now and again she would pull out her gun and check the magazine, all the while making sure that the safety lever was engaged. The only giveaway of her nerves. But the way she handled it was expert, her hands moving smoothly and freely over the weapon, her fingers trained and precise.

She holstered the gun for a final time. She pulled down the sun visor and wiped her eyes clear of smudged mascara with spit on her fingers, and swept up the loose hairs that had escaped. As she pushed the sun visor back into place, she held out her left hand and instructed Ben to pull into a small lay-by, tucked into the edge of the pavement.

"Just pull in there," she said as she waved her hand out to the left. "Take the first space so that there is nothing in front of you, and leave a bit of room in front too." He followed her instructions without question and left at least three feet in front of him where he could easily swing the car out if necessary. He turned the key in the ignition, shutting down the engine. As it slowed into silence, he knew this would be the moment that she would leave him. Potentially this was the last moment he would see any of the people from his old life.

"Hannah, what do I do now? Just wait? Just wait here?"

"Yes, Ben." She nodded, her words calm and cold as if she were talking to a stranger. The void between the woman he knew as his wife and the woman sitting before him seemed to grow wider as she slipped back into her role. She snatched at his hand, held without emotion as nothing more than an access point to view his watch. It was a quarter to five, and the first shadows were beginning to appear as the sun fell. "Ten minutes, and I'll be calling you. When I do, drive straight up this road and take the last right. I will be with Matthew on the pavement walking towards you, away from the glass fronted building with all the steps. Don't stop the car until I am next to it." He nodded in agreement, desperate to emit an air of steadfastness, commitment and belief. But his fear of failure would not leave him. It's heaviness in the air made him feel like he was choking, and yet Hannah seemed to suffer none of the same difficulties. She was composed and calm. Ready to move.

"What do I do if you don't call me?" His words were small, and apprehensive. He wanted to take them back as soon as he had said them, as he bowed his head away from her. He had hoped to hide his fear, but he could not. She took his chin in her hand and gripped his face.

"Don't you dare think that way, Ben. It's not an option for me not to be there. It's not an option for me not to call you. In ten minutes time I will be walking out of that building with Matthew in my arms and towards a new life together. A real life, where I don't have to lie to you anymore. Don't you dare imagine that not to be possible." She didn't wait for his agreement. With her hand on the door handle, she stopped only as she felt Ben's hand against her arm. As she turned to tell him to let go she felt his other hand on her face, holding her, his fingertips brushing past her ears. He placed his lips against hers, and kissed her passionately, his lips never once breaking contact. It felt like the first time, but knew in reality it might be the last.

"I love you, Hannah," he whispered to her, his words like drops of heaven to her ears. She closed her eyes as she heard him say the words, words that she had feared she may never hear again. Yet here in the intensity of their situation she felt his forgiveness, and faith, and promised herself that she would live up to it. She promised herself that she would make his sacrifice count.

PART THREE

EIGHTEEN

THE LAST TEN MINUTES OF Mark's life had been like the polar ends of two magnets. When Captain White told him that Agent Mulligan and her team had slipped off the grid, he was certain that could only spell trouble. It took only a quick glance at the screens in his office to confirm the news, and he wasted no time in dashing to the Surveillance Centre. He slammed open the double doors, immediately casting a silence over the room.

"Forrester? Forrester, where are you?" A small in stature man stood up from amongst a large collection of monitors in the amphitheatre shaped room. He was short and hunched over, a result of sitting at a desk for fifty years. He had lived almost his whole life in secrecy, often not leaving Headquarters for weeks on end. But his years on naval warships operating radar had left him partially agoraphobic, and so the Agency served him well. Some people wanted to hide from the rest of the world.

"Sir."

"Forrester, what has happened to the signal from Mulligan's vehicle? How the hell could you have lost them?"

"Sir, I have run every test that I have, and all of my equipment is fine. I have every other system tracked and identified. On my last count I have one hundred and six agents all accounted for. Five agents, one of which is your trusted Miss Mulligan, have simply disappeared as if their signals have been, shall we say, deactivated." Mark looked to Captain White, who was shuffling uncomfortably on the spot. "There is no logical explanation from my point of view as to how I can lose one vehicle and five individuals who are all travelling together, and not have lost another agent if it is my system at fault."

"Agent Mulligan would not turn off the tracer. It's unthinkable. Find the error."

"Sir, you don't seem to understand me. It's unthinka......"

"Find them," Mark bellowed. "You have everything at your disposal. Wherever they are, you find them. I don't want to hear about another member of this agency failing!" Mark turned in Captain White's direction, who felt the eyes from around the room fall upon him. He prayed for time to stop, for the seconds to stop ticking, so that he could escape his own discomfort unnoticed and slip away from their judgment.

Forrester sat back down in his chair. Mark could hear whisperings coming from the workstation, but he didn't know if it was from Forrester or another colleague. Short of watching the red flashing lights on the screen, he was lost when it came to tracking his agents. He relied on everybody to do their job. If they failed, so did he, and failure was not an option he wanted to consider.

"Sir, could you take a look at this please," a small voice called out from behind a computer screen. Mark watched as Forrester straightened himself up, before shuffling towards the voice. Mark watched him, his irritation growing with each slow step.

"What is it, Thorne? What do you have?" he said as he approached. He rested his hands down onto piles of paperwork that in Mark's opinion would have been better off being filed appropriately. It reminded him on Ben's handwritten notes, and he didn't want to think of either of those things right now.

"Well, Sir, I thought I'd scan across different channels and look at a few different frequencies. By doing so I picked up a weak signal. I have tracked it with GPS and triangulated it to a position on the river, east of the city. The trace has the same signal as Stone's mobile phone."

"Forrester?" Mark's attention had been gripped by the mention of Stone's name, and he almost ran towards them. "What have we got? Have we got him?" Forrester ignored Mark as he crouched down to look at the signal with his own eyes, recalculating the position of the signal for himself.

"Good work, Thorne. Well done." Forrester turned to look at Mark. "I'd say that we have a strong chance of having found our target."

Mark turned to Captain White. "I want you to get things moving. I want every agent we have got at that location. Get him here now."

"Sir, I can't pull everybody. What if it's wrong?"

"White, are you questioning my authority? My decisions? After what happened with Sadler? He has slipped through everybody. Wait," he said as he stopped to answer the telephone that was buzzing on his belt. They all stopped to listen as they heard their leader announcing success, before it seemed to Captain White that it was even within reach. He slipped his telephone back into his pocket before looking back up to Captain White. "I don't want to take any chances. Anyway, that was Mulligan and her team is accounted for. They have had an accident and it screwed up their signals. There is your answer, Forrester. Now, get that location downloaded to every GPS we have, and get our agents on it."

Mark turned to leave the room, and headed back to his office. He saw the first of the reserve agents running from their desks in order to coordinate the strike. He clapped his hands together, as if cheering on a child at school sports day, all the while shouting 'let's go, let's go'. This was what he had been waiting for. Since the first day that he had taken this job, he had been waiting for the day when glory would land at his feet. He thought that it had happened yesterday, and it had hurt to learn that his celebrations had been premature. When he walked in through the main front doors yesterday he had been so convinced of his own success. He couldn't wait to celebrate the fact that he now had in his possession the intelligence to engineer an army, a weapon, a warfare so advanced. His legacy would continue in war for generations to come. But he had been too quick to congratulate himself. Now it was time. It had to be.

He slammed the door behind him, his face overwhelmed by broad but cautious smiles as he walked into his office. They were the type of inappropriate smiles that make an appearance when you least want them to, when you hear a sad story but yet somehow still see the funny side. *He died how? He was run over by a mobility scooter? The driver was drunk? How terrible,* and then the smile that strips you of authenticity. You can't hide it. You feel the shame but the smile is defiant. He needed a whiskey to calm his nerves, or excitement, whichever of the two it was that he could feel in his belly.

He loosened his tie, and pulling it away from his neck he threw it onto his desk. He breathed for what felt like the first time all day. *Just half an hour to wait, no more than that.* He would have word that Ben had been picked up. Once he knew he was bound in plastic grip ties, with muffles across his ears and blacked out goggles strapped to his face, he could relax. Once they had him secure, Mark would order his execution.

He poured a generous amount of whisky into a neat little glass and took a large sip. He pulled out the oversized desk chair and slumped into the cushioned leather seat. The padded backrest massaged his knotted-up muscles as he leaned back. He hung his head backwards, before rolling it left and right to ease the tension in his neck. He took a large glug of whiskey and set the glass down on his desk and opened the drawer underneath. He flicked the small latch and pulled open the drawer to the left of his knees. He took out Ben's, *no wait, my files,* and placed them down onto the desk next to his whisky. Inside the drawer there were other beige carton files that had nothing written on them, the only exception the emblem of The Agency; a small black triangle with an old Latin phrase. 'Serviamus Humiliter'. He had always thought it a rather inadequate description of the provisions offered by the Agency, and was not a motto that he lived by. He did not aim to *serve humbly*, as the phrase suggested, and he had preferred his own motto of *achieve and succeed* to govern the rules by which he would live.

He pulled out the first of the unmarked files from the drawer and dropped it on the desk in front of him. As he turned the cover, facing him was a small picture of Catherine Mulligan. It had been taken many years previously, before she had known Ben. The file and photograph were dog-eared and tatty. The picture had been taken on her registration day as a fully trained agent. There was no hint of a smile on her face, as there had been when she had graduated university. There was no father at her side, proudly smiling in awe of his child's success. Just Catherine Mulligan, wearing a black polo neck sweater, her hair tied back without care into a tight ponytail. She stood emotionless, as she had been trained to do, her face disclosing no secret or fact. She didn't even have an identity, for it was this day that she had chosen to forego her own.

He leafed through the extensive file. Inside it contained everything that one may wish to know about the life of Catherine Mulligan. It detailed how she was born in Ireland, and shortly afterwards travelled to England once her father's return was demanded by his home country. Her early memories were happy, according at least to the psychological researcher that compiled the earliest of personality assessments and history recollection. Her training was extensive, at first in driving, and then in weaponry. After her first homeland assignment, she had made a request to work as an Operations Officer. She hadn't wanted to work in homeland security, but rather spread her wings and move around the world. She wanted to be the agent who worked with local dissidents, collecting assets in the shape and form of other humans that strived for an alternative world to the one in which they found themselves. Her degree in economics and fluency in several foreign languages had made her an excellent choice, and she was set to go on her first foreign mission only two weeks after Mark read her file for the first time and changed everything.

When Mark first read this file and saw that her mother had died after one of her father's missions became compromised, he knew she was the right choice. Catherine had been present in the house when the back door flew open. She had heard the first gunshot and scream. She heard her father's words stream into her head. *Catherine, if ever you are scared, do as I tell you, OK?* She did exactly as her father had instructed. She didn't make a sound as she crept silently into the nearest hiding place. She opened the cupboard door in the dining room and sat inside, concentrating hard to control her breathing, fiddling with her buttons. She heard the footsteps of the intruder pass by the cupboard door. She waited in fear, surrounded by the scent of wet paper and urine until somebody came close enough to the door of the cupboard and knelt down, telling her to release the internal lock.

She had been there for two days, and it was after this point that they secluded themselves away with her grandfather. That was the longest summer of her life, wondering where her mother had gone, and why she didn't want her anymore.

Mark knew firsthand how the death of Ben's father had both simultaneously destroyed and cemented Ben's life path. He believed that this shared grief would secure their partnership, and provide an authenticity to her placement that the previous attempts had failed to achieve. She was beautiful too and he knew that Ben would like her.

He closed the file and picked up his glass of whisky. He pulled the glass up to his lips and knocked back another measure, the warmth of which slipped down his throat, burning him with a sense of masochistic pleasure. It was impossible to think of Catherine without thinking of the man he once called his best friend. He couldn't think of Ben without admitting to the sense of loss and guilt that hung over his success.

Like Catherine, Mark too had taken choices that were difficult to live with. His appointment into the position of power that he occupied had been questioned time and time again by those that sat underneath his umbrella of control. They always questioned if his background in science and position of trust was enough to counteract his lack of military experience. He promised himself when he took the position that he would make the right decisions, and that he would consider the aspirations of the Agency above his own. That he would stifle his guilt and do what was necessary.

In all truth, everyday life had changed little. He went to work, called Ben regularly, and played football with him and Matthew most weekends. They still hit the bar together at the end of a long day. Ben still watched as Mark fooled around with any woman naive enough not to realise that behind the expensive suit, hid a married man who offered them nothing more than a quick fumble and a morning full of regret. It was as it always was. He celebrated the birth of Matthew, even though it was his very existence that almost threatened the whole operation. It even brought his choice of agent and her ability to maintain her role into question.

But it was during quiet times when he was alone that he couldn't prevent the aimless wanderings of his mind. He couldn't help but consider the friend he had lost, and the future they wouldn't share as the bells rang in his success. He wondered once Ben was truly gone how his life might be. He knew the casual trips out and beers in a bar would be nothing but a memory. The fun would be gone. But maybe he could still see Matthew? Perhaps that would be possible. He could be there for Matthew, and that would help make up for what he had lost......wouldn't it?

He knew that with Ben's death part of him would disappear too, but trusted that the loss would make room for success, for money, and for the power that he craved. He would take Ben's research and build it as his own. NEMREC would become known as Mark's work, as his creation, for it would be him that would deliver it to its true and faithful purpose.

He stood up and pulled open the door. As he pulled it shut behind him he made his way up the corridor and back to the Surveillance Centre. As he turned the corner speed of the other body travelling in the opposite direction startled him, and he felt his heart skip as her presence took him by surprise. In unison they both gasped.

"What the hell?" Mark breathed a sigh of relief as his cognitive senses kicked into action, delayed by the influence of the two large whiskies. "I thought you'd had an accident?"

The response was almost automatic as she smiled. "We really weren't very far away. I came in by the underground to get here quickly. I left my agents there." She hoped that her thinly veiled lies were not detectable. She relied on the same training that the Agency had taught her, using it to cover the truth and lie convincingly. She was so good at it that not even the people who loved her could tell the difference between what was real and what was fabrication.

"Oh right, okay." He glanced down at his watch and she tried to remember if she had told him where it was that the false accident had occurred, and if there was any conceivable way that she could have managed to arrive already. "I'm heading back to the Surveillance Centre. You don't need to be here when they bring him in. You are staying in one of the safe houses, right?" She knew the plan. An isolated house far away from the city, where she was supposed to await further instruction with Matthew.

"Yes, and I was hoping to take Matthew now if you deem it a good idea. Unless there is anything you need me to do first?" She had learned a long time ago never to try to intervene with Mark's assumption of power, and at all times to positively reinforce his level of control. Given any chance to ask his permission to ensure the completion of a task that she already knew that she would do, or to ask his approval for something that didn't need it, she would take it. Posing her own ideas as his also worked in her favour. Many times she had managed to avoid an unwanted conflict or situation, or to secure a more favourable position based on this one technique alone. With her training and his lack of it, Mark was very easy to manipulate, and she wondered just how it was that more people didn't seemingly take advantage of him in his senior position. She hoped this time her plan had not backfired, because the simplest request for her time now would throw everything away.

"Yes, I want you to take Matthew. It's not appropriate for him to be here when we bring him in. Follow the plan. We will have you escorted to the safe house."

"No, no," she interrupted, hoping that she hadn't made too rash a response, or in her haste belittled his ideas. "It's an unnecessary use of resources when we have him being captured as we speak." She knew it had worked when she saw hi nodding. He checked the time on his wrist watch, and promptly moved past her, suggesting the conversation was already coming to a close.

"Yes, quite right. I can't afford to spare anybody for you. Get on with it yourself," he said as he waved his arm towards the direction of Matthew's room. "I'll make a call to let them know you are coming. You'll have to organise the car yourself." He pulled his mobile from his pocket. "Mulligan is on her way to collect him." He hung up and turned to Hannah with a smile. "It's done. Go pick him up," he said as he was already starting to walk backwards on the balls of his feet. He called out to her as the distance between them reassuringly grew. "He'll be okay you know. I spoke to him earlier. It'll be hard at first, but he will adjust. We'll speak tomorrow. I'll call you." He turned and disappeared behind the next corner.

With that, Hannah hurried towards the opposite end of the corridor whilst Mark smiled to himself and stepped towards the Surveillance Centre. Pushing open the large double doors he announced his arrival with an immediate question.

"So where are we? What have we got?"

Forrester looked over his glasses and towards the back of the Surveillance Centre towards Mark. Mark didn't notice Forrester's exasperation as he took a coffee from the refreshments table, pouring himself a large mug of oily black fluid, and tipping in a couple of sugars. He could really feel the effects of the alcohol that he had just knocked back, and he wanted a clear head. He began walking towards the station where Forrester was working, considering each step and proceeding one at a time.

"Sir, the first team will be within one hundred meters of the transmit site within the next minute, and the rest are only minutes behind."

"Good. Have them stand by and await their colleagues. Wherever he is holed up I want a perimeter around him. No chances for escape this time. This time he is ours. This time, he is dead." Mark listened as Forrester relayed his instructions to the teams as they drove through the outskirts of the forest. He sipped on his coffee and pulled up an empty seat alongside Forrester. He wanted a prime viewpoint to watch the birth of his success. He watched the screen as the blue marker flashed, marking the newly detected signal. The *Ben* signal. They all watched as waves of red lights circled in, each representing a field agent. Mark could feel his pulse racing as he listened to the radio transmission from the leading team.

"Jedi twenty one, do you read me? Over."

"Loud and clear Jedi, what is your position? Over," relayed Forrester, speaking as he held down the transmit button of the intercom, clearly in his element. One of the few days he lived for.

"In position, approximately twenty meters from target. It's a boathouse. I repeat. Boathouse. Over."

"Standby, Jedi twenty one. Standby. Over."

Mark sipped his coffee and stood up. He began to pace around the workstation, clearly annoying Forrester who was listening to a steady relay of messages. Each workstation gave its signal. Soon enough he had ten teams in place, over half of Mark's company, and more than enough to encircle the boat house. Forrester looked across the room towards Mark, who was standing with his arms folded, one thumb brought up apprehensively tapping on his lips. He looked again at the blue marker flashing in the same position. It hadn't moved. *Could he be asleep,* Mark wondered. He imagined Ben sleeping, trying to rest after the events of the day. He sensed the first thoughts of pity, and as fast as they arose he brushed them aside.

"Sir, we have enough teams in place. We have the target surrounded. Whenever you are ready."

Mark looked up at Forrester knowing that it was time to fit the final piece of the jigsaw in place. "What about the satellite? I want the satellite images." Forrester looked towards his assistant for an update.

"About five minutes Sir," said a bespectacled head from behind another workstation. Mark looked back up to the primary screen which filled almost a whole wall in front of them. He saw the blue marker, surrounded by red dots, the other side bordered by the river. Wherever they were, there was no way out.

"What the hell is taking so long with it?" Mark's patience was wearing thin. *Was it really necessary to have the satellite images? Did he really need them?*

"He is surrounded, Sir," coaxed Forrester, trying to divert the heat away from his aide. He was eager to see the strike. It wasn't often he got a day like this, and his impatience was poking him. *It wasn't necessary,* Mark thought. *They could manage without it.* "There really is no way out this time," Forrester offered. It was the last push Mark needed.

"Okay," Mark said. He took a deep breath. "Give the order."

He watched Forrester pick up the intercom and press the transmit button. He listened as the static faded away. In its place he heard a jumble of muffled words as they rolled off Forrester's tongue. He sat back down at the workstation with his fingers interwoven like the strands of hair in a braid, pulled tight and captive, and he rested his lips onto them. He didn't hear as Forrester gave the order, and there was no machismo left. Instead he quietly and privately closed his eyes, said goodbye to Ben, and prayed for forgiveness for what he was about to do.

NINETEEN

IN THE NEAR DISTANCE, THE white walls of the small cottage glistened as if they were neon. The daylight was beginning to fade and the only light was the first rays of moonlight scattering down through the dusky sky. The moisture from the forest floor was rising, a carpet of mist which clung to the abundant ferns. One by one, the agents constructed their circumferential border between the cottage and the real world, and now whatever lay inside its wooden walls belonged to the Agency. The team leader positioned himself with his knees in the broken undergrowth, and he listened out for the breaking of twigs around him. Each snap indicated another agent in place who would be ready at his command. He watched a faint heat signal inside the cottage on his monitor, stationary and weak, perhaps secondary to the damp air. There was no smoke rising from the chimney, and the signal was too weak to be a fire. It had to be a person, one that was cold and wet, probably hypothermic.

He raised his finger to his ear, pushing the ear piece further in to hear the instructions as they were relayed to him.

"In position, approximately twenty meters from target. It's a boathouse. I repeat. Boathouse. Over."

"Standby, Jedi twenty one. Standby. Over."

His calculations were accurate, and he had a good complement of men forming the border that they had created. He stood by as instructed. He reached down to his thigh, feeling for the handgun as it sat holstered to his leg. His fingers knew exactly where it was; trained well for speed and accuracy they would move to the gun without the need for sight or conscious thought. In the dead of night, in the blackest of rooms, he knew each member of his team could handle the weapon strapped to them as if it were an extension of their hand. His silent breath formed small clouds in front of his face which served to camouflage him further in the rising mist.

The rattle of metal and plastic filtered through the dusk as each agent checked his weapon. When the time came there were no questions asked. Each agent wanted to be ready. They would rally to their commander's signal, weapon in hand and ready to shoot. No guilt allowed.

The team leader raised his fingers to his ear once more as he heard the break in static. He listened as Forrester gave the instruction. Without delay he raised his arm and clicked his fingers, forming a right angle with his fingers pointing at the sky. With two short strokes forward, his fingers indicated to the men that it was time. They relayed the message up the line, the signal spreading as fast as fire through dry woodland. The leader stalked like a wildcat, his legs low, creeping silently through the land. He crept towards the target. On point, his team fell into line behind him, a death snake winding towards the cottage. Standing at the side of the front door, the point man waited for the rest of his team to fall into place, their arms loaded and minds alert; nothing would get past them this time. They had only one instruction.

Shoot to kill.

Other agents swarmed around him, encircling their leading man to take up their positions. Others slipped into place around the sides and back of the building, and he waited until the final men were in position. The building was surrounded. Those at the front knew their destination once that door was open, left or right, push forward or hold back. The final agent climbed the steps leading to the porch taking, bringing him within striking distance of the front door. He was holding the battering ram in his hands, nose blunt and hanging low. The rest of the agents held their weapons up near their shoulders, stacked in next to each other in two rows either side of the door. The agent moved moved in close and began swinging the ram back and forth, feeling the inertia of its weight. The leader took a final confirmatory look around. With his finger on his ear piece listening out for instruction, he raised his eyes towards the agent stood expectantly at the door and gave a single sharp nod of the head. The agent lunged the ram at the door with all of his might behind it.

He delivered the blow just underneath the door handle. The silence of the forest was shattered as the wood splintered, but the door remained in place. One more recoil and delivery, and the ram smashed into the door once more. The wood burst open like sparks raining down from a firework. The agents filtered into the room to take up their positions, improvising by finding security behind settees and the very chair where Ben had sat only one hour before. The two most advanced agents scanned the front of the living area, circling the kitchen units and small cottage style dining table. There were some scattered pieces of tissue on the table and the floor which attracted their attention. Another agent clicked his fingers, motioning to the pot of congealed red gunk left on top of the cooker. One by one the agents filtered through the house, clearing each room, smashing in doors and opening cupboards as they conducted their search.

"What did you find?" the leader asked as he walked into the living room and saw his most senior agent returning towards him, empty handed.

"Sir, there is nothing here. We searched the whole place."

The leader placed his fingers to his ears and spoke into the small headset mouthpiece.

"Nothing?" Forrester asked as he heard the relay that the search had proven futile. The team leader checked his screen for the signal trace again.

"We are still reading the signal. Is there a basement?" he said as he looked up to the agents which surrounded him. Several agents started another search for a trap door. They knew that there was no internal door left unchecked so the only thing left would be a trapdoor in the floorboards. They pulled the settee and chairs back, kicking them away to reveal nothing but solid floorboards. Another team in the bedroom simultaneously lifted the weight of the bed frame as if it were no heavier than a book, and again confirmed the absence of an escape route.

"There is nothing here, Sir," replied the leader over the headpiece, confirming that the search of the bedrooms had proven fruitless. Then an agent on his knees spoke.

"Sir, take a look at this."

The agent was holding up a small black box that could have been a speaker, or a child's walkie-talkie. But he recognised it as a transmitter. He had seen them hundreds of times before, and used them just as many. As he took the device and released the transmit button he heard a voice in his ear from Headquarters. It was Forrester.

"We've lost him."

"Sir, I think that this is our heat signal." Another agent held up the large pot of red dough like mixture, still warm from the preparation of the smoke bombs.

The leader tossed the transmitter aside in frustration, sending angular shards of plastic scattering to the floor as the lightweight transmitter shattered into pieces. He held down the transmit button on his earpiece and waited as Forrester took receipt of his call and cleared his secure line.

"Sir, the signal is just a transmitter. The target remains unsecured. I repeat. The target remains unsecured. Over."

"What?!" Mark jumped to his feet as if his chair had caught alight, and sent it toppling behind him. "Ben wouldn't know the first thing about what to do with a transmitter. They have lost him!" he bellowed as he pointed an accusatory finger at the red lights on the main screen. Mark scrambled his fingers across the desk in front of him looking for a head-set with which he could communicate directly to the team. He caught another communications officer by surprise as he took the headset from his head. Ramming it into place, he bypassed Forrester and spoke directly to the field agent.

"Jedi twenty one, this is Mark Ballantyne. What exactly have you found?"

Forrester staggered towards Ben. "Sir, you are risking security," barked Forrester. But Mark ignored him. He didn't care anymore.

"Sir, we tracked the signal, but it's coming from a transmitter. There is nobody here. Somebody was here, but they left."

"Surveillance to Jedi, do you read me, over?" Forrester interrupted, livid at the flagrant loss of anonymity across communication channels.

"Copy that. Go ahead, over."

"Can you confirm for me what's there at the scene? What type of transmitter have you found?"

"Is Mr. Ballantyne still there?" said the agent, having no other choice but to use his name.

"We are both listening," confirmed Mark.

"The transmitter. It's one of ours, Sir. Over." Mark looked at Forrester, who mirrored his expression of gormless astonishment.

"Jedi, what are you saying? That it's our equipment there?" Mark couldn't believe that. Who would be there from his team?

"That's what it looks like, Sir." Mark raced over to the station where the technician was still desperately working to get the satellite up and running. He wanted to know where they were. Exactly.

"I want eyes on the ground. Get me that location," he ordered as he approached the workbench. Forrester was joining him, and as respectfully as he could with his frayed patience, he nudged the technician out of his seat and took over. Within moments he could see the clarity of the image improving as the pixels increased in number, bringing the cottage into view. "Where is that?" asked Mark.

"Just a moment, and we'll have it better." Forrester played with the settings, and sure enough, his years of experience were put to good use as the image of the white cottage came into view. As the picture loaded and Forrester rotated the image in order to bring the walls and the once perfectly constructed front door into view, Mark took an audible breath in as he realised the familiar sight before him. "Where is that?" Forrester asked.

Mark didn't have time to answer as he pulled the headset from his ears and tossed it back down on the table. Racing up the steps he burst through the double doors, leaving behind him nothing but a room full of confused faces.

TWENTY

WITH EVERY STEP THAT MARK took towards his office, his anger grew to a capacity that he had never expected or felt the presence of before. As he paced through the bright white corridors devoid of life with almost the whole department on the tail of nothing more than a transmitter, there were no other sounds to muffle the clip clop of his footsteps. They ticked along like a second hand counting down time, a constant reminder that it could be too late.

As he turned the corner into the corridor which connected to his office, he breathed. At the other end of the corridor stood Hannah, Matthew in her arms, his legs wrapped around her waist. Mark quickened his pace, and he saw that as he inched closer towards her, she too took longer strides. But Hannah was burdened, and Matthew slowed her down.

There was only one set of stairs between them, and it looked to Mark that he was closer than she was. The brow of the stairs became his only focus, a way to block her exit. His best weapon for negotiation was in her arms, and there was no way that once he had her, that she or Ben would escape him again. He knew it was Hannah that had betrayed him.

As Mark reached the top of the staircase Hannah hesitated, realising she would no longer be able to get there before him. Her pace stuttered and she almost tripped over. Her feet came to a sudden stop only a meter and a half away from the stairs. It was her only safe exit. She looked at her watch. She had less than five minutes left.

"Catherine, are you in a hurry?" His voice was kind, amiable, but the simplicity and softness of his words was a mere mask. The ice cold sensation they instilled as they picked up the hairs on her arms seemed more menacing than anything she had experienced in his presence before. She knew something was wrong immediately.

"Um, no. Not in a hurry," she lied. "Just want to get this little man home." She smiled a half smile and ruffled Matthew's hair. His fingers gripped like claws around her shoulders. As Mark approached them she instinctively took a step backwards, but it was foolish for it betrayed her fear and simultaneously her guilt. Matthew however had no such guard, and giggled affectionately as Mark reached out to touch his face.

"You're a bit of a big boy to be carried aren't you?" he said to Matthew. From the grumpy frown that spread across Matthew's face, he agreed with Mark's sentiment.

"Mummy said I had to be carried." He hung his face to cover his shame at the overbearing nature of his mother's control.

"Come on," Mark said, as he reached out to place his hands under Matthew's armpits. Hannah held on tight and took another step backwards. She hitched Matthew upwards and as her hand cupped the back of his head, she pulled his face in towards her.

"I just want to get him home, as you said. It's best for him now."

"Sorry, Catherine," he said as he took another step closer. "We have a few minor details that need to be rectified before you leave." His eyes lingered on the back of Matthew's head as he picked at the locks of his hair with meticulous precision. He turned back to face Hannah. "Before either of you leave."

"Mummy," Matthew asked, "why is Uncle Mark calling you Catherine?"

"It's just a silly game, baby," she said, smiling as much to reassure herself as Matthew.

"No, Matthew, Mummy is wrong. It's not a silly game." Matthew, encouraged by his inclusion in the conversation fought against the weakening grip of his mother, squirming with the willowy flexibility of youth. Soon Matthew was looking at Mark, but found no common meeting point, and instead saw that Mark's eyes were fixated on Hannah. Matthew looked back up to his mother's face, white as an Ionian villa. He was too young to recognise the presence of fear in the face of another, but her pallor and latent expression made him uneasy. "But she will realise her mistake now, and will come with me so that we can solve our little problem. Anyway Matthew, you must have missed Daddy, and he is on his way now to meet us here." Before she could summon the diminishing strength in her arms, Matthew had contorted his way free, wriggling wormlike to the ground.

For a moment she watched in shock as Mark led Matthew away, dumfounded and clinging to the rail of the stairway that should have been her getaway only moments before. She looked at her watch. Four minutes. She had no choice but to follow Mark. Up until now she had pushed forwards like a rampant tsunami wave, pushing onwards bringing forth destruction, flattening any object that stood in her path. Yet now as she stood as a lifeless victim watching Mark spirit away her son, she was the one left behind amongst the debris, the tatters of life laying scattered about her feet. But with their backs to her and some distance between them it gave her enough space to think, and reconsider a new path. It gave her enough time to remember the steel holstered on her hip, and how she was faster than Mark every single time. She picked up her pace, and with only a hairs distance between them, she drew her weapon.

"No further, Mark. Stand where you are." He heard the familiar click as she slid back the top section of the weapon, engaging the bullet in its rightful position. She pressed the barrel of the gun into his side, pushing it deeply, directing the nose of it up inside his shoulder blade. She angled it so that in a single shot she could strike his heart with a trajectory that would miss Matthew in any of the scenarios that she calculated. He stood still, but Matthew had not comprehended the situation, and looked back towards his mother. "Matthew, don't turn around. Close your eyes."

He did instinctively as his mother told him, whipping his head back and squeezing his eyes shut, wrinkling up the youthful skin around them. Mark also turned his head, just enough to get a side eye glimpse of Hannah. He could see her bent up arm and clenched jaw, and the pushing that he felt in his side was unmistakable as she thrust the gun in a little harder. It was a sensation that he had never felt before, but knew without any doubts what it was.

"Do you think I am stupid, Catherine?" He allowed a tiny smirk of a smile to creep over his thin lips, and the sight of them made her feel physically sick. "Actually, don't answer that," he scoffed. "Just take a look underneath my jacket, on the left." Her first thought was that Matthew was also on the left side of him. Immediately she feared what she may discover as she realised that Mark's right arm was not hanging by his side, but instead was wrapped around his belly in the direction of Matthew. She lifted up the flap of his jacket to see his milky white hand curled around a gun, his bony fingers placed on the trigger and the nose angled towards Matthew's body. Every thought of escape fell away from her, peeling away like old paint and crumbling to the floor. Her right hand fell away from Mark's body, knowing there was no more room for negotiation. There was a gun aimed at her son. No matter what else happened, she could not so blatantly risk his life.

"That's better. Matthew," he said, as he ruffled his fingers through his hair, "you better open your eyes now." He stood there, eyes clenched, disobedient of his command.

"It's okay, baby. Do as Uncle Mark says." Her words repulsed every fibre of her body as she told her son to obey his command. She watched as Mark patted his fair curls back into place, and then rested his hand down onto Matthew's shoulder. Matthew opened his eyes, and for a moment Hannah felt she could see the look of understanding on his face, that somewhere in the moments of blindness he had seen the truth, and that Mark was not to be trusted.

"Now you run towards my office and go and sit in the big chair. My chair. Mummy and I are following." He handed Matthew his access card and told him to swipe it against the screen outside the door. Matthew looked towards his mother, who nodded her head reassuringly, and although he remained hesitant, Matthew walked towards Mark's office. Mark turned to face her, the real Mark, the one she had never known existed.

"Catherine, get the fuck in my office."

He pulled her forwards and she began to followed Matthew. She sneaked a glance at her watch and could see that she had only three minutes left until she was supposed to call Ben. She thought about him sitting in the car, the three passports to a new life in his hands, watching his wrist as the seconds ticked down. She thought about the plans of the building which she had studied extensively as a student and tried to recall all of the exits and the corridors that potentially could lead her to safety. She knew that with Mark behind her and Matthew just entering his office her options were limited.

Matthew stood and watched his mother only meters behind him, and turned to her for approval before he entered the office. Before she could nod her head, Mark was at her side, and gripped her arm in his fist.

"In you go," he shouted to Matthew. Mark pulled Hannah forwards, and within seconds they were all in the office. Matthew ran as instructed and sat in the oversized leather chair, and Mark pushed Hannah's shoulders with just enough force to make her sit down in one of the smaller, more uncomfortable visitors chairs. Matthew sat still, his knees together and feet dangling beneath him, his hands gripping the armrests. Mark slammed the door shut behind them, encasing them in the office.

Mark peeled off his jacket and threw it against the leather sofa that lined the far wall. It fell in a heap, but it left a trail of tension that hung over the room like an oppressive smog. He placed Hannah's gun on top of the cabinet in the corner of the room, amongst photographs of important political figures. He holstered his at his side. Mark had beads of sweat forming on his brow, and he turned, one hand placed on his hips, the other across his mouth. He looked at Hannah first, and then towards Matthew, who was staring back, wide-eyed and terrified.

"Matthew," he began as he sat on the edge of the desk, facing him. "I'm going to tell you a story. It's very interesting, and it's about a little girl called Catherine Marie Mulligan. Have you ever heard a story about her before?" Matthew shook his head in denial. Mark turned to Hannah, and with a false sense of shock, cupped his hand across his mouth. "You never told him about Catherine Marie Mulligan? Well, Matthew, let me tell you about this very clever little girl.

"Catherine was born in Ireland. You know where that is don't you?" He nodded his head. "Catherine's daddy was a very important man, and he did lots of very important work. And do you know, Matthew, that her daddy was so clever that the Queen of England asked him to leave Ireland and come back to England to work. In this very office. He would come in everyday, do lots of important things that helped to keep lots of people safe, and Catherine and her mummy would stay at home. Sometimes Catherine didn't even have to go to school."

"Every little girl has to go to school, Uncle Mark."

"Not if they are extra special. Like you, Matthew. You haven't had to go to school this week have you?" Matthew thought for a moment, and shook his head. "Because you are very special too. Like little Catherine. But she had a problem, Matthew. Do you know what that problem was?" Mark stood up and placed his hands on the desk and leaned in so that he could speak quietly. He looked at Hannah and then back to Matthew. "Secretly, Catherine's daddy was a bad man. He was a very, bad man."

"But the Queen asked him to come to England. She wouldn't ask a bad man to come to England."

"But she did, Matthew. It didn't matter that he was bad, as long as it was a secret. But he forgot that it was supposed to be a secret, and Catherine's daddy made lots of other men very angry." Matthew looked towards his mother, who sat uncomfortably in her visitors chair as she relived the story of her youth, which had an end that she had no desire to recollect.

"That's enough, Mark. Matthew doesn't need to hear this." Hannah looked down at her watch. The ten minute window that she had was almost up, and she thought of Ben sitting in the car checking his watch, counting down the last moments.

"I'll decide that. Matthew wants to hear the story, because afterwards he will get to see his daddy again. You want that, don't you, Matthew?" Matthew was nervous, his smile sheepish. He was excited at the prospect of his father's reappearance but he was uncertain if he should really trust Uncle Mark. But he was scared enough not to question him. He nodded. "So one day, when little Catherine Mulligan was playing at home, a very angry man came into her house. Catherine was very clever though, and she hid away in a cupboard so that he couldn't find her, and she stayed there for two days."

"Like Harry Potter."

"Yes, like Harry Potter, Matthew. You've got it." Mark crouched down at the side of Matthew's chair and his knees creaked like an old door as he leaned in closer to whisper in Matthew's ear, loud enough for Hannah to hear. His eyes fixated on Hannah who squirmed in her chair. "But do you know what happened to her mummy?" Matthew shook his head, uncertain that he wanted to hear the end of the story.

"The bad man took her away. Forever. Do you know why?"

"No."

"Because she wouldn't tell them where Catherine's daddy was. All she had to do was tell them where Catherine's daddy was, but she wouldn't." From inside the desk Mark revealed a beige cardboard file, and instantly Hannah feared it to be her own. He turned it around and slid it across the desk, his hand stretched out, pushing her past towards her, imprisoning her with it. He opened the file, and confirming her worst fears she saw her own young naive face staring back at her. He leafed through the papers, turning them over for her to see. She had no time to read them, but she didn't need to, she knew what was there. It was her whole life in written form. As he worked through the paperwork, she saw the photographs tucked underneath the psychological assessments. She saw records of her schooling, her university days, old boyfriends and extended family. First job. First car. She recognised the image of her father without a second glance, when he was younger and larger, and didn't live in hiding. She saw the photograph of the boathouse cottage just coming into view as he moved other papers from the top of it. Matthew was watching a scene unravel before him which he didn't understand, and he fiddled with the armrests for a distraction, picking at the leather trying to make a hole as if he were Alice and could escape down it.

"Matthew, I don't know where your daddy is. That's the truth. But I want to know. I want to help him see you again. Your mummy doesn't want to tell me where he is. She doesn't want me to help him."

"Mark stop it." He ignored her plea.

"She doesn't want to tell me. Do you remember what happened to Catherine's mummy when she wouldn't tell the bad man where Catherine's daddy was?"

"My daddy is not a bad man like Catherine's daddy was." Pride and fear for her son welled up inside of Hannah. She looked at her watch and knew ten minutes had passed.

"I need to know where he is though. And only your mummy knows. She has to tell me, Matthew."

"My daddy is not a bad man," Matthew repeated, summoning all of his bravery, his teeth clenched, chest puffed out. He could barely breathe. "Why do you want to know?"

Mark leaned in closer still, almost resting his chin onto Matthew's shoulder as he whispered again in his ear. "Because your mummy has been very bad, and if she doesn't tell me where he is, you will never see her again."

As he uttered the final words, he turned his head back to

look at Hannah who he expected to see sitting at the desk opposite him. He wanted to make sure that she had heard every single threat that peppered his lies. Instead he found an empty chair. Hannah had slipped out of it and with her had taken the agency regulation paperweight from the desk. She raised her hand in the air, but Mark lunged backward, unsteadying her, sending the paperweight tumbling to the ground with a heavy thud. He thrust his hands forward and took her by the neck, his fingers slipping around the shape of it, forcing her backwards onto the leather settee. They fell together, him on top of her, his knee falling heavily into her side, winding her.

"Where is he, Catherine!" he screamed, as he pushed harder into her neck. He felt her struggling for breath beneath him. "You're playing with your lives! It's over, just tell me!" Suddenly aware of movement behind him, he turned to see the door that leads to the underground bunker closing behind him. "No!" he screamed as he leapt up to catch it. In his haste he tripped over Hannah's foot, and as he fell to the ground he landed on the sharp edge of the paperweight, opening up a gash at the level of his ribs. Through the small opening that was gradually closing he saw Matthew running down the white corridor towards the safety of the bunker. He had discarded Mark's access card on the floor of the corridor, just out of reach. Before he could get to his feet the door had locked shut, sealing Matthew away from either his or Hannah's grasp.

"Matthew!" Hannah choked as she realised what had happened. She turned to Mark, still lying on the floor as she scrambled to her feet. "Mark, open the door!"

"I can't," he said as he struck his fist into the ground.

"Open it," she screamed, grabbing the gun from his hip as she knelt on top of him, tearing open the fresh wound. He recoiled. "Open it now!" She trained the gun at his head, and with her other hand rubbed at her bruised neck.

"I can't!" he repeated, as he pushed his way out from underneath her, kneeling up in the face of his own gun. "I can't open it for another ten minutes. He has my card," as he pointed at the door.

"You can override it. I know that. Do it." She was standing above him, and held the gun in a strong grip aimed at his face.

"I just told you, I can't! Not for ten minutes." He sat back on the settee and leaned his head against his hands. Hannah moved in closer towards him. "It's a safety mechanism."

Hannah could feel the effects of the adrenaline charging through her system, and her hand was shaking as she held the gun out in front of her, and so she gripped it a little tighter with both hands. She was trying to think of another way out. She knew that there must be an exit from the bunker other than through Mark's office. It was only logical, but she didn't know it. "Get up. Come on." She waved the gun towards him, its nose hovering around in front of his face. She motioned for him to move towards the desk. "You must have plans for the bunker. Show me them."

"There are no plans. Why would there be plans?"

"Because there are plans for everything in this place. I've seen them before. Nothing is left unplanned."

"Not this. This place is supposed to be a secret. Its existence is only known by a handful of people. I'm your only hope down there, otherwise he will never find a way out." She looked towards the door as tears swelled in her eyes, unable to cover her terror at the thought of his entrapment. "Now stop being stupid, and tell me where Ben is. I'll let you go if you tell me where he is."

"Never." The first one fell, streaming down her cheek.

"Catherine, I just don't get it. Two days ago you were set to hand him over. What the hell changed?"

"Shut up, let me think." She looked again at her watch.

"Catherine. Your son is trapped. You just have to tell me where Ben is and you and Matthew can walk out of here like nothing happened. I won't even try to stop you. I'll let you go."

"I said shut up," and she looked at her watch again.

"Why do you keep looking at your watch? Is he waiting for you? Is he close?" The excitement in his voice almost got the better of him, before she interrupted him again.

"I said shut up," she repeated as she hit the side of his head with the barrel of the gun. He recoiled a little, and clutched at his head. As he brought his hands away, there was a streak of blood across his finger tips.

"Fuck, Catherine," he spat through gritted teeth, pain and anger smothering him in equal measures. "You know if they come in here and find you with a gun at my head, they'll shoot you on the spot. They won't think twice. Then Matthew will have no parents. Do you realise what you are playing with? He'll be an orphan." The words burnt her like acid.

"I can't let you have him. Either of them."

"Why? It's so easy. Just tell me where he is. If he is close it can all be over in minutes."

"No. You see, you don't know me as well as you think. You think I am just a cold bitch that joined this agency to make up for the past. To avenge the death of my mother. You thought that I could just live with him and not feel anything. You think that I am the same person as I used to be."

"You are, Catherine. You are the same. You are the same girl who walked in here who said that she wanted to kill the same people who killed her mother. You think every bullet that you have fired, every person's life that you have taken somehow makes up for the loss of her life. And you are right, Catherine. It does."

"It doesn't. You're wrong. It just destroys my life, and Matthew's life."

"And Ben's life." It was a blameless sarcastic response, as if he was an outsider looking in, judging her from his ivory tower of morality and perfection. *Look at what* you *did. You. All you. How could* you *live with yourself?*

"You won't take them from me."

"I will, Catherine. You are holding that gun up to my head shaking like a little girl, pretending that you'll shoot me. But you won't, because you need me. And you need this. This agency. This life. This is all you know. It's not Ben you need. It's me. You won't shoot me. Tell me where he is." She looked at her watch again. At least six minutes had passed since the door had closed and sealed Matthew inside the cocoon of the underground bunker.

"Open the door," she stammered.

"I'll open the door when you tell me where Ben is."

"Open the door, or I'll shoot you now."

"If you shoot me you'll never get in and you'll never get Matthew back." Mark started to stand up, forcing her backwards.

"Open the door." She pushed the gun into his forehead unsteadying him a little, and he felt the cold metal hard up against him.

"I said tell me where Ben is and I'll open the...." Suddenly Mark let out a gut wrenching scream as he felt a bullet pierce his flesh just underneath his shoulder. The force shot him backwards, landing on the settee.

"You fucking shot me!" he said as he clutched his right hand across his left shoulder. He doubled up in agony pushing the heel of his hand into the open wound. Blood oozed out through the gaps between his fingers. He pulled his hand away to reveal a perforating wound which had ripped through his skin.

"And I'll shoot you again. Open the door." She pushed the tip of the gun back against his head, steady this time, without the shakes. She hoped that he wouldn't call her bluff. She knew as well as he did that without him that door wasn't going to open. But she also knew that after making a bullet sized hole in his shoulder and threatening his life, the balance of power was in her favour, reinforced by every nervous transmission of his pain and fear. He raised his head and watched her staring at him. All it took was for somebody to walk through the door, but the chance of that happening without his express invitation was unlikely. He knew that he was cornered and that he had to go along with her plan. He had underestimated her.

He limped upward and Hannah backed away as he sat down at the computer.

"Show me what you are doing." He clicked on an icon on the screen and tapped out a series of numbers.

"Do you have your access card?" She nodded and reached inside her pocket. "I need the numbers from it," he said as he took the card from her. "It needs two people to override it. My access code and that of another agent. It's supposed to make the person inside the bunker safer." He copied in the numbers as they appeared before him. As he pressed the enter key, she heard the mechanism inside the door clicking into life and after what seemed like an age, she saw the green light appear and the red one shut down.

As she stood up behind him, her eyes caught sight of the pile of files on the desk. She recognised Ben's handwriting on a sheet that was slipping out to the side, teetering on the edge of falling. She pulled the first file towards her and opened it up. Seeing it was Ben's notes, she turned to look at Mark.

"Why do you have these here?" She pushed for an answer, encouraging it out of him with the tip of her gun in the base of his neck.

"I'm still a scientist, Catherine. It's really quite remarkable, although I don't understand it all just yet. He, and NEMREC really are quite brilliant." His praise tasted like the false success of a cheated victory, and she wanted to shoot him all the more. Instead she gathered the files close to her and took the telephone from her back pocket. As Mark tried to step forth from his seat, she pushed the gun back towards his head. "Wait there," she said as she dialled Ben's number. Before even one ring was complete he answered, and she could sense the desperation in his voice.

"Oh God, Hannah. Are you there, shall I come now?"

"No, not yet. There has been a delay." She could see Mark watching her, itching to know where Ben, the scientist and friend who he loved, hated and admired in equal quantities, was located. She could see his hatred chipped into the wrinkles around his eyes as they became a little more prominent as he listened to them speak. She wondered who he hated more, Ben for his brilliance, her for her deceit, or himself for his failure to see the operation through to what he would describe as a successful end.

"What delay? Do you have Matthew?"

"There is a change of plan. Meet me at the docks. You are looking for dock two. Look for the boat from earlier, and get on it. We will meet you there. Bring the documents."

"But Hannah, wait."

"No, Ben. Things got fucked up, and you need to meet me there instead. No questions. Go now." She hung up the telephone, not giving him time to question her instructions.

She heard the latch of the door handle to Mark's office engage as somebody placed their hand the other side.

"Careful!" Mark shouted as he too realised that somebody was about to enter and wanted to warn them about his trigger happy captor. The door flew open as Captain White put the full force of his boot behind it. Hannah fired off a couple of shots, hoping to put some delay between her and their approach, and dropped to the floor concealing herself behind the side of the desk. She saw Mark cower behind the desk as Captain White returned fire. The bullets struck the wall, sending small clouds of plaster dust tumbling across the regulatory furniture. Hannah fired off a few return shots and then wedged her back up against the side of the desk whilst trying to keep an eye on Mark. She grabbed a smoke bomb from her inside pocket and taking the lighter placed a spark on the homemade fuse towards the base of the bomb. She waited for the first plumes of pink smoke to appear, before hurling it towards the entrance door. Soon the smoke filled the office, and she saw Mark trying to scramble over the desk to safety and into view.

"Don't shoot," he shouted as he hauled himself forwards. She knew that Captain White wouldn't risk firing a misplaced shot into his boss's chest. She lit another smoke bomb to buy more time. As she threw it towards the door, she pulled back hard on Mark's leg, and he yelped in pain as he fell backwards. She paid no attention as he slumped into a pathetic heap clutching the oozing wounds on his torso. She squeezed the trigger again and a solitary bullet left the gun, before she heard the click of an empty chamber. Tossing it to the ground she gathered up the files, and crawled along the floor to where the entrance door to the bunker lay. She snatched up her access card as heard the first of the random bullets sailing her way as Mark gave the order to fire at will. Keeping low, she pulled herself as fast as she could into the open space of the doorway, shoving in Ben's files first. The bullets continued to rain in her direction, quick whipping sounds as the metal pierced the air, followed by the blunt thud as they struck the reinforced walls. As she forced the door behind her, she could just hear Mark shout the instruction to *get to the docks, number two.*

As the door closed it brought with it near silence, the only sound the occasional hollow thud as a random bullet struck the other side of the wall. She collected the files into a neat pile, and counted ten, each filled with Ben's written words. Finding the files was a small victory and one that in no way could powder over the cracks of what was lost. But she hoped that their reclamation would be a comfort to Ben, and more importantly prove her allegiance.

***

"Get a team to the docks," Mark screamed at Captain White as he pulled him through the open door from a nightmarish haze of pink smoke. "Dock number two." Captain White was more interested in the wound that Mark had sustained to his shoulder, and whilst praying that it was not attributable to his own hand he focused his efforts on trying to get some pressure on the gaping hole. There was a fine trickle of blood from the rear exit wound. It was a fact that would have satisfied Hannah a great deal should she have seen it. By pulling himself across the desk he had opened up the wound, tearing more fibres apart.

"Sir, you need to lie back. Come on, Sir," Captain White said as he tried to exert some pressure to force him to lie down. Mark slumped against the outside wall of his office, no longer able to sustain his protest. He mobilised his unwounded shoulder to punch his frustration against the wall behind him, striking it three times in short succession. "Get a medic here," Captain White called to one of the office workers who was rounding the corner after hearing the commotion, attracted like a magpie to silver as the plumes of smoke billowed out.

"White, get the teams moving. They cannot let him get away."

"Sir, all the teams are across the other side of the city. They are almost half an hour away." Mark recalled with self-reproach his decision to send every agent chasing after the cottage that had proven to be nothing more than a false transmission. *Idiot!* "Then get that door open," he snapped. "I want that bitch back in here to answer to me. Me! You hear that. She shot me! She's a fucking dead woman."

"You need to rest. You are bleeding heavily. You must stay here," Captain White said, relieved to hear that the hole in Mark's shoulder was not the result of one of his stray bullets.

"Get that door open. Now. And get the teams on the way." He pushed Captain White's hand away and motioned for him to re-enter the smoke filled office and work at getting the door open.

"Sir you know that there is a delay."

"Just get on it. When it'll open, I want it open."

Captain White stood to his feet and took his telephone from his belt clip to call to the Surveillance Centre. Mark listened as he relayed the instructions to get the teams en route to the docks, and followed by asking them to work on getting the bunker door open. As Mark pulled his chin back to get a better glimpse of the entrance wound on his chest, he reached his fingers in a spider like fashion across his shoulder to investigate the bullet's exit route. He discovered an irregular, corrugated edge to an otherwise warm cavity, the feel of which made him think of Ami. The hot poker-like pain seemed implacable, and he could smell the faintest whiff of burnt skin. He promised himself that there was no way in the world that Catherine would get away with what she had done. Capturing her and seeing her lose her life would now almost be as satisfying as watching Ben do the same. In his propensity for gleeful revenge, he never once considered Matthew, the bounds of the Agency within which he worked, or how it might be that he could learn to live with himself after the consummation of the plan that was forming in his mind.

TWENTY ONE

HANNAH RAN ALONG THE UNWINDING corridor, a brilliant white slope which steadily descended, all the while clutching the cardboard files to her chest. As she passed each door, she used her elbow and her body weight to lever each handle in her search to locate Matthew. She pushed each door, slamming them open and shouting his name over and over in the hope that she would see his familiar blond curls. After a futile search through at least six rooms, she arrived at a fixed circular table aligned with the central axis of the room. Twelve satellite stools were fixed in position around it. Bursting into the room like a rogue meteor from the depths of another solar system, she dropped the files onto the table and continued searching the rooms that branched away from the central chamber.

Indistinguishable in every static detail, every surface white. The only variation to the colour scheme was the beige trim of the folded up blankets that sat neatly on the end of every bed, unused and sealed in a plastic airtight bag. The white metallic cupboards reminded her of school lockers, with small slits across the front panel. Room after room, the same scene was repeated.

As she turned back to the table after exiting the last replica room, she couldn't begin to see a way out. More importantly she had covered each room and her search for Matthew had proven fruitless. Each room was an isolated pocket, and the only corridor that seemed to lead anywhere was the one that went directly back to Mark's office. She snatched at her telephone and prayed for a signal. There wasn't even one bar.

Beyond desperation, she threw the telephone down onto the table and slumped onto one of the small white plastic stools beneath her. She rested her head into her hands in an attempt to stop them shaking. She suppressed her tears, determined not to allow her desperate predicament to be the reason that her mind shut down. She pressed her cheekbones firmly and rhythmically, pressed her lips together. She told herself to think logically and to formulate a plan, steadfast that somewhere in her mind was the education to find a solution. She nibbled at the skin around her thumb whilst she subconsciously stroked the files on the table with the other hand. In that moment she felt something familiar brush at her side. It was the gentlest displacement of air in an otherwise static and sterile environment and it indicated that she wasn't alone. It was a familiar feeling, followed by a grip so gentle that nothing could replace it, and something that she could never mistake.

"Matthew?" She flew up and round in one fluid motion, like a lazy sail whipped into life by a passing breeze on an ocean tide. He stood at her side, his hand resting onto her arm, his eyes wide as caverns and hopeful for the security of his mother. With no further words, she grabbed him and squeezed him close to her chest, his natural smell a remedy for her fear. "I looked everywhere for you. Where were you hiding?"

"I hid in the cupboard like Catherine did." She dropped down to her knees to be at the same level, desperate to get as close as she could to him.

"Well done, baby. Well done." She cupped his face in her hands, turning him left and right, back and forth, pulling at the skin on his cheeks and around his eyes as if she would be able to find signs of trauma or pain in the freckles and curves of his face. "Are you okay?" He nodded, and with his confirmation she felt the surge in purpose, the need to fight. Sitting at this table was useless. She held him to her chest, feeling the rapid gallop of his heart drumming against her own. His face looked physically intact, but the muscles that held his eyes in place appeared to have relaxed, his mouth hung open just a little as if dumbfounded. "What is it baby?" she asked

"Uncle Mark is a bad man, Mummy."

"Yes. He doesn't want to help us. We have to run away from him. We have to run far away with Daddy where we will be safe again." She stroked his face as he nodded his approval. "Stay here, Mummy has to find us a way out of here." He hung on, staring at her.

"You were going to hit him with that big thing you picked up from the desk, weren't you." His judgment of her actions hurt almost as much as the thought of the gun held by Mark in Matthew's direction only minutes before. She saw him catch sight of the second gun on her hip which Mark had failed to discover. She wondered how best to answer, and had no idea what the right thing was. She took a chance on the truth.

"Yes. I would have hit him because I knew that he was a bad man, and I didn't want him to hurt us."

He nodded, smiled a little, and she knew that was the most she could ask for right now. She picked him up and sat his exhausted and apathetic body down on the table. She ran back into each room knowing that without the anxiety of Matthew's absence she would find the methodical and rational approach to reveal another exit. It was impossible to consider that such a bunker would not have a secret and concealed exit installed, because without an exit it would simply be a waiting room for the inevitable ambush from above. She searched frantically, but with a calm caution to not miss some minor detail of importance. She searched all of the cupboards looking for concealed crawl ways and hidden doors.

At first there was nothing, but as she ran into the final room, she realised that it wasn't just a bedroom. It had the same single sized bed and pile of fresh plastic wrapped laundry at the end of the bed. But on the far wall there was an indentation which suggested the shape of a doorway. As she pushed against the recessed area of the wall she felt the slightest disturbance in its position, which only served to strengthen her instincts that this was a possible exit. She traced her fingers across the perimeter of the recess, searching for any discrepant bump that may indicate the presence of a button or concealed handle, but found nothing. As she repeated the same process on the wall to the side, her smooth fingers detected a small dimple in the plaster work, something pliable to compression. Wasting no time, she pushed the area in and sure enough the door opened outwards, and she saw light bursting through from the other side.

She saw what reminded her of a multi-storey car park, with three black cars lined up facing a wall. She scanned her eyes around the room, allowing them to settle on a button which read 'Activate'. Looking inside the cars, she could see that there was a set of keys in the ignition of the one closest to her, and after finding the door unlocked she turned the key. The overwhelming satisfaction of the engine's roar couldn't have offered greater fulfilment than the symphony of an orchestra. Smiling with relief, she ran back towards the central room for Matthew and Ben's research files. Matthew was sitting where she left him and after scooping him up, and taking the files in her other hand, she ran as fast as she could back to the waiting car.

The sound of the engine filled the small room, bouncing back from the walls like gas molecules in an airtight container unable to escape. She couldn't hear her own footsteps, or those in pursuit behind her over the din of the engine. Opening the rear door she ushered Matthew inside and secured his seat belt. In the foot well of the front passenger seat she tossed the files and slammed the door shut. Matthew watched as his mother pushed the activation button and walked back towards the car.

What appeared to be a normal wall withdrew into a recess, exposing a ramp and the last shards of daylight just visible in the distance. She sat down and turned to Matthew who was motionless behind her, resting his hands into his lap, staring at his mother. He regarded her in the same way in which Ben had regarded her earlier on in the day, when he realised that there had always been a side to her life that he knew nothing about. She looked like his mother, sounded and smelt like her, but yet was somehow different. The mother he knew didn't carry guns for a start. The mother he knew didn't attack people with heavy paperweights, or leave bullet holes in the chests of friends. The look in his eyes as his brows crunched together suggested that he was waiting for the real version of his mother to show up and expel the imposter. It was the same expression on Ben's face at the safe house earlier on that day, when he had still thought that to shoot a man was the worst thing that could have happened to him. It was disappointment, and it hurt her more than any pain she had felt before.

"We are going to get Daddy, and then we are going on a big adventure on a boat." He didn't say anything, but he nodded obligingly. He didn't smile, but she chose to ignore it. "Mummy is going to drive quite fast, so I need you to hold on tight. Okay?" A small grin reached his lips, slight but she detected it, and it gave her hope that one day he might forgive her for the pain that she had caused him and Ben. Before she could turn around, she saw the smile on his face fade. She followed the path of his gaze and found Mark standing before her. She thought of running him down, but the knowledge that Matthew was with her made such an act difficult, and she had no choice but to wait to see his next move.

He walked to the car with the steady controlled pace of the soldier that he never was. Each step was deliberate and well placed, but there was a sallow look on his face, and she couldn't help but notice the blood streaking and seeping its way down his shirt. Hannah looked around towards the exit back to the all white bedrooms, but even as she looked she knew that there was no hope in that direction.

"Keep your hands on the wheel Hannah, where I can see them," she shouted. He was only inches from the car, and too close for her to pull the gun from behind her, the one that he had failed to consider as he had confiscated her other weapon. He was holding a matt black gun which she recognised as her own, and its sight was trained at her head. She doubted he would use it, because to use it now would end the hunt for Ben, but she appreciated the intrinsic risk in making assumptions like that when she was responsible for the bloody wound beneath his shoulder. She reprimanded herself about how she should have shot him in both shoulders, or better still, have killed him as soon as he had opened the door to the bunker. He opened the car door, and slipped inside next to Matthew. She knew that the wound must be hurting him.

"I will let you go. Both you and Matthew," he lied, "just as soon as I have Ben." She knew he was lying, and it was only now that she considered the likelihood that the car was reinforced and that his bullets would not have penetrated the glass work had she refused to get out. She wished again that she had killed him, or at least ran him over repeatedly instead of blithely waiting for him to act. Her thoughts flipped back and forth between Matthew and her wasted opportunities to put this to bed.

I should have killed him, she said to herself. He sat back into the car and closed the door. She saw Matthew's face pushed up against the window, steam forming as his hot breath passed against the glass.

"Come here, climb over," she said as she beckoned him into the front seat. Mark raised his arm as if he was about to stop him, but she was quicker, and she blocked his reach. Matthew did as his mother said, stepping over into the front seat as if he had been sat on a spring ready and waiting. She reached over and fastened his seat belt, kissing him on the cheek, and stroking her fingers down the side of his face. She tried to place all of her fear, and all of her worry to the back of her mind, and allow nothing but positivity and strength to move across her face in the warmest most honest smile she could muster. Matthew smiled nervously back, and she planted a soft kiss on the tip of his nose. She placed her hands over his ears, and just before she sealed them shut, she told him to close his eyes. He did so, and as she pressed down against his small ears she turned to Mark.

"If you hurt a single hair on his head, I will fucking kill you. I promise you that."

"And yet it's me that is holding a gun to the back of your chair. So I think it is up to you to do as I say." She considered the concealed gun that she could feel pressing uncomfortably into her back, but realised there was no hope to use it now with Matthew in the car.

Not in front of him. I can't. I just can't.

"Take us to the docks," Mark spat. She looked down at her son, who was staring back at her and pushing back further and further in his seat and towards the door to keep as much distance as possible between him and Mark, a man who until only minutes before he had trusted implicitly. She smiled again, and as she released the handbrake and heard Mark's sarcastic congratulatory remarks regarding her submission to his will, she thought of Ben. She hoped that he was already at dock two and waiting on the boat. She trusted the man in charge of the boat, and knew that he would do all he could to keep her husband safe. It was her time now to focus, and her only job was to protect Matthew.

TWENTY TWO

BEN DROVE THE CAR TOWARDS the detailed Victorian gateway which marked the entrance to the old docks. Turning in through the red brick columns between which would have at one time stood a wrought iron gate he saw one of the last workers leave. The docks were quiet now, and had been for years, receiving only one or two small deliveries or exports a day. He knew that there was another dock yard across town, over half an hour away, and as he drove through the deserted road over the broken tarmac and labyrinth of sewerage covers, he couldn't quite shake the thought that this might be the wrong place.

As the car toppled over the bumps in the largely disused road, he passed the near derelict buildings on his right. The once terracotta coloured bricks were now thick with a layer of dirt, covered in the filth from the industry that once made this a thriving town within a town. Many of the windows were broken. There were remnants of graffiti left as the mark of wayward teenagers who would break in and stake a claim on the place overnight. In the centre of the building a striking tower rose up, the merlons and crenels that created the saw tooth pattern of the parapet more suitable for a medieval castle fortress than an abandoned dockyard. There was a small round space on the tower, free of grime where a clock had once sat, guarding the working hours. It had long since been removed.

The manmade ground gave way to the natural landscape pushing its way up from underneath. In places the road had been smothered by a mixture of grass and moss from above, and Ben became lost in the thoughts of his possible mistake. There were no signs, no guidance. He pushed the occasional tormented theory that it could all still be an elaborate trap to the back of his mind and kept a look out for a signpost.

Just as he began to contemplate the idea of turning back, the wheels of the car jumped as he drove over the old disused train tracks that led to the old wheat store. The looming image of an old Caisson, once used to close the mouth of the docks formed an impressive shadow as he drove past the wall of steel, rusted and defaced by more graffiti. As he passed the old ship, he finally saw a sign that read 'Dock One', and figured he must be on the right track. The light was fading so he pushed down harder on the accelerator and picked up his speed. Soon, after passing more broken lumps of concrete and discarded metal implements for which he had no clue of the purpose, he saw the sign for dock two. The car splashed through a series of puddles, and sure enough as he neared the end of the broken land, marked clearly with a series of steal lumps fixed solidly into the ground, he saw a small white boat, tethered onto a set of broken white railings. The same boat on which Hannah had saved his life.

He pulled up the car a few meters from the edge and killed the engine. He picked up the three passports, and regarded the boat for a moment. There was utter silence in the dockyard, with not a single worker left to interrupt the peace. Everything around him was cast in a deep shadow, courtesy of the disappearing sun, making the whole scenario seem even more terrifying. Nobody questioned him, and nobody called out to complain at his intrusion. There was not a soul around but for a sole man on the boat, whom he had no idea if he should trust or not. From his appearance he guessed that it had to be the man who had delivered the car. His best option was to give him the benefit of his incredible doubt.

Ben stepped out of the car, keeping his body behind the door, shielded from view. He looked down at the passports and squeezed them, taking courage from Hannah's planning and help.

Her track record in trust had proven to be less than flawless, and images of the four agents lying dead on the ground were at the forefront of his mind. But he reminded himself that he believed that she loved him. Without that belief there was nothing left; no hope for the plan to work and for them to find an escape, no hope for Matthew or his chance to savour another day with him, no hope at all for a future. Any future.

He had lost NEMREC and the ideals by which he had lived his life for so many years had been idly stolen from him with barely a glimmer of conscience. Without his family he had nothing. He had to remain strong in his belief that she loved him, otherwise he was left with nothing but a past full of lies and a meaningless chance at a life without worth. He didn't want to lose anything else. Or anybody else.

He reached down to his hip and patted the gun that he had placed there earlier and felt in some bizarre way reassured by its presence. As if carrying a gun was a normal thing for him. He thought back to the bag of weapons in the boot of the car, and wondered how a person might react, and in particular the man standing before him on the boat, if he opened the boot and pulled a machine gun as his backup plan.

He closed the door and took a tentative step towards the boat, moving around to the front of the car. The engine felt warm as his hands rested onto the bonnet as he crept his way forward. The man on the boat remained cool and as motionless as an ice statue.

There was nothing but open water ahead. The only interruption to the heaving mass of the endless ocean was the patches of sea foam, lit by the weak light of the rising moon. There were no street lights, and the first stars flickered into view above him. It was hard to make out if the man was holding a gun in the shadow of dusk, or if he just had his hands on the controls of the boat, but it unsettled Ben and he could feel himself hanging back. He knew he must look as suspicious as he felt.

"Where is Hannah?" the voice called from the boat. It was a soft voice, firm but the edges were rounded into a southern Irish accent.

"She got delayed in Headquarters. She told me to meet her here." The man held his hand up and for a panic stricken moment Ben thought that his worst fears had been confirmed. Instead he raised his hand to his ear and Ben realised that the boatman was holding nothing more threatening than a telephone. He could barely hear the words as the man on the boat spoke quietly into the mouthpiece, but he was sure he could make out the name Hannah. Ben stood waiting at the car, not wanting to assume a rite of passage towards the boat, and not wanting to risk disrupting any plan that Hannah may have put in place. He was not supposed to be here on his own, and he reminded himself to tread with caution.

The man on the boat tucked the telephone back into his pocket, before proceeding to climb from the boat and onto the dock. He walked fast, and straight towards Ben, almost as if he were set to embrace him and offer comfort. But as he approached he swerved around the side of him and headed straight towards the back of the car. He was heading for the boot which contained the concealed armament.

He remembered Hannah placing the bag in the car, and he remembered quite clearly what was in it. The idea of this stranger suddenly having control of the multitude of weapons was a frightening concept and a new thought came into his mind. It was strong and superseded all others in that moment. *Escape. How am I going to escape? Into the water? The car? Under the car? Use the gun?* He saw the lid of the boot open and the man from the boat disappeared behind it. Ben felt instant fear and became paralysed to the spot as if his toes had sprouted roots. His terror prevented him from employing any one of the random acts of restraint that had taken over his ideas of escape, and instead he watched as the man pulled the bag of weapons from the boot. He didn't take out any of the guns or threaten him. He started to walk back around the front of the car towards Ben, whereby he stopped and stood in front of him to speak.

"Hannah is in trouble. She's on her way and she has Matthew, but something is wrong. I think Mark is with her."

She has Matthew. This was the first thought that Ben processed, but the joy of the boatman's words was short lived, and soon everything else that he had said registered. *Hannah is in trouble. Something is wrong. Mark is with her.*

"What's wrong? What did she say?" Ben was overcome by the need to protect his wife and son, and with renewed vigour he reached out and snatched at the man's jacket sleeve. The man looked up, startled by the tenacity of the grip, but Ben stood his ground and he firmed up his hold of the man's arm. His fear of this unknown character was outweighed by that which he suddenly felt for the safety of his family.

"When I asked her if she was okay, she answered by saying yes twice. And quickly. It means she is in trouble, that something is wrong." He paused for a moment and trained his eyes unsympathetically towards Ben. "Again."

As Ben caught sight of his face, he knew that he had seen it somewhere before. The cap pulled over his forehead and the light beige coloured coat reminded him of the underground station earlier on today, when he had shot the agent and agreed to go willingly with Hannah. This man had stood at the other end of the platform, relaying guidance and instructions.

"Wait, I know you. You were at the underground station."

"Yes I was there. I work with Hannah."

"But you didn't come with us. You weren't at the safe house where Hannah took me to."

"No," he said, as he tried to free his arm from Ben's grip. "I don't work for the Agency."

"What were you doing there?"

"I would have thought that was fairly obvious by now." He snatched away his arm from Ben's grip. The boatman continued to walk towards the vessel, his arms outstretched to balance out the weight of the laden weapons bag.

"What does that mean?" Ben asked as he started after him, deciding not to push him any further on his presence at the underground station. "What are we going to do now?"

"What are we going to do?" the boatman replied, emphasising the *we* in his sentence. Continuing with the same cynical distain, he told Ben, "We are going to do what we are supposed to do. This whole plan was to get you out, and that is what I am going to do."

"And Hannah? Matthew?" Ben couldn't believe his ears. Would they really just leave Hannah here to face up to what had happened in the knowledge that the Agency knew that she was a traitor?

"Hannah made it quite clear back at the cottage," he said as he walked back to where Ben was standing with a more sympathetic and amiable approach. "My aim is to get you out and that if anything was to go wrong for her, I should continue as planned." He looked at Ben properly for the first time, with his dishevelled and sweaty hair falling lankly onto the creases in his forehead, partially covering the cuts on his face. He had the expression of a man determined yet frail, keen to make his last stand, his last charge in a battle where the odds were stacked so high against him that he was certain it would also be his last act in life.

"There is nothing I can do for Hannah right now. It's you they want. Not her. Not Matthew." The boatman shrugged his shoulders a little bit as if to suggest he was incapable to help or resolve the situation. "If they come here with Matthew and you are here, there is nothing that Mark won't do in order to capture you. Your escape is his ruin. Don't you understand that?"

"But what if my escape is Matthew's ruin? Or Hannah's?" Ben closed his eyes momentarily as if the mental image that his mind had conjured up was playing out in reality and he couldn't bear to watch. "It's because of me that they are even at risk."

"That's not true, and you know it." The boatman started to walk towards the edge of the dock and Ben followed automatically, listening as he spoke. "Hannah was involved in something that she saw as wrong. She tried to fix it. We are here because of her actions. And her actions have done you good. You'd be dead if not for her." The boatman placed a set of keys which he had been rolling around in his fingers into his jacket pocket and fastened the small zipper to prevent them from falling out. "If you die, all of it has been for nothing."

"But if they die, it is still for nothing," Ben tried to remind him, again touching his arm, but this time encouragingly rather than forcefully, in search of his understanding.

"I am going to take you away to a safe house as was planned before," the man said, ignoring his pleas. "From there, you'll wait. When we can, we'll get you, and get them, out to safety."

"But they know now. Before, Hannah was relying on the fact that they had no idea that it was her helping me. Mark knows now. He'll kill her. He'll kill them both."

The boatman listened, and whilst he fiddled at the ropes of the boat for a distraction, he knew that somewhere hidden within Ben's plea there was truth. Reluctantly, he knew Ben was right. If any of them died, everything was for nothing.

"He won't let them go without me. If I'm gone, somebody will pay the price. It will be Hannah, and most likely Matthew too. I can't be responsible for that. I may as well be dead if that's what will happen."

The boatman stopped untying the knots that secured the boat and stood back up straight, turning to face Ben again. "The only way of getting them on this boat is if he has you. Then Hannah will feel that she has failed."

"But what if there was a way to get them on the boat, and for him to think that he has me."

"If he thinks he has you, it's because he does have you," the boatman scoffed. "He might shoot you the second he see's you."

"He won't shoot me. He'll trade me in, but he won't kill me.

Not with his own hands." Ben thought back to all of the times in their history when he had stood at Mark's side, or when Mark had stood at his. There was a unity in their friendship, which he understood had been stretched to the limits, but just like Hannah, who he knew beyond any doubt that she still loved him, he knew Mark could not look him in the eye and take his life with his own hand. It just wasn't possible. *The past had to count for something.* "He won't be able to do it."

"Ok, let's say he doesn't shoot you as soon as he sees you." The boatman smiled a little at the willingness of his trustee. He tasted the sweet flavour of glory that would prevail in the event of such an impossible success. "What do you have in mind?"

TWENTY THREE

HANNAH HAD PURPOSEFULLY CHOSEN A long and winding route to the docks in the hope of giving Mark the false impression that they were heading in the direction of the new dock yard. She regularly looked around towards Matthew and made eye contact with him, smiling each time she did so and resting her hand on his knee, where she could feel him trembling. Occasionally she would catch him staring at Mark, his hands gripped onto the seat, and his eyes peering backwards in judgement of a man who he had both loved and trusted. It broke her heart to watch him learn the deceitful and fraudulent nature of people.

She sensed the impressive scale of Matthew's judgment as he stared at Mark. She could sense Mark's discomfort as she watched him fidgeting, avoiding eye contact with Matthew. The scorn of a child's condemnation was an unexpected and unpleasant complication that he had failed to foresee. His preoccupation and mental torment had served Hannah well, and it was only as they passed the once elegant gates to the old dockyard that Mark realised his mistake.

"Where are you going?" he asked, his words sharp and dangerous, like broken shards of glass.

"The dockyard."

"The old docks?" He hit the door in frustration and underneath her hand she felt Matthew flinch as Mark grunted and swore. Momentarily, Hannah enjoyed his displeasure, and praised the twist of luck that his misunderstanding had bestowed upon her. But she knew before long that he would divert the agents towards them, and he was already reaching for his telephone. But she hoped that she had bought them enough time in which to make their escape. At least Mark was isolated from the rest of the Agency, and that gave her a degree of hope. On one hand she was praying that Ben had already left. But at the same time she couldn't help but selfishly pray he had waited for her. For them.

Before long, the car jolted as the wheels bobbled over the grassy, abandoned train tracks that Ben had crossed only half an hour before. The image of the old Caisson was cast in shadow, almost invisible as it began to disappear and blend into the low light. The moonlight reflected in the broken windows casting anthropomorphic shadows in the derelict old building, and as she passed them, she could see the black saloon car up ahead close to dock two, lights still on. The wheels of their car rolled through the giant puddles, the heavy reinforced walls thundering over the broken ground. As the distance between her and the stationary car grew smaller she saw the passenger door of the car had been left open, and that just to the side of it only feet from the docks she saw the body of a man lying face down on the ground. She tried to stifle her shock, but she had reacted automatically before she had had the chance to control herself, and it alerted Mark to the presence of the body.

"Pull up over there, near that body," he said, pointing his arm between the front seats. Matthew tried to sit forwards in his seat, urged on by his curiosity to get a better look. Scanning the ground where it lay, she looked at the beige jacket and flat cap, and by estimating his size she knew it wasn't Ben on the floor. Relieved and saddened but not in equal measures, she did as Mark instructed and pulled the car up parallel to the dock side.

"Turn off the engine," he instructed. They sat for a few moments in silence. Hannah scanned the dark in search of Ben. *He should already be gone,* she thought to herself as her frenetic eyes caught sight of the edge of the white of the boat bobbing in and out of view behind the dock wall.

"Mummy, where are we?" Matthew asked, but as she tried to reassure him, she heard Mark shush them both from the back of the car.

"Matthew, get out of the car," Mark demanded. Matthew looked to his mother, who in turn was staring at Mark.

"What do you want from him? Leave him alone."

"Shut up, Catherine. We are all getting out of the car. Come on, move." He gave his order and they both followed, Matthew by clambering over the gear stick and into the security of his mother's arms. As soon as they stood up and Mark had closed his door she felt the tip of a gun poke into her side. Mark grabbed her shoulder with his other weakened hand. She reluctantly stepped forwards as she felt him pushing her with the nose of the gun. They inched towards the prone body, near silence surrounding them. She cast her eyes out like a giant sea net, capturing image after image, discarding each when no trace of Ben was found. She desperately searched for clues to explain the bizarre scene in front of her. She stared at the boatman, face down in the mud. The boat still moored at the side of the dock. She covered Matthew's eyes as he struggled to take a glimpse, wriggling his face out from her shoulder.

"Who is it, Catherine? Do you recognise him?"

"No," she lied, not wanting to complicate her situation any further than she knew it already was. By choosing to help Ben she had drawn a line underneath her involvement with the Agency, and there was no choice for going back. There was only one way out now. There would be no severance pay for her silence as had been agreed. There would be no pat on the back for her excellent service that had resulted in the most significant development in warfare in the twenty first century. NEMREC he had told her, reciting words that she knew to be a bastardized representation of Ben's own beliefs, would mark a turning point in biological weaponry development, and a reclassification of the order of the human race. It would not be possible to consider the human race as equal anymore, he had explained.

She understood now as they stood on the edge of the dock together that he would string her up and publicly shame her, like a village witch burnt on an agency endorsed stake as an example to others. She would become the face of anarchy, the face that fought against the Agency in a foolish yet gallant manner, but whose choices could always be seen as inappropriate and poorly judged. Her demise would be taught to future generations of agents as they became familiar with their weapons and pledged their allegiance to a force that they did not fully understand. Only once they had learned what being an agent really involved would they remember the lesson of Catherine Mulligan. Her horrible death would be the push to get them back in line.

"Check him. Is he dead?" Hannah stepped forward, temporarily freeing herself from Matthew's grip. He stood on the ground next to her. He clung to her leg, as if they were one and the same. He was forced to let go of her as she leaned down to see the face. The mouth of the boatman was resting on the edge of a dockside puddle, and she could see the ripples on the water as his breath brushed past the surface. As she angled her gaze towards his, she saw the faintest of twitches in his eye. She knew from Mark's position that her body would be blocking his view, and she watched as one of the boatman's eyes peeled open and turned to look at her. She followed his line of sight as he directed his open eye across the puddle towards his hand, in position just underneath his head. The boatman tapped his forefinger on the well concealed gun. Then he held one finger up and pointed to the direction of the boat, lying low over the dock. But the boatman's continuation to play dead gave her the sign that she too should play along. She placed her fingers on his neck as if to check for a pulse.

"He's dead." She turned back to Mark to see that he was now standing with Matthew at his side, his hand resting on his shoulder. The blood from the wound that she had inflicted was following the course of gravity and dribbling down onto Matthew's jumper. Mark's face was sickly grey, and she assumed from the blood on his clothes that he must have lost a lot, and the wound was still oozing. The thought of his blood on her son repulsed her, and she felt the bitter taste of bile rising in her stomach. She stood up and motioned for Matthew to come towards her, but Mark held him back with the remaining strength in his wounded arm.

"He stays here, Catherine. Now where is Ben?" She could see Matthew struggling and squirming again. There was a mixture of fear and anger on his face, his eyes scrunched together, his lips loose and unable to speak.

"I don't know," she said genuinely, tears hovering in her eyes as if all they were waiting for was an introduction to fall. "Please let Matthew go."

"He's here. This is all part of *your* plan, remember?" He tapped the shaft of his gun against his trouser leg just to remind her that he had it, and she was just thankful that it wasn't aimed at Matthew. She could see from the contortions of his facial muscles that Matthew's squirming was eliciting an inordinate amount of discomfort in Mark's shoulder wound, and it seemed to be this very motion that had reopened the once stemmed flow of blood. Matthew was forcing him to use his muscles in this arm and the loosely knitted tissues and early clotting of the wound were being washed away by fresh, bloody flow.

"This isn't part of the plan, Mark. I am blind now. It was never meant to be this way." She held out her arms and pleaded with him again. "Let Matthew go. Let him come to me, please."

"Ben!" Mark shouted. "I know you're here, Ben," he said with a smug tone that reminded her of playground games that Matthew should be playing. "Come out come out wherever you are. I've got your son, Ben. I'll shoot him. You know it."

It was Matthew's tears that finally released her own. She could see a dark patch forming on the front of Matthew's trousers, and she wanted to shoot Mark right then. She thought again how it might feel to have your son watch you shoot somebody. This time she promised herself that she would take the pain of watching her son recoil from her, that she would deal with his nightmares, and that everything was possible as long as he was alive. She began to reach her hand around her hip, Mark too distracted to realise. Just as she was about to rest her hand over the gun she saw Ben appear from behind the dock wall. He rose up, a gun held in both hands outstretched and pointing at Mark.

"That's enough, Mark. Let him go. Let him go to Hannah." Ben wanted to jump out of the boat and snatch Matthew in his arms, especially since the rocking of the water made his aim less than steady, but he tried instead to remain focussed, moving the guns in rhythm with the movement of the boat, all the while his sights trained on Mark. Mark found the whole scene hilarious. From his words to the guns, Ben seemed to him like a caricature of a movie hero, a fancy dress version of Billy the Kid, water for bullets. A full belly laugh erupted, curtailed only by the pain of his bleeding shoulder.

"Daddy!" Matthew shouted over Mark's laughter. Relief ebbed onto his face, before receding as he once again felt the grip of his captor from behind.

"It's okay, baby. Daddy's here now. I'll protect you." Ben felt every inch of his skin contract, from the soles of his feet right up to the round mass that was his skull. His flesh was goose pimpled and the small hairs on his neck were standing to attention. He swallowed the wave of nausea and focussed on ignoring the continued laughter from Mark.

Several moments passed when it seemed nobody made a sound. The laughter ceased and not even Matthew spoke. The scene became paralysed, a moment of life captured in an oil painting. The realisation of Ben as a tangible entity had stunned Mark, and once the nervous laughter had worn thin he was faced with the reality that he was the only one left to do the job. He was alone and had nobody to hide behind. No desk, no office, no agent, no hierarchy or agency to command. He was faced with only Ben before him, their history between them, and his directive willing him forward. The realisation of his efforts was no more than a single bullet away from being claimed. He took a step forwards and firmed up his grip of Matthew.

Mark broke the silence. "You, my friend, have proven difficult to trap. But it would seem you have had quite the little assistant doing your bidding for you." He looked towards Hannah whose eyes flicked between the two men. "You wouldn't have survived a second on your own." Mark raised his gun in Ben's direction again. Both Hannah and Matthew squealed in unison.

"I survived your first attempt to shoot me, Mark," Ben reminded him, as he thought back to the shooter on the rooftop of the laboratory. Mark was pushing forwards and guiding Matthew with him. But he no longer looked steady. He almost looked like he was using Matthew as a human crutch. "How could you do it? How could you sell me out?"

"It was easy enough. Enough money, enough glory, we will all trade what we have for something that we want, for something we crave."

"You would trade me for that? Mark, I can't remember life without you." Ben's voice sounded fractured, as if it could shatter into a million broken-hearted pieces at any moment.

"And now you'll never have to. I'll take your work and I'll be the fucking genius for once. No more of life in the shadows. No more comparisons."

"You're just a pawn Mark," Hannah stuttered. "Just like I was. There is no glory for anybody in the Agency."

"You're wrong, Catherine," he said arrogantly, not at all convinced by her theories. "There is. Once I turn you in," he said as he took another step towards Ben, "your work is mine."

"Even if that were true, it's too late." She inched her way forwards towards Matthew and smiled at him, holding out her fingertips in an effort to narrow the abhorrent distance between them. "You don't have the documents anymore."

"What?"

"I took them. They are destroyed. They were all on your desk, and I destroyed them."

"That's a lie." He tried to think back to his office, full of smoke and hard to negotiate. Were the files still there? Had she really taken them? He couldn't be sure.

"It's the truth. I'm sorry, Ben," she said as she looked for forgiveness. "I'm so sorry about everything."

As the man lying on the floor listened to the conversation above him, he waited patiently for Ben's move.

"Mark, give me Matthew," Ben said ignoring Hannah's apologies. "You can't use him like this. Let him come to me. Let him come now."

"Didn't you hear what I said? There is only one way this is playing out. My way. My way!" He gripped onto Matthew harder whilst pressing down on his shoulder for support, as more blood began to ooze from his shoulder. Matthew's cries grew louder, Hannah's too.

"Mark, don't..." Ben said.

"Move away from the boat, Ben," Mark screamed in a guttural and threatening call to listen.

"Mark, please..."

"Get off the boat," he screamed again as Matthew shook beneath him. It was time to end it. He was tired of Ben's pathetic defiance. *Couldn't he see it was useless? Couldn't he see who was in control?* He took the gun and thrust it towards Matthew's chest. Matthew screamed out as he felt the barrel push between his tiny ribs like a doctor's exploratory finger.

"Ben!" Hannah screamed, as she pulled her own gun and pointed it at Mark. Time for thought was over. There was no space for anything but action. She had left it too late. There was a gun trained on Matthew. *I'm too late! It's too late!*

Immediately Ben abandoned his guns, holding them up in the air.

"Alright. Alright, Mark, you win. We'll trade. Me for Matthew. Just let him go."

"That's what it took, huh? That's the only thing I had to do. Finally you have come to your senses." Mark's voice was calm, like a flat line of death. "But you have more fight in you than I thought you would. More stupidity, too, for such a fucking genius." Ben threw the guns on the floor of the boat and took a grip of the small ladder. Pulling himself out of the boat and standing on the edge of the dock, he held his arms outstretched releasing a series of perpetual pleas, begging Mark to forsake his weapon and free Matthew. "Get over here."

Ben stepped past the boatman as Mark instructed. When Ben was within reach Mark relinquished the gun from Matthew's chest, raising it at Ben's temple. Matthew ran to Hannah. She scooped him up and fell to the rough ground, cradling him like a small baby. He gripped her body with his tiny fingers. The smell of urine coming from his trousers took her straight back to the cupboard where she had sat for days as a child after the execution of her mother. She rocked him back and forth as he lay paralysed in her arms, and she told him over and over that nobody would ever hurt him again.

"Finally, it's over," Mark said, as he smirked at Ben standing before him, dropping the gun and enjoying a moment of triumph. "Get in the car."

"You're not going to kill me?" Ben knew it was a risk, but he figured if he wanted to shoot him he could have already done so ten times over. He had to push him. He had to know.

"And give up the chance to drag you in, take the glory? I'm not gonna miss that. Now walk."

"Give me a chance to say goodbye. Please."

"I said walk," Mark shouted, pushing Ben forwards with the nose of the gun. Mark waited for him to take the first steps forwards towards the car. Hannah watched helplessly as he marched Ben forwards and away from her forever. She wanted to react, but she couldn't stop herself from thinking about the boatman who was alive just metres away. They must have a plan. *They must*, she pleaded to herself. *Do something!*

212

"Mark, you know you are taking Matthew's father away from him. You realise that don't you?" Ben said.

"Oh, just shut up, Ben." Mark didn't want to listen to his ramblings. He had done it. He had got him. "It's over now."

"You know I could never let you do that." For all he had done, and all that he had become, Ben wanted to hate Mark. He saw remnants of the friend who had been there through his darkest moments, the one he had loved and never thought he would live without. Part of him, the old Ben, wanted to sit him down, help him get to hospital and protect him. He wanted to believe that the boy who had put his arm around his shoulders as he wept for a lost father was still there. But he wasn't. He was so sorry for what he was about to do, but even sorrier that the Mark he loved was already gone. Finally he realised. There was nothing left to grieve for.

"You don't have much choice," Mark sneered.

"Yes I do." Ben's comments were cool and collected, and had Mark not have been so intoxicated on his own glory he would have been more alert as Ben shouted, "now!"

The boatman rolled over. His perfectly trained eye found the sight of the gun and with only a split second between turning and firing, he pulled the trigger, releasing two rounds which fired through the air towards Mark. Mark swung round just in time for the first of the bullets to plant itself in his side, and the second in the right side of his chest. Ben jumped forwards and dropped to the floor, turning as he did so kicking up a small dust cloud from the dry ground. He saw Mark land next to him, his eyes wide and vacant, and his body limp and heavy. A split second of sadness gripped Ben, followed by an immediate sense of relief as if somebody had reached inside of him and pulled out the fear. As he staggered back to his feet he raced towards Matthew and Hannah where he fell to the ground and into her arms. He held them, and for the second time today he cherished the sense that Matthew's life had been saved. First from disease, and secondly from Mark. He promised himself that in whatever life it was that they now had, there would never be anything of greater importance than his

213

family again.

The boatman was also quick to his feet and raced over to them. "Come on Hannah, there is no time to waste." He pulled Hannah to her feet and Ben took Matthew from her. He kissed his face repeatedly and made the same promises to him that Hannah had made only moments before.

"Get him to the boat," said Hannah, pushing them forwards. "Do you have the passports?"

"They're in the boat already." She nodded and smiled at him, and grabbing his face in her hands she kissed him passionately on the lips. As their lips met and she felt the wet warmth of his skin, all she wanted to do was get on the boat and leave. But she had one more thing to do. She had to try to make up for the hurt. She had to try to destroy the plans of the Agency. She hadn't stolen the files for nothing. She ran back towards the car. She looked back briefly and saw Ben carrying Matthew to the boat, lowering him in. The boatman was reaching up and took Matthew from him before Ben also stepped into the boat. She smiled to herself as she reached in and collected the files. She held them tightly to her chest and took her first steps past Mark into a future that seemed so full of promise. She could see Ben talking to Matthew standing in the boat looking as perfect as he ever had. She had done it. She had saved him and in the process somehow managed to save herself.

As Ben stood upright and looked back towards Hannah he saw Mark pushing himself up, disabled but not stopped by the two bullets and with a gun gripped in his hand. He was turning to face Hannah.

"Hannah!" screamed Ben. He reached down to grab a gun from the floor of the boat, but he heard the shot ring out above him. He snatched the gun up from the deck of the boat and raised it up and over the dockside. He fired two shots which struck Mark in the chest. The gun dropped from Mark's hand and his head fell to the dirt. As he clambered over the ladder for a second time, he saw her lying face down and motionless on the ground. He fell to his knees as he reached Hannah, without a second thought for Mark. He could see the wound in her back, just to the side and around where he knew her liver to be. He turned her over, hoping to see weakness and pain rather than the silence of death. Her breathing was brusque and staccato, but she was alive. She was still clutching the files, hanging on not for the research but for a chance of forgiveness and a second chance at unity with the man that she had almost killed.

"Hannah," he whimpered as he hovered above her, stroking her face and brushing her blond hair away from her eyes. He pulled the files from her arms, a bloodstained bullet hole scarring the folders. He realised that suddenly they were not as important as he had imagined them to be. They had stopped him living his life in the present, and every day had served as a reminder of his painful past. He wished that he had realised before this moment. He bent back down towards Hannah, and after sliding both arms underneath her, he scooped her up. Her head flopped into his chest and he felt the warmth of her breath against his skin.

"I got your files, Ben. I did it. I got you, and Matthew." Only now did he recognise that nothing held greater importance to him than his wife and child. Not even NEMREC. He ran with her in his arms back to the boat and lowered her in with the help of the boatman, the same way he had Matthew only moments before.

"Get us out of here," he shouted as he pulled off his jacket and tore at his shirt for something to press against the wound. She couldn't die. He couldn't lose anything else. As the boat sped away, nobody looked back. Matthew crouched on the floor, holding his mother's head, whilst Ben shouted *faster, faster* to the boatman. He applied all of his weight and all of his strength to the wound on his wife's body, screaming at her to stay alive.

As they sped across the waves, the boat tipping up and down as it crashed against the billowing swell of the open water, Ben knew he had only so much time. Hannah had saved his life, she had saved Matthew, and NEMREC too. He had no intention of failing her now.

TWENTY FOUR

SITTING IN THE UNEMBELLISHED CORRIDOR listening to the blinking of the overhead strip lighting, he realised that he was third in line. He had discarded his shirt just like everyone else as he waited his turn, naked from the waist up. His muscles were tight and tattooed. But the banter between the five soldiers stopped as soon as their Captain walked in. When he stood before you, there was no place for stupidity. It led only to punishment.

The five soldiers stood to attention in front of the imposing figure as he inspected their muscles and prosperity of youth. He walked towards the door and beckoned for them to follow as he led the way into the five bedded room. They each took a space, and after being instructed to do so removed their shiny black boots. They tucked them neatly under the bed as they each had thousands of times before.

He regarded his captain and his fellow soldiers as they readied themselves, half naked standing proudly at the side of their beds. He wondered what they thought of him, if they thought that he deserved it. He knew why he had been chosen, but what about them? Perhaps he would trust some of them. But he also knew that others would remain loyal to their Captain and sell him out if they found out his plans.

They sat down in unison swinging their feet up on to the

beds, organised in a round, their feet all facing inwards to a central point like a clock face. They eyed each other in silence as their Captain stood to the side of the door, keeping watch over his flock.

The nurse joined them, pushing her trolley in front of her, arriving at the bed space of the first soldier. They all watched him wince as the large gauge needle was inserted into the crease of his arm. The soldier flexed his arm back into a tight bend as the nurse pulled the needle from his arm. The pain was visible as he writhed about. One of the other soldiers began to snigger, but it was short lived, remembering that he was also waiting his turn for the same treatment. She stuck a couple of gauze swaps over the hole left by the needle and taped them down. She told the soldier to *hold it in place*, to *press down*. She pushed the silver trolley towards the next bed space. There were four more prepared syringes. The first batch. The only batch. It was the first NEMREC injection in history.

As she was finishing with the second soldier the door opened. From the shadows stepped an aged man, sporting a grand looking white moustache and a well kept head of silver hair. He wore a green hat which donned a red band and impressive insignia. He wasn't unsteady on his feet but he was slow, and the seventieth birthday that he was rumoured to have celebrated last month was no surprise to most. He nodded his head briskly to the nurse, who now appeared nervous for the first time, and she stood politely aside to allow him time to pass.

For a moment he stood at the side of the third bed and looked upon the soldier propped up against the headrest, much like a father would a son during a moment of pride and satisfaction. "Finally," he said, and he rested his hand onto his shoulder and patted his skin.

"Yes, General White. Finally." The old man smiled at the soldier's formal response, and looked upon the well defined body with delight, as if was his own work that had achieved such near perfection. "If you don't mind my saying, Sir, it's not before time."

The old man gestured the nurse to come forward and she brought her trolley to the side of the bed. The General watched her work. She took the soldiers arm and cleaned the crease of his elbow, wiping the small alcohol-laced cotton ball repeatedly over the injection site. "You are right, you have waited patiently. But as of today, the wait is over."

She inserted the needle, piercing a large hole in the surface of his skin. The soldier was brave and said nothing, eliciting no reaction. He didn't wince, flinch, or complain. None of his company would have known that he felt anything. Those still to receive the injection looked disparagingly upon the first two soldiers, unfairly judging their outward display of discomfort.

The serum burnt as it travelled through his system, each muscle tingling as it skirted through his body like a microbe taking swift control of its host. He clenched his jaw, eager not to demonstrate how much it hurt. The general eyed the nurse's work closely, and as she removed the needle General White smiled softly at the soldier. "Two weeks, and this will all seem like a distant memory, and all of the years of waiting will be worth it."

The nurse taped the gauze swabs to his arm and placed the fingers of his other hand on top of them, politely instructing him to press down on the wound.

"When can I start physical training again?" the soldier asked. "I don't want to miss much."

"We'll have you up and moving soon enough, Matthew. Don't worry. In two weeks time, once this has done its job," he said as he pointed to the empty syringe that had just been inserted into Matthew's arm, "it'll be like you never stopped training." General White held up the syringe and turned it in his fingers, glancing over the word NEMREC-1. Matthew rubbed his arm as the serum burnt its way into the cells, travelling first over his shoulder and then across his chest and towards his heart. The General turned to walk away, stopping only as he heard Matthew speak.

"General White, Sir." A genuine and heartfelt smile graced Matthew's lips. In contrast to the contempt he felt for the rest of his company, a simple and easy hatred, with White it was different.

IDENTITY X

It wasn't so simple. "Thank you for recommending me. Without you I wouldn't be here today. I wouldn't have this opportunity."

The General smiled. "Matthew, without your parents' efforts to preserve your father's research all those years ago, it would never have been possible. They paid the ultimate price, God rest their souls. You too. The Agency owes them, and you, a great debt."

As he turned to walk away Matthew rested his head back on his pillow and decided to stop fighting. He succumbed to the burning sensation as it took over the muscles in his other arm and delved painfully into his hips. He closed his eyes and bit his lip, acceding to the discomfort as the old man left the room. In two weeks time it would all be worth it. By that time the serum would have done its job. He would become exactly what they intended. He would be stronger than anybody else, including the four others lying beside him, the last of which was moaning as the nurse forced the painful serum into his arm. He would prove to them what NEMREC was. He would show them what his father created. He would become exactly what they intended.

He promised himself that he would make each and every one of them pay their debt.

The End

ABOUT THE AUTHOR

Thank you for purchasing this novel. If you would like more information regarding future work, or wish to sign up to the mailing list, you can visit my website. I'll even throw in a free book as a thank you!

www.michellemuckley.com

and before you go....

Please consider leaving a review for Identity X on Amazon

Printed in Great Britain
by Amazon.co.uk, Ltd.,
Marston Gate.